MOUNT HOPE

SARAH PRICE

REALMS

Most CHARISMA HOUSE BOOK GROUP products are available at special quantity discounts for bulk purchase for sales promotions, premiums, fund-raising, and educational needs. For details, write Charisma House Book Group, 600 Rinehart Road, Lake Mary, Florida 32746, or telephone (407) 333-0600.

MOUNT HOPE by Sarah Price
Published by Realms
Charisma Media/Charisma House Book Group
600 Rinehart Road, Lake Mary, Florida 32746
www.charismahouse.com

Unless otherwise noted, all Scripture quotations are from the Holy Bible, English Standard Version. Copyright © 2001 by Crossway Bibles, a division of Good News Publishers. Used by permission.

Design Director: Justin Evans

Visit the author's website at sarahpriceauthor.com.

Library of Congress Cataloging-in-Publication Data:
Names: Price, Sarah, 1969- author.
Title: Mount Hope / by Sarah Price.
Description: Lake Mary, Florida : Realms, 2016.
Identifiers: LCCN 2016031864| ISBN 9781629987569 (trade paper) | ISBN
   9781629987576 (ebook)
Subjects: LCSH: Amish--Fiction. | Christian fiction.
Classification: LCC PS3616.R5275 M69 2016 | DDC 813/.6--dc23
LC record available at https://lccn.loc.gov/2016031864

First edition

16 17 18 19 20 — 9 8 7 6 5 4 3 2 1
Printed in the United States of America

❧ A Note About Vocabulary ❧

THE AMISH SPEAK Pennsylvania Dutch (also called Amish German or Amish Dutch). This is a verbal language with variations in spelling among communities throughout the United States. In some regions, a grandfather is *grossdaadi*, while in other regions he is known as *grossdawdi*.

In addition, words such as *mayhaps*, the use of the word *then* at the end of sentences, and, my favorite, *for sure and certain*, are not necessarily from the Pennsylvania Dutch language/dialect but are unique to the Amish.

The use of these words comes from my own experience living among the Amish in Lancaster County, Pennsylvania.

❧ *Prologue* ❧

NOT ONCE IN her ten short years did Fanny ever think of any place but Colorado as *home*.

She loved waking up in the mornings and seeing the white-capped Sangre de Cristo Mountains from the small window in the room she shared with her sister. Often, she awoke early, just so that she could stare out the window and watch the sky change from dark blue to gray to a steely white as the sun rose and cast shadows on the mountain. She would lie in her bunk, her face turned to the window, and wonder what, if anything, lived on top of the mountain. *One day,* she thought, *I will climb to the top of that mountain.*

It was a ten-year-old's dream.

Since the time when the Amish community first settled just outside of Westcliffe, Colorado, more than thirty new families had left their homes in Indiana, Ohio, and even Pennsylvania to join their community. Most of them were young couples with small *kinner* who moved west for the promise of land with limited exposure to the outside world. Fanny Price's parents had been among them just eight years prior.

Her parents had moved there for very different reasons. Fanny's father chased his dream of purchasing a larger farm than what he could afford in Pennsylvania. Fanny's mother followed because she was his wife.

With the help of the *g'may* he built a small, three-bedroom log cabin on an inexpensive tract of thirty-two acres in the San Luis Valley at the base of those beautiful mountains. Everyone admired the view, remarking on how the snow at the top of the mountain range contrasted sharply with the beautiful, lush evergreen trees at its base, trickling into the green valley where Fanny's parents had settled. Yet, as far as Fanny knew, despite the majestic beauty of those mountains, not one member of their church district had ever built farther than the tree line.

From the other room Fanny heard her father starting to move around. Clearly it was time for morning chores. With a sigh Fanny shut her eyes and waited until she heard the creak of her parents' bedroom door and her father's footsteps heading to the kitchen. She knew that, if she waited three minutes (not two and not four), she would hear her mother's footsteps next. While the baby was still nursing, her father got up earlier to fetch his own coffee. It would be ready by the time *Maem* joined him in the kitchen.

Usually Fanny waited until she heard her older *bruder*, William, stirring from the boys' room before she slipped down from her top bunk and, in the cold of the morning, shivered out of her nightgown in order to dress for the day. She didn't like going into the kitchen unless William was already there. His presence felt like an added layer of protection to Fanny, especially in the days following the birth of baby Ruth.

"You up, then?"

Fanny lifted her head, her long brown hair tousled and covering her face. She pushed it back and looked at the door. To her surprise, it wasn't *Maem*; it was William. "*Ja.* Are you?"

He gave her a silly look. "No, goose! I'm just standing here talking to you in my sleep!"

She giggled and slid out from under the quilt, careful not to wake her younger sister Susan, who shared the bunk with her.

"You best hurry," he said. "I heard *Maem* and *Daed* talking about Pennsylvania again."

Fanny stopped herself from dropping to the floor. Her heart began to beat rapidly. "Oh, help," she whispered. She felt frozen in place and not just from the chilly autumn air.

"Hurry," he whispered one more time before following his own advice and scurrying back to his own bedroom to change.

For two months Fanny and William had watched their parents whispering about something. They did not know what it was, but they sensed that it involved them, since more often than not, *Maem* and *Daed* would glance in the direction of their two oldest children when they whispered. Several times William heard them talking about their other family back in Lancaster County and would pinch Fanny to stop fidgeting so that she wouldn't distract him from eavesdropping.

In the barn they would speculate what their parents were talking about and they could come up with only one thing: the family was going to move back to Pennsylvania and give up on the whole idea of farming in Colorado. The past eight years had not been kind to the Prices. The other Amish families who lived in the valley began to relocate farther south of the town. As they moved out, more *Englischers* moved in, wanting the comfort of land without the sacrifice of being too far from the town proper.

Despite his fruitless attempts at farming in the dry, arid soil, *Daed* refused to follow the others who began to leave. He loved the house that he had built and knew that, one day, his crops would finally prosper. That day had yet to arrive.

"What else could it be?" William had asked her just last week, abnegation in his voice as they mucked the small dairy shed.

The higher altitude of Westcliffe had made it next to impossible to maintain a large dairy herd. The paddock grass was not rich enough to sustain the number of cows that their father needed in order to make enough money to sustain the family. And the season for growing hay was too short to supply enough forage for the winters. Little by little, the herd had begun to shrink, with one cow after another sold or butchered until there were only ten cows left. And then it came: the drought.

Fanny responded with a sneeze, wiping her nose on her sleeve.

"You sick again?" William asked, forgetting about Pennsylvania for the moment. "You need a better jacket, Fanny Price! Winter isn't even here yet! You'll catch your death from it, that's for sure and certain!"

But Fanny ignored him, knowing only too well that she would not get a new jacket that winter. She didn't complain about it to her parents, knowing that they both had enough on their mind trying to figure out how to feed and clothe their six children. Susan was born soon after they moved to Colorado, then the twins, Jerome and Peter, arrived three years later. While *Daed* struggled to make ends meet, *Maem* raised five small children largely on her own. By the time baby Ruth arrived, the sixth (and hopefully final addition to the family), a hard tension seemed to linger over the Price farm and its household.

Clearly decisions had to be made and the logical one— the *only* one, in fact—was for the family to cut their losses, sell the three-bedroom log house and barn, and return to Gordonville. At least they had some of *Daed*'s family living there who could help them restart.

Neither William nor Fanny thought there was any shame in that. They were both rather excited about the prospect. The Amish community in Westcliffe was so spread out that they usually didn't see another Amish person for days, even weeks. *Maem* homeschooled them since the schoolhouse was too far away for daily journeys, and they missed most church services since they had only one buggy. Often Fanny and her mother took turns missing it so that the others could attend.

Yes, Lancaster County seemed like the answer to everyone's prayers.

So when William and Fanny slipped into the kitchen, quietly joining their parents at the kitchen table where two cups of hot chocolate waited for them, their parents' announcement came as quite a surprise.

"Fanny girl, you need to pack up your things," her father said, staring at her over the top of his mug, the steam from the hot coffee creating a foggy barrier between them.

Confused, Fanny blinked, her brown eyes looking first at her father, then at her mother. If she first thought that she had misunderstood *Daed*, when she saw that her mother was avoiding meeting her questioning gaze, Fanny knew she had not. "Me?" she said in a frightened voice. "Just me?"

Daed looked at *Maem*. She stared down at the floor, the dark circles under her eyes giving her a tired, haggard look.

William spoke up, breaking the silence between their parents and asking the one question that lingered in the air. "You mean all of us, *Daed*, ain't so? We are all to pack."

"*Nee.*" *Daed*'s response was curt and emotionless. Now he too no longer looked at his oldest daughter. "Just Fanny."

Fanny's hands began to shake and she spilled hot chocolate on the table. Normally her mother would snap at her, but this time she merely pushed a dirty dishcloth in Fanny's direction.

"Where's Fanny going, *Daed*?" William had always pushed the limits with their father, and for a second Fanny feared that William's sharp tone might land him behind the woodpile having a man-to-man "talk" with *Daed* and his belt.

But not this time.

"Ohio."

Once again, Fanny thought she did not hear her father properly. *Ohio?*

"Ohio?" William cried out. "What's in Ohio? Our family's in Pennsylvania!"

Maem took a deep breath and, without raising her head, looked at her son. "William!" she cautioned.

It surprised Fanny that her father did not reprimand William's insolence. Questioning their parents was simply not something that the children did. But her father looked tired, the dark circles under his eyes speaking of many sleepless nights. Surely this decision had not come easily to either of her parents.

"Your *maem* has family in Ohio," *Daed* explained. "Fanny's going to move in with *Maem*'s *schwester* for a while."

Fanny glanced at William, the color drained from her cheeks. They had never met *Maem*'s sister in Ohio. She would have preferred returning to Pennsylvania instead. At least she knew more about her father's family, even if she didn't remember them from before the family moved.

"My *schwester* Naomi is married to the bishop," *Maem* contributed. "His children are grown and she has none of her own. And she lives on a small property next to my other *schwester*, Martha." For the first time *Maem* forced a small smile at Fanny. "Your *Aendi* Martha has two *dochders* just about your age, Fanny. And two older stepsons from her husband's first marriage."

"Why am I being sent there?" Fanny asked, her eyes still large and frightened as she tried to understand what exactly was happening.

"You'll help them with their basket-making business," *Daed* explained.

"Baskets?" Fanny asked, more out of disbelief than as an actual question.

"They could use your help."

Fanny wasn't so certain that this was true. She knew nothing about these two sisters in Ohio and their basket-making business. In fact, on the rare occasions her mother received a letter, Fanny had just assumed they lived in Pennsylvania. And, even more disturbing to Fanny, she knew nothing about basket making. How helpful could she truly be to this family? Fanny suspected that she was being sent away so that her parents could provide for her other siblings.

William shook his head. "You can't send Fanny without the rest of us!"

Maem's hand fluttered to the back of her neck. Fanny stared at her, silently begging her mother to say something—anything!—that would indicate that this whole discussion was a mistake. But as she looked at her mother, she saw how tired she looked. While she had only just turned thirty-two, she looked almost fifty years old. Her hair was already thinning and turning gray at the roots that were just visible beneath her stiff white prayer *kapp*.

"Please, William," she said in a soft, pleading voice. "This is hard enough as it is."

"I...I don't want to leave," Fanny whispered, her dark eyes wide and frightened. "Don't send me away."

"You both know we are struggling," *Maem* replied, once again averting her eyes. "Just can't make do out here no more."

"But I thought we would *all* move back to Lancaster!" William cried.

"We would if we could," *Maem* said. "But we've too much money invested in this place. Fanny's going to return and help out the *aendis*. My older *schwester*, Naomi, offered to take her in. That will help us all and be better for Fanny anyway."

While neither Fanny nor William had ever met this Naomi, they had certainly listened to *Maem* read the sporadic letters written to her by her oldest sister. Her husband had been selected by lot to become a preacher, and within two years, he was elected the bishop of his church district. It was clear that Naomi saw this as a sign of divine appointment rather than selection by lot. Often the letters spoke disparagingly of the situation that her younger sister had fallen into when the Prices moved to Colorado. It wasn't surprising to Fanny that Naomi had poked her nose into the family business once again. That seemed to be what this Naomi person did best.

As for *Maem*'s other sister, Martha, her letters were even more infrequent and consisted of nothing more than a list of recent activities: gardening, washing, quilting, and prayers for health for the Prices. On the few occasions that *Maem* read them out loud, it sounded as if the letter could have been written to a complete stranger rather than her very own sister. That made it even more surprising whenever *Maem* commented about how Naomi and Martha were as inseparable as two peas in a pod. Their personalities seemed as opposite as fire and ice: the former fiery hot and the latter emotionlessly placid. Fanny could never imagine that she'd ever have *that* type of friendship with baby Ruth, who was ten years her junior, or especially with her sister Susan, who was only two years younger.

But neither Ruth nor Susan were forefront in her mind. Instead, Fanny sat before her parents, trying to register the fact that she had just learned she was being sent away from the only home she had ever really known.

William scooted his chair close to his *schwester*'s and put his arm protectively around Fanny's shoulders. "I won't let you send our Fanny away!"

Finally their father had enough. He slammed his hand, open palmed, onto the top of the table and exclaimed, "Quiet, William!" Then, his eyes narrowing as he scowled in the direction of his son, he added, "'Sides, your turn will come next week."

William's arm stiffened and Fanny squeezed his knee under the table.

"What's that supposed to mean, *Daed*?"

Daed remained emotionless. "William, you're going to have to go to your *onkle* Aaron's in Lancaster County."

At this announcement William jumped to his feet, accidentally knocking down the ladder-back chair on which he had sat.

"Sit down!" *Daed* commanded, his voice booming, which made Fanny shrink farther into her seat. "You'll be learning the carpenter trade from my *bruder* Aaron and returning here to help me when you turn sixteen."

At their father's words, equally as surprising as what he had said earlier about her being sent to Ohio, Fanny felt William's arm drop from her shoulders. He slid his hand under the table and sought out hers. When he found it, he squeezed her fingers so tight that she thought they might turn blue.

"When shall *I* return, *Maem*?" she asked, somehow finding the courage to speak up.

But her mother did not answer her. The baby began to cry from the cradle at the foot of their bed in the master bedroom and she jumped up, hurrying to fetch Ruth. Her father merely gave her a look and advised her to pack, and pack quickly, for the driver would be arriving within the hour and it would be best for the younger siblings if she were gone before they awoke.

Without further discussion, *Daed* stood up and gestured for William to join him outside to start on the chores. Fanny watched as her older brother stood up and slowly followed his father outside, pausing at the door to cast a long look over his shoulder at Fanny. And then, after a sharp word from *Daed*, William turned, and with his head hanging down, he disappeared into the lingering darkness of morning.

Alone and stunned, Fanny somehow managed to make her way into the bedroom and in a robotic fashion took her three dresses and nightgown from the hooks that hung from the wall. She folded them and placed them into a small canvas bag along with her few toiletries, undergarments, and stockings. When she finished, there was still room for more. The only problem was that she had nothing more to take.

The next day Fanny found herself seated in the back seat of a passenger van, her bag clutched to her chest as she stared out the window. The van pulled down a long, winding driveway lined with white fencing, and headed toward a large farm nestled in a wide valley between two hills.

Fanny's eyes grew wide at the sight of the extensive farm that was set off the road. Since the driver had turned off the highway and started driving through Holmes County, Ohio, Fanny had noticed that most of the farmhouses there were set just off the main roads, not back in the center of the farms like her parents' home. And, as far as this farm went, with four buildings on the property—the barn clearly dominating the others—it was certainly the largest farm that Fanny had ever set her eyes upon.

Beyond the drawn-out driveway, the fencing—no longer white but just regular post and barbed wire—seemed to stretch for miles. The herd of cows, mostly black and white Holstein cows with a few creamy-colored Jerseys mixed in, grazed on the lush green grass expanse. Their udders seemed full and their bellies fat. No scrawny bones on their hips, nor any patchy, dry grass to be their only grazing material. Fanny tried to count them but gave up when she reached forty, twice as large as her father's herd had ever been.

Forty cows! If milking one cow took ten minutes, forty would take almost seven hours, an impossible task for a single person, let alone doing this two or three times a day! With such a large herd, her uncle was truly blessed to have two grown sons.

Before leaving Colorado, the driver had picked up two other families, a young couple who had recently married and an older couple with two teenage sons. They were moving back to Lancaster for the very same reason that the Prices were sending Fanny and her *bruder* away: there simply were limited ways for an Amish family to make a living in the Colorado community unless trade was their occupation. During the two-day journey, the van had stopped only four times to refuel and allow the travelers to use the restrooms. For food Fanny had a small cooler of sandwiches, water, and fruit her mother had packed. When the driver got sleepy, his companion took over so they could drive straight through.

The drive from Westcliffe, Colorado, to Mount Hope, Ohio, had taken over twenty-one hours. By the time the van arrived in Mount Hope, Fanny felt tired and cramped, her stomach bloated and her head pounding. She had never liked traveling in a car, although she hadn't much experience with it. To be thrown headlong into an almost twenty-two-hour drive only solidified her partiality to the horse and buggy over these motorized boxes.

Fanny was their first stop, and as the van pulled to a stop by the barn, she felt her nerves begin to unravel—and not for the first time. Although quite mature for her young age, she knew nothing about Ohio. And she knew very little about her aunts, uncles, and cousins beyond the little she had gleaned from the infrequent letters *Maem* had read to the family.

She had known better than to question her parents. The last thing she wanted was a trip out to the woodpile to become her departing memory of the Colorado farm. But when she asked, for one last time, when she would be returning, her mother had averted her eyes and quickly returned into the house.

Fanny suspected what the answer was: never.

Now, as she stood in the driveway, her canvas bag and small cooler by her feet, she stared at the farmhouse and wondered what to do next. The house loomed large, a massive two-story structure with multiple porches and doors. She wondered how many rooms it contained. Certainly many more than her parents' small four-room house in Colorado.

Near the red barn was a smaller building with a large, wooden sliding door that opened into the horses' stalls. She could see two of them staring at her as they chewed on their hay. Three gray-topped buggies were parked between the horse barn and the house, forcing Fanny to panic once again. Just how many people live here, she wondered. After all, her family of eight had only one buggy!

"Fanny? Fanny Price!"

Startled at the sound of her own name, Fanny looked in the direction of the voice that called to her. A robust woman stood at an open doorway of the house. She looked the same age as her mother, and Fanny knew instinctively that it had to be *Aendi* Naomi. The woman took a step onto the porch, holding the screen door open with her hip as she waited for Fanny to come to her. Without being told, Fanny bent down to pick up her bag and the cooler before walking toward her aunt, whom she had never met before this day.

"You're a full half-day early!" the woman said by way of a greeting.

The hostility in her voice, so fiery and sharp, confirmed Fanny's suspicions about which aunt she had just met. No hello. No embrace. Not even a compassionate smile. *Definitely Naomi*, she thought with a heavy heart.

Appraising the young girl with narrowed eyes, her aunt did not seem pleased with what she saw or, perhaps, it was the change of arrival time. "My word! Didn't the driver stop to give you a rest?"

Intimidated by this aggressive greeting, Fanny responded by merely shaking her head.

"I can't imagine why not!" Naomi clicked her tongue and scowled. "*Ja, vell*, nothing to be done about that now, I reckon. You're here, so that's that."

Clearly Naomi was irritated by her early arrival, which was Fanny's first indication that her aunt did not like unexpected changes to plans. Not wanting to aggravate her further, Fanny stood before the woman and waited for instructions.

Once again, her aunt gave her a quick study. Her eyes narrowed and her lips pursed as if she was disappointed by what she saw.

During the long drive, Fanny hadn't changed her dress, so she knew it was wrinkled and stained from where she had dropped her sandwich the previous afternoon. Her stiff cap was barely pinned to her pulled-back hair. When a light breeze brushed her cheeks, a stray strand of hair fluttered and stuck to her mouth. With the back of her hand Fanny pushed it back.

"Not too much to look at," her aunt said, "but I reckon that some good hearty meals will put meat on your bones." Then, stepping onto the porch, the door finally shutting behind her, Naomi walked past Fanny and headed toward the other side of the house where a large archway protected the doorway. Pausing at the steps, her aunt turned around and saw that Fanny still stood in the same place. "Come along then, Fanny! No sense dilly-dallying!"

Obediently Fanny obliged her aunt's request and carried her things toward the porch where her aunt stood impatiently waiting for her.

"You best not be an idler," Naomi remarked. "Might not have much to do in Colorado, but there's plenty of chores to tackle on this here farm."

Already this was off to a bad start, Fanny realized, as she took a deep breath before stepping inside the house.

It took a moment for her eyes to adjust to the dim lighting in the vast kitchen with the open gathering room. She stood there, staring at the large table and expanse of kitchen counters and cabinets. The walls were painted a pale green, and dark green window shades kept out the natural sunlight. Two green sofas and two reclining chairs were on the far end of the room, along with a white painted bookshelf full of books and knickknacks.

The room was bigger than her parents' entire house, she realized.

The sound of footsteps coming down the stairs made Fanny look in that direction. Another woman appeared and, unlike Naomi, greeted Fanny with a soft smile. "My, my!" She crossed the room and stood before Fanny. There was a gentle way about her, and despite the difference in age from her own *maem*, Fanny knew that this must be her other aunt, Martha Bontrager.

"Let's have a look at you, Fanny!" the woman said, ignoring Naomi's scoff. "I reckon that I *do* see the resemblance to your *daed*." She paused. "I trust your *maem* is doing better now?"

Fanny didn't know what she meant or how to respond.

Naomi, however, did. With a disapproving roll of her eyes, she snapped, "Of course not, Martha! That's why the child has been sent here!" She clicked her tongue and shook her head. "What could you expect from that *schwester* of ours, anyhow? Running off with that man to Pennsylvania and then moving to Colorado! Such nonsense!"

Clearly the rebuke stung Martha, for her smile disappeared. "*Ja, vell*, no sense in dredging that up, I reckon." She stared into the distance.

Still remaining silent, Fanny looked down at her shoes.

"You must be hungry after such a long journey, *ja*?" Without waiting for an answer, Martha hurried to the counter and picked up a plastic container. She popped off the top and carried it back to Fanny. "Set your things down by the door and come have a cookie," she said.

Naomi held out her hand to stop Fanny from moving. "*Nee*, child. Go set your things by the stairs."

Stopping mid step, Martha raised her eyebrows and faced Naomi with a quizzical expression on her face. "But, *Schwester*, she's to live with you, *ja*?"

The look that was exchanged between the two sisters made Fanny wish she could shrink into herself. It was bad enough that her parents had sent her away without any indication of how long she would be gone, but to realize that neither of her aunts truly wanted her was almost too much for Fanny to bear.

But, as always, she remained silent.

"I cannot have her stay with us," Naomi said in a stern voice. "With the bishop being so busy these days, he can't have disturbances." She paused and lifted her chin with an air of self-inflated importance. "It *is* baptism, communion, and soon the wedding season, after all."

Martha pursed her lips and contemplated what her older sister had said.

"Besides, you already have children here. *We* do not." The way Naomi emphasized the word *we* made it clear that she was done with the conversation.

Martha, however, did not let it rest. To her credit, she lowered her voice when she said, "That is the very reason,

Schwester, that our niece Fanny should reside with you at your house. My husband's sons live here..."

With a heavy sigh of irritation, Naomi dismissed her concern by interrupting her. "Oh, help, Martha. Not that old argument again. Why! We discussed this. The child is clearly far behind in all aspects. Growing up together she'll be more like a little *schwester* to all. The two boys will be long settled down before she's of age for courting."

Fanny's eyes grew wide at the mention of courting. She was only ten years of age and they were talking courtship?

"It's rather inappropriate, Naomi," Martha whispered in what appeared to be a last-bid attempt at swaying her sister's mind.

"Oh, fiddle-faddle! Even if she does fill out and become pretty in the face, they are less likely to court her if they've always known her as a younger sister." She paused dramatically as if to reflect on her own words. "*Nee*, Martha, having them grow up together is much better."

Martha glanced at Fanny, who hadn't moved from the spot where she stood. "It wouldn't be such a terrible thing anyway, I reckon."

At this comment, as if completely unaware that Fanny remained in the room, never mind privy to the conversation, Naomi waved her hand dismissively at her sister. "Oh, come now, Martha. We shall do no more than raise this child under the righteousness of a proper *g'may*. That, and that alone, shall secure her a proper future with a suitable enough man. That is, after all, our only familial obligation!"

Once again Martha seemed to give in to Naomi, her shoulders sagging just enough to tell Fanny more than she cared to know. Martha's submissive reactions reminded her too much of her mother, while Naomi had more of a take-charge personality. The fierce determination in her eyes indicated that she was not to be trifled with.

Martha, however, was clearly the softer of the two women, perhaps due to a stronger maternal instinct. She knew that she was more partial to the younger aunt already; a fact she confirmed when she returned her attention to Fanny.

"Never mind those particulars now, shall we?" she said in a soft, light voice. "We'll sort all of that out later. Besides, your cousins are looking forward to meeting you!" She gestured toward the table for Fanny to sit before hurrying to the bottom of the staircase in the back of the room and calling out, "Thomas, Elijah! Come down now and meet your cousin. Fetch the girls too, if they are up there."

Within seconds, the sound of footsteps could be heard as Martha's children came tromping down the hardwood stairs. To Fanny, it sounded as if a herd of horses was stampeding at a full gallop towards her and she shrank further into herself, her shoulders rounded forward and her head hanging so that her chin almost pressed against her chest.

"Why, look at her! She's just a wisp of a girl," one of the boys said, only to be shushed by his mother.

"That'll do, Thomas!"

He gave a lopsided grin, one that was full of mischief. Fanny saw it out of the corner of her eye. She knew right away that he was a handful. From the looks of him, he was in his late teens and, most likely, on his *rumschpringe*— the time in an Amish youth's life when they are permitted to explore the world outside of the confines of the church and community. Fanny had only heard stories from some of her church friends about their older siblings going through

19

their own *rumschpringe*. In Colorado most of the youths met once or twice a month for singings. She couldn't help but wonder what the Amish youth in Ohio did during their running-around period.

Two girls who appeared to be only a year or two older than Fanny leaned their heads together, one whispering to the other, who responded by giggling.

"Miriam! Julia!"

They looked at their mother, forcing a look of innocence on their faces.

"You are being unwelcoming to your cousin who traveled quite a distance to come stay with us," Martha said with a heavy sigh of distress. "Whatever will I do with you?"

"Her *kapp* is funny looking," one of the two girls said in a loud voice. "I don't see what's rude about that!"

Before Martha could reply, the second son stepped forward and stretched out his hand toward Fanny. "I'm Elijah, and I'm happy to meet you, Cousin Fanny," he said in an even tone. He appeared to be six years older than Fanny, about sixteen, his shoulders not quite filled out and his face not weathered from seasons working outdoors. Unlike his older brother, Elijah's cheeks were not pot-marked with acne and he had kind eyes, dark chocolate orbs that stared at her with curiosity.

Despite the welcoming gesture, Fanny eyed his hand suspiciously. After the reception from his siblings, she worried that Elijah was up to something. But when he stood there, his hand lingering in the air between them, she finally reached out and shook it. "*Danke*," she whispered.

He leaned forward and, in a voice loud enough for everyone else to hear, whispered, "And I *like* your prayer *kapp*."

His older brother gave him a push with his elbow and the two sisters giggled before running away. Elijah started toward his brother. When Thomas darted away, following his sisters, Fanny suddenly found herself alone in the room with her two aunts. She stared after the Bontrager children. Regardless of what her aunt had said, Fanny knew that she was an unwelcome addition to their household. As she sat at the table, listening to the sounds of laughter that filtered in through the open window, her heart felt heavy and she longed for the comfort of her own home and her own siblings.

———————

From the moment that Fanny entered the small one-room schoolhouse, situated on a fenced-in plot of land adjacent to the Bontragers' farm, she knew that she would not fit in with the other children from Mount Hope, Ohio. Without exception, the other students, about twenty in all, stared at her, some with their mouths hanging agape as they saw her stiff, cup-shaped prayer *kapp* that was so different from their own. Self-consciously Fanny reached up her hand and touched the side of her *kapp* by her ear, which caused two of the younger boys seated in the front of the room to begin giggling.

"Jonah! Benjamin!" the teacher scolded.

Miriam and Julia had deserted Fanny, already taking their assigned seats with nary a look in the direction of their cousin. Clearly she was on her own.

"You must be Fanny Price!" the teacher said, a warm smile on her face as she walked between the desks and down the center aisle to greet her. "Your aunt told me all about you, and I'm so eager to hear about Colorado." She glanced at her other students. "We've been studying the maps to see just how far you have traveled, haven't we, class?"

Fanny looked up at the teacher and decided that, even if the other students thought poorly of her, she had an advocate in the lovely young woman standing before her. "*Danke*, Teacher," she whispered.

Placing her hand on Fanny's shoulder, she guided the newcomer toward the front of the room. "Now, tell me about your schooling so far, then," she said, her words spoken in a singsong way.

Fanny bit her lower lips, embarrassed to admit that she had never attended school. Instead, her mother had taught her what little she knew. "I know how to read and write," Fanny said, her voice so soft that the teacher had to lean forward to hear her. "And some sums. My older *bruder* helped me with that."

"Oh, *ja*, I see."

A few of the children snickered and the teacher frowned in their direction. Then, returning her attention to Fanny, she smiled once again. "We shall have a lot of fun working together to make certain you get caught up to the others," she said. "Now, there is an empty desk in the second row. You can sit there."

With the eyes of the other students upon her, the walk to the empty desk felt as if it took minutes instead of seconds. When she reached the small wooden desk, Fanny sat down and slouched, wishing that she could just blink her eyes and wake up from the horrid dream she was living. Had it really been only two weeks ago that she left Colorado?

Since her arrival in Mount Hope, Fanny spent most of her days alone. Both Thomas and Elijah worked with their father, Timothy, in the fields. Even though it was autumn, there was still a lot of work to be done to harvest the corn and squeeze in one final hay cutting. Miriam and Julia went to school, but thankfully, Martha had insisted that Fanny stay at home awhile to acclimate herself to her new surroundings.

Fanny quickly learned that Martha was extremely easygoing and gentle while Naomi was a force to be reckoned with. Staying home with Martha was a nice way to get to know her aunt, but whenever Fanny heard Naomi walk through the door for her daily visits, she scampered outside and hid in the dairy barn.

Five days after Fanny's arrival, Naomi finally convinced Martha to enroll Fanny in school with no further delay. Martha appeared reluctant, having grown to enjoy Fanny's company. Secretly Fanny had hoped Martha would come to her defense; the idea of attending school, with a strange curriculum and even stranger people, intimidated her. But Martha had finally given into her older sister's demands. Naomi had a way of making others see the logic in her point of view, even if they didn't always agree with it.

Now, as Fanny slid into her seat behind the small wooden desk, she felt even smaller and more insignificant than she had at her arrival at the Bontragers' farm.

The rest of the morning passed slowly, the other students familiar with the daily routine of reading Scripture and singing hymns before focusing their attention on reading, writing, arithmetic, and English. Fanny, however, spent most of the morning looking through a reader that, she soon happened to learn, was for a much younger student. Behind her, Fanny thought she heard one or two children snicker when Teacher handed her the reader, but she suspected that she might have imagined it, being that she felt so self-conscious.

However, during the break for the noon meal, she didn't want to expose herself to any more ridicule. Instead of eating with the other children, she slipped around the side of the schoolhouse and hid away from everyone's line of sight. She felt safer in her own company, especially since the only two people she knew, Miriam and Julia, made no attempt to include her within their own group of friends.

She was still sitting there when a horse and buggy came along the road. The noise of the horse's hooves and the gentle rattle of the buggy wheels caught her attention: it sounded familiar and she took comfort in that. But when the horse stopped near the schoolyard and someone called out her name, she startled.

"Fanny Price!" a young man's voice repeated when she did not respond at first.

It was Elijah. He sat in the open buggy, watching her sit by herself, her back pressed against the side of the outhouse building.

Fanny placed her napkin into her small red and white cooler before scrambling to her feet and hurrying to the fence that separated the schoolyard from the road. She leaned against it but said nothing, not quite knowing why Elijah was at her school in the first place.

"What are you doing, Fanny, sitting all by yourself?" he asked as he deftly held the leather reins in his hands. The horse took a small step forward and the buggy wheels rattled, but Elijah stepped harder on the brake. "You didn't make any friends yet, then?"

She shook her head and looked down at the ground.

"*Ach!*" The word sounded guttural and she thought he might reprimand her. Instead he smiled at her and quickly jumped down from the buggy, pausing only to untie the lead rope that was around the horse's neck and fasten it to a fence post. "Come along now, Fanny," Elijah said and jumped over the fence. "Can't make friends hiding back here, can you now?"

He started walking toward the other side of the building, pausing just once to make certain Fanny followed him. Only then did she do so, her heart pounding with the mixed emotions of both embarrassment and joy that Elijah had taken note of her.

Several of the older boys noticed him right away and stopped playing baseball to run over to him. After all, it had only been two years ago that he too had attended the school.

"You coming to play some ball?" one of the boys asked.

"*Nee*, Amos," Elijah answered. "Too much work for folly."

The boy made a face at him. "You sound like an old farmer during harvest, now!"

Ignoring the gibe, Elijah glanced over their heads and scanned the schoolyard. "You've seen my sisters?" Just as the words left his lips, both of his sisters left the small group of girls near the tall oak tree and hurried over to him.

"Elijah! Is everything all right at home?" Julia asked.

"*Ja, ja.* I was just passing by." He shifted his gaze to Fanny. "Saw Fanny sitting all by herself. Thought I'd check in to make certain you were introducing her to the other girls."

The silence that followed his statement clearly indicated their response. He sighed and scowled.

Fanny glanced at him, noticing not for the first time how striking he was. In many ways, he reminded her of William, who with his protective nature and kind heart always stuck up for her. She did not see his uneven hairline from a poorly given haircut, nor his dirty black trousers with the hole by his pocket. Instead the fact that, once again, he had come to her rescue—something he had done on numerous occasions since her arrival—made him look larger than life in her eyes.

"We were just going to look for her," Miriam said, the flicker of guilt in her eyes giving away her lie.

"I reckon you were," Elijah said, a stern look on his face as he waited for Miriam to take Fanny's hand. With great show Miriam led her over to the small group of girls near the rusted metal swing set.

Fanny paused, pretending to stumble over a rock so that she could look back at Elijah. He continued to watch her as he slowly walked to the fence where he had tied the horse. She saw him smile at her and raise his hand, an encouraging gesture that she remembered long after his horse and buggy had disappeared down the road.

❦ *Chapter 1* ❦

O H, COME NOW, Fanny! Please! Just for today!"
Fanny finished wringing out the last pillowcase
and, with all of the patience she could muster,
stooped to pick up the basket of damp clothing before
walking past Miriam toward the door. She wasn't surprised that Miriam followed her, still begging her for help.
After eight years of living with the Bontragers, Fanny had
learned to expect nothing more from her cousins Miriam
and Julia. When the mood suited they included Fanny in
their conversations and, occasionally, some social outings,
but, as of late, both Miriam and Julia seemed far more
focused on obtaining the attention of men and were using
Fanny to achieve this goal.

"I don't see why you won't do this for me," Miriam
whined. She wrung her hands before her as if to emphasize
her plight. "Just once!"

Fanny smiled to herself as she dropped the wicker
laundry basket on the corner of the porch. She leaned forward and reached for the little brown bag of clothespins
that hung from a nail on the trim. Clearly her cousin's
memory was failing her if she thought the request was a
new one. "That's what you said last time, *ja*?" Fanny was
still smiling, even though her back was to her cousin. "And
the time before that, if I recall."

Stomping her foot, Miriam crossed her arms over her chest. "I would do it for you," she said. "And I have!"

This time Fanny laughed, a soft sound and without any malice. "*Ach*, Miriam!" She pinned the edge of the pillowcase to the clothesline that stretched from the edge of the porch roof and across the yard to the top of the barn. "I reckon you would," she said, and after a short pause, glanced over her shoulder, "only I've never asked!"

"Oh! What would *you* understand, anyway? You haven't been courted yet!"

The disparaging observation might have jarred another but Fanny merely returned her attention to hanging the wash. At twenty-one, Miriam's desperation to marry was well known within the church district. A pretty, young woman with a round face and bright hazel eyes, she had caught the attention of several young men, many of whom had come calling on her. While Miriam never spoke outright regarding her courters, Fanny had once heard the sound of a horse and buggy leaving the farm at four o'clock on a Monday morning. She had thought Miriam would be married soon afterward. Yet, for no apparent reason to Fanny, not one of them had asked Miriam to get married.

Thinking about how Miriam must feel being the only unmarried woman—besides her younger sister, Julia—from her group of friends, Fanny remained silent as she hung another pillowcase on the clothesline. Nearby, two red chickens made some noises, and a rooster strutted along the walkway. Fanny paused to watch it, seeing the rooster lower his wing toward the ground and dance protectively around one of the hens.

That's what Miriam needs, Fanny thought with a sigh. When she reached down for a sheet, she gave in. "Fine, Miriam. I will make that order tonight so you may go early to the gathering!"

Miriam jumped up and down, clapping her hands before she quickly hugged Fanny. "Oh, *danke*! It won't take you long anyway, Fanny! It's just the one basket and you are so good at it!"

As Miriam hurried back into the house, Fanny shook her head, the smile slowly fading from her face. In the past eight years, ever since she had moved to Ohio, she had never become close with either Miriam or Julia. It wasn't that they were really unkind to her. No, they tolerated her well enough. However, there was always so much work to be done at the farm. Thomas and Elijah worked alongside their father, either milking the cows or working in the fields. The responsibilities for tending to the house and garden as well as making and selling the baskets were left to the women.

It sounded like a simple division of labor. But it wasn't.

Unlike in Colorado, the garden at the Bontragers' farm was productive. Unfortunately that also meant it required much more effort to maintain. Between fast-growing weeds and scratching chickens, the garden's needs were as demanding as the chores inside the house. Dirty clothes and linens were washed three times a week—a never-ending chore since clothes were soiled every day with only one or two other outfits to replace them. The men often wore the same clothes two or even three days in a row while the women had enough dresses to rotate.

The other hardship was the food preparation. Since their farm was off a back road and Timothy Bontrager didn't like Martha to shop in town, most of their food was grown on the farm and prepared in their kitchen. Baking bread, making pies, and plucking chickens for the evening meal were not uncommon practices. With so much to do, there wasn't time for socializing with her two cousins. And now that Miriam and Julia were well into their courting years, they did what they could to off-load as many of their chores as possible to Fanny's care.

It wasn't that Fanny minded; no, that wasn't it. She just felt the yearning for real sisterly companionship. She often thought about her own siblings back in Colorado, wondering what they were like and if they ever thought about her. From the few letters that were addressed to her, Fanny doubted it.

"What was that all about, Fanny?"

Startled, Fanny dropped the edge of the sheet and it fell toward the ground. "Oh, help!" She tried to grab the corner, but it landed in the dirt. She sure hoped that Naomi wasn't staring out the kitchen window of the *grossdawdihaus*.

"You scared me, Elijah!" she said as she stilled her heart.

"I did now, did I?" He laughed at her, leaning against the four-by-four post that held up the roof of the small weathered overhang. For a second, he stood there watching her as she wiped away the dirt. "You must have been knee deep in thought then if you didn't see me walking from the barn!"

Fanny put her hand on her hip and tried to scowl at him. But with Elijah she could not even feign irritation.

"Let me guess," he continued. "Miriam is pawning off her chores so that she can go riding with Jeb."

Fanny suppressed a smile. "However did you guess, Elijah Bontrager?"

In response, he made a low, guttural noise, indicative of his disapproval. "You really ought not let her do that, Fanny. She shouldn't shirk her chores. Besides, she'll have *plenty* of time to spend with Jeb after they marry in November." The way he emphasized the word *plenty* made Fanny laugh at last.

"I didn't think anyone knew about her courting Jeb," Fanny remarked. "Do you really think they will marry?"

"Quite certain," he admitted as he brushed some straw from his white shirt, dirty from working in the barn all morning. "I overheard Miriam whispering with *Maem* just the other day."

This was news to Fanny. For several months she knew that Miriam was occasionally riding home from singings with Jeb. In early spring Fanny would sit on the porch, gazing into the sky to look at the different constellations—something Elijah used to do with her when they were both younger—when Jeb's buggy would pull into the driveway to drop off Miriam.

If Fanny hadn't known who the driver was, Miriam certainly made it clear that it was none other than Jeb Riehl. She'd say good-bye to him just loud enough so that the neighbors on the next farm probably heard it too.

Jeb was certainly nice enough, *mayhaps* too nice in Fanny's opinion. The few times when Fanny attended social gatherings or was in his presence, he often seemed as if he tried just a little too hard to fit in. His laughter sounded forced and his willingness to go along with everyone made him appear overly accommodating. Miriam, however, seemed more than pleased to ride home with him after youth sing-ings. Unlike the other courters, Jeb wasn't one to ask to come into the kitchen and sit on the rocking chair, holding Miriam on his lap until the wee hours of the morning, as was the undiscussed—but encouraged—courting custom in their community.

But to marry him? *Such a short courtship and so little in common*, Fanny thought.

As if reading her mind, Elijah sighed. "He's a dull one, this Jeb. And Miriam is so lively. Why, then! He even brings her home directly from the singings. I doubt he's ever taken her for a long ride down back roads or really had a good long talk with her!"

Fanny held the edge of the sheet to her chest and stared at Elijah. Was that what happened during courtships? She wouldn't know and had never thought to ask. And as she stared at Elijah, whose attention was elsewhere and not on her reaction, it dawned on her that Elijah too must have courted a girl or two. How else would he have known?

"You should give him a chance, Elijah," Fanny said at last. "*Mayhaps* he's not as..." She paused, searching for the right word. "...lethargic as he seems."

Turning to look at her, Elijah chuckled at Fanny's care-fully chosen word. "Lethargic? Oh, Fanny, your heart is so pure and kind." He reached over and helped her with the sheet she had begun to pin on the line. "Why, I reckon Miriam would have no interest in your 'lethargic' Jeb were it not for the 150-acre farm he's set to inherit!"

"One hundred sixty acres," Fanny corrected politely, which only made Elijah roll his eyes.

"One hundred sixty acres, indeed! She sure does mention it enough; I should have remembered!" Teasingly he bowed before her to indicate that he stood corrected, a gesture that made her smile. When he straightened up again, he took a deep breath as if filling his lungs with fresh air. "It's a gorgeous day anyway. What has she asked you to do for her, then? Hopefully something outside."

"Weed the garden. And feed the calves." The truth was that Fanny didn't mind taking over Miriam's chores. She much preferred to work with the sun on her back and the comforting feeling of the earth under her bare feet. The sound of singing birds and the occasional neigh from one of the horses in the fields gave her a happy feeling, not that she was generally unhappy. Without those chores to keep her busy, she'd be forced to sit inside with Martha and Naomi, the former often lounging on the sofa and napping while the latter complained about it. *No, thank you,* Fanny thought. Being outside was so much better.

"*Mayhaps* later we can go for a ride then?"

Fanny's eyes lit up and she almost bounced on the balls of her feet. But she was too old to show her enthusiasm in such a childish manner. Instead, she nodded her head as she tried to contain her excitement. "Oh, *ja,* Elijah, that would be *wunderbarr!*" There was nothing she enjoyed more than riding bareback through the fields on Penny, the chestnut, hackney mare that Elijah had bought a few years back. Neither of his sisters liked to ride, and Thomas was far too busy tending to his own affairs—which often included disappearing with his *Englischer* friends. Fanny, however, loved to accompany Elijah; although she wasn't certain whether she favored riding the pony or just being in his company. *Perhaps both*, she thought.

When Elijah purchased Penny, he had presented it to Fanny with great fanfare, although no one else was around. He already had another horse, a thoroughbred that caused his parents to frown when he had purchased it. Such a horse was not very practical on a farm, not fitted for doing field work and certainly too high strung for driving a buggy. However, since neither of their sons had taken the kneeling vow, neither Timothy nor Martha could discipline them: not Elijah for his high-spirited horse nor Thomas for his high-spirited lifestyle.

Fanny suspected that would change when Elijah became a baptized member of the church in October.

"Elijah! Fanny!"

They both turned toward the smaller *grossdawdihaus* that was attached to the larger main house. Naomi stood on the small landing outside the door, her black dress fluttering around her ankles from the breeze. As usual, she wore a fierce expression on her face.

"*Kum vonct nah!*" she called once she knew that she had their attention.

Elijah and Fanny exchanged a look. Ever since she had moved there, Naomi rarely invited anyone to her house, especially the Bontrager children. When the children were younger, she had complained that they tracked in too much dirt, a complaint she continued even now that they were adults and more mindful of their manners. Fanny suspected it was because her aunt didn't like cleaning. Period. But, as usual, Fanny never expressed that opinion, even when Miriam and Julia joked about Naomi's refusal to host guests.

Once Elijah and Fanny entered the kitchen, after repeatedly wiping their feet on the doormat, they were surprised to see the entire Bontrager family gathered there.

"Has something happened?" Elijah asked, concerned by the unexpected look of a family meeting. He directed the question pointedly to his father.

"*Nee*, Elijah," Timothy said, quick to reassure him. "But I have news. News that I wanted to discuss with everyone."

Fanny couldn't help but wonder why they were called to Naomi's house when their own kitchen was much better suited to accommodate everyone. Once again, she kept her thoughts to herself.

"I must leave for a while," he said. With his hands behind his back and his head held high, Fanny suspected that whatever was taking Timothy away from the farm was certainly not a frivolous reason.

Elijah stepped forward, standing before his father. "Something *has* happened," he insisted.

This time, Naomi responded. "Your *daed* needs to go to Pinecraft, Elijah."

For a long moment, no one spoke. Pinecraft, Florida, was where Timothy's father lived with his second wife. Fanny had never met Timothy's father or stepmother, but like a dutiful ward, each year she had signed every birthday, Father's Day, Mother's Day, and Christmas card that the Bontragers sent to them.

Timothy cleared his throat. "There has been…" He hesitated. "…an accident with your *grossdawdi*."

"An accident?" Julia raised her hand to her chest, covering her heart. While overly dramatic, the gesture was not contrived and Miriam put her arm around her younger sister.

Timothy leveled his gaze at his two daughters. "*Grossdawdi* fell and broke his hip."

Fanny noticed that Martha barely reacted, obviously privy to this information prior to the discussion. Because she stood behind Elijah and Thomas, Fanny saw that both of them lowered their heads at the announcement. No one asked the one question that was lingering, unspoken, in the air.

"Is it serious then?" Fanny asked, no longer able to contain herself.

Naomi frowned at her. "*Ach*, Fanny! Such a question!"

Timothy, however, responded with a curt "Serious enough to take me to Florida."

Martha spoke in a more even and reasonable tone. "Fanny, dear, nothing for you to fret over, I'm sure."

Ignoring his wife and sister-in-law, Timothy turned his attention to both of his sons. "There is no telling how long I shall be gone. Thomas shall accompany me. And I am expecting you," he said, leveling his gaze directly at Elijah, "to manage the farm."

"I will, *Daed*," Elijah replied, casting his gaze downward in humility.

If anyone was surprised by Timothy's announcement, no one made a display of it. Fanny's eyes flickered in the direction of her eldest cousin—for, even if only related by marriage, she thought of him in those terms. Thomas seemed to stand a bit taller and his eyes narrowed, just enough to indicate that, while not surprised, he was irritated with his father's announcement. Despite the wild streak that he still harbored, Thomas knew better than to challenge Timothy's words.

Thomas's absence would not make much difference for Elijah. The oldest Bontrager son tended to wander away and sometimes not come home until the wee hours of the morning. He ran with a group of friends that caused a great deal of angst to his father. Fanny suspected Thomas was to go along so that Timothy could try to convince him to settle down into a calmer, more peaceful way of life, and to finally join the church as Elijah was that autumn.

Thomas's departure meant that Elijah was responsible for completing both his and his brother's chores. Timothy couldn't leave Martha in charge, her inability to exert herself far too apparent, although Fanny wasn't certain if the reason for that was from her ongoing summer cold or from years of living in Timothy's overbearing presence.

"And see to it the morning and evening prayers are conducted," Timothy added, a stern expression upon his face, "as well as ensuring everyone attends worship service."

Fanny wondered why such a request needed to be voiced. After all, of the four children, Elijah had always been the most righteous and studious of Scripture. Clearly, with Timothy leaving and Thomas accompanying him, Elijah was the only man left to manage more than just the physical labor; he should preside over the fulfillment of doctrinal duties too.

However, when Fanny saw the humble slump of Elijah's shoulders, she realized that the fact that Timothy made a point of voicing the appointment was an unspoken—and rare—compliment to his son.

If so, no one could be happier than Fanny. The compliment was well deserved.

She loved listening to Elijah read the Bible at night, his voice deep and smooth, unlike Bishop Yoder, who spoke in a high-pitched monotonous tone. Besides, even if Thomas had remained at home, his father surely would not have bequeathed these responsibilities to him. Thomas hadn't attended a worship service in almost two months and had made no indication of wanting to take his kneeling vow anytime soon. It was a family disappointment that no one spoke about, but the scowl on Timothy's face every other Sunday said more than words ever could express.

Timothy took a deep breath, pacing before the children and reaching up to tug at his long, wiry, white beard. "Naomi has volunteered to oversee the farm, ensuring that everything runs smoothly," he said, "and also to help your *maem*."

The slightest smile, triumphant in nature, crossed Naomi's lips, while Martha expressed no visible reaction—whether favorable or unfavorable. Instead, she stood there, her hands clasped before her stout waistline and her eyes gazing out the window behind her husband's shoulder. The forced smile on her face had neither grown nor shrunk with any of Timothy's words. To Fanny, her aunt looked distracted and uninterested in the conversation.

"As I said, I have no idea how long I shall be gone," Timothy repeated. "I expect everyone to do their part to help Elijah and obey Naomi's requests. During my absence, her word is as good as mine."

Now Fanny understood the reason behind calling the meeting in Naomi's house. With Timothy leaving to tend to his father, he wanted to establish the line of authority during his absence.

Ever since Naomi's husband passed away five years ago, she had taken on a new role within the household. The bishop's unexpected death—at the dinner table no less— had created an interesting shift in the family dynamics. Unlike most women, Naomi used her husband's death in much the same way as she had used his life: to achieve her own superiority over others.

Immediately after his death and burial, Naomi sold their little house and moved into the *grossdawdihaus* on the Bontragers' farm. She refused to transform into a quiet widow, accepting visitors on Saturday and Sunday evenings from the comfort of her rocking chair and spending the rest of her time knitting blankets to sell to tourists. Instead, she continued to rule over the household. And while Naomi could no longer use her now-deceased husband as the backup for her decisions, she certainly referred to his former role within the church to substantiate *her* authority.

Fanny wasn't certain which was worse.

And, for some unknown reason, Timothy tended to defer to Naomi's opinions more than anyone else's. Naomi's jurisdiction was not just limited to the house, either. She often shared her opinion with Timothy over the basket-weaving business as well as the crop rotation in the fields.

The only lesson that Fanny took away from this shift in household power was that Naomi's power consisted more in the overbearing conviction of her tone than in the wisdom of her actual opinions.

"You will, most likely, have to help with the autumn harvest," he said, leveling a stern look at his two daughters.

"The harvest? You'll be gone *that* long? But what about my wedding?" Miriam stared first at her father and then her mother. If Elijah hadn't forewarned her, Fanny would have been more startled. Clearly Jeb and Miriam had indeed finalized their plans to wed in November. Normally such plans were not openly discussed until closer to the actual wedding.

Timothy held up his hand, an indication that she had no need to worry. "Please, Miriam. Harvest is well before wedding season. I'm certain there will be no delays with your marriage to Jeb."

Fanny glanced at Timothy too aware of the irritation in his voice. With Miriam, it was always about herself. Even now, with her grandfather injured in Florida, Miriam spoke and thought of one thing and one thing only: Miriam.

"Julia," Timothy said, pausing before her. She looked up, her large chocolate brown eyes similar to Miriam's but betraying less selfishness. Timothy made a noise deep in his throat as if clearing it. "Your *aendi* will approve any social engagements for you," he said. Fanny glanced at Martha, who bore no reaction to this responsibility being assigned to her older sister, despite Julia being her own daughter. Instead, she turned her head and coughed into her hand.

Julia bent her head in acknowledgment of her father's instruction.

"As for Fanny..." Timothy paused. *"Ach,* where is she now?"

"Here," she said in a small voice, stepping forward so that she was not so hidden from his line of sight.

He glanced over the top of his glasses at her as if surprised to see her standing there at all. *"Ja,* there you are indeed, Fanny." Timothy seemed to study her through narrowed eyes as if noticing her for the first time since she had entered the room.

Fanny brightened at being addressed at all.

He didn't seem to notice. "Your *aendi* Martha's weak constitution requires you to stay with her." He cleared his throat and tugged at his beard. "No market, no visiting. I don't want her alone, is that understood?"

Fanny couldn't help but look over at Martha. She had noticed Martha was more lethargic than usual, but she wasn't certain what Timothy meant by a *weak constitution*. Was Martha ill? Had something happened that no one had shared with her? The color drained from Fanny's cheeks. If anything happened to Martha, she would only have Elijah to protect her from Naomi's sharp tongue and criticism. Surely with Miriam to wed in November, Julia would soon follow. And with Elijah committed to taking his kneeling vow in early October, in all likelihood he would marry as well, although Fanny did not know whether he was currently courting anyone.

"I understand," she replied softly.

Timothy started to walk away but quickly changed his mind. "*Ach*, I almost forgot. Your *bruder*. William, *ja*?"

At the mention of her brother, Fanny immediately raised her head and stared at Timothy. While she wrote to her brother every week, she had not seen him, or any member of her immediate family, since her departure from Colorado eight years ago. "My *bruder*?" she asked, her voice full of eagerness. She longed to hear anything about her brother since his letters came less frequently and certainly not as regularly as she sent hers.

"I understand he is to visit the area and will stop by in a few weeks. Should I not be here, you have my permission to welcome him at our farm. I daresay that I had hoped he would see his sister much changed after so many years of righteous living in our household," he went on, his eyes giving her one last critical study, "but I'm afraid he will not."

The excitement faded from Fanny's face and she felt her shoulders sag under the weight of Timothy's words. If he noticed the crestfallen expression that covered her face, he gave no indication. She blinked her eyes rapidly, feeling the all-too-familiar sting of reproach from the closest thing she had to a father. She'd save the crying for later when she would have the luxury of retreating to the privacy of her own, small bedroom.

From the corner of her eye, she noticed that Elijah shifted his weight from one foot to another as if he felt uncomfortable with his father's words. While Elijah often jumped to Fanny's defense when faced with injustices inflicted by his sisters, he had never stood up to his father. Fanny did not think less of him for that; in fact, she *would* have thought less of him if he did, since honoring thy father and mother was one of God's commandments.

She did not profess to understand why Timothy remained so critical of her. Instead, she bottled up her emotions and sought wisdom in the one book that held all the answers: the Bible.

While she never could find out what she had done—or continued to do—that offended him so, the prospect of a respite from his overbearing presence was enough to help her shake off the sting of his comments.

❧ *Chapter 2* ❧

THE RAIN ALWAYS made Fanny feel invisible.

On days when the sky was gray and little puddles formed in the driveway, no one lingered outside. Instead all of the Bontrager women would hurry through their outdoor chores—or in the case of Miriam, complain of aches to avoid them—so that they could stay inside the warm kitchen. On these days no one paid any attention to Fanny, more content talking with each other, especially when Naomi joined them, complaining that the noise of rain hitting against the windows gave her a headache.

With the main room so full of people, Fanny could sit in the wooden rocking chair on the sitting porch. A nearby bookshelf, filled with devotionals and other Timothy-approved reading material, blocked Fanny from the kitchen. As she was hidden in plain sight, no one thought to look for her, at least not while they hovered around the kitchen table or sat near the kerosene heater while they crocheted blankets or worked on making baskets.

Fanny preferred to make baskets. There was something about the gentle weaving of the willow branches that relaxed her. She enjoyed the feeling of the sticks as she wove them around the spokes, the slightly concave base forming before she focused on weaving the sides. Her focus on basket making did not go unnoticed by the others, and rather than complain, the other young women often tried to persuade her to help them make their quota.

"Looks like it might be clearing up," Martha said as she peered out the window. "How fortunate!"

Naomi followed her sister's gaze. "Hadn't read that it was going to break! Those weather people! They don't know a forecast from a rotten tomato!" She pressed her lips together, making a firm line on her face. For a few seconds, she focused on her crocheting, her fingers moving so quickly that even Fanny couldn't figure out what pattern Naomi was making. "If that sun comes out," Naomi said, not even looking up, "you best be heading over to the Yoders."

The statement, though spoken to no one by name, was clearly directed at Fanny.

One of the local Amish stores carried the baskets made by the Bontragers, especially the small baskets that Fanny often made. Apparently the tourists purchased them for holding their pens or loose mail, or so Fanny was told by Barbara Yoder, the elderly woman who ran the store.

So once a week Fanny would find time to go into town, a box filled with the baskets resting in the rusty basket on the front of her bicycle. Even though town was three miles away, some of it requiring her to go both up and down hills, the ride was never long enough. An occasional buggy would pass by, the driver lifting his or her hand to acknowledge Fanny. She would return the gesture with a solemn nod of her head, unless she knew the person, in which case she might smile.

For Fanny, the long journey to town was a welcomed break.

"Wait until the rain stops, Fanny," Martha added, glancing up from her work and giving her a soft smile. "No need for you to get sick."

"No danger of that," Fanny responded. "But I'll wait until there is a break in the weather."

"*Mayhaps* you could stop at the store, then," Martha added. "I could use some more sugar and tea."

"Honey," Naomi added. "We're all out of honey. And with your cough, Martha, you can never have enough honey." She turned toward Fanny. "And make sure it's local and not one of those *Englische* brands! Lord knows what they put in their honey."

Fanny nodded but did not reply. Naomi hadn't needed to remind her about the family's policy regarding food: fresh, local, and organic. It was a rule that had been drilled into Fanny's head each and every time she was sent to the store.

By the time the clouds began to break up and a hint of sun started to peek through, it was almost two in the afternoon. Fanny grabbed the rusty bicycle from the shed, noticing that the buggy was already gone. She hadn't heard Elijah was going somewhere today; he usually mentioned it at breakfast or, at least, the noon meal. As she pedaled down the short driveway, she wondered where he might have gone on a Wednesday afternoon.

Only a week had passed since Timothy and Thomas had left for Florida. No letters had arrived yet, although Fanny suspected that neither her uncle nor his eldest son were much in the way of letter writers. With Timothy gone from the farm, Fanny had a newfound freedom, despite his forbidding her to leave Martha's side if no one else was around. His demand for his wife to have constant companionship was not an onerous one. Out of the entire Bontrager family, Martha was the kindest, second only to Elijah.

During the past few months, when an early summer allergy had turned into a lingering sinus infection, Martha had come to depend on Fanny. Fanny didn't resent the constant neediness of her aunt. If nothing else, Martha vocalized her appreciation for the things Fanny did.

"Ach, Fanny Price!"

No sooner had Fanny leaned her bicycle against the side of the Yoders' store than Addie called out to her from behind the front counter. Through the open doorway Fanny could see the older woman waving at her.

Fanny smiled back as she entered the store.

"Where've you been of late?" Addie wiped her hands on her black apron. A stout woman with thinning white hair, Addie Hostetler was kind and outgoing, her large, wide smile a frequent gift that she bestowed on Fanny. While she attended a different church district from the Bontrager family, Addie knew most of the people from the surrounding communities, and she always managed to make every person who entered her store feel as if she had been expecting them. Now, she reached for the box that Fanny carried and said in a light tone, "Thought you might have gone off traveling with Timothy!"

"Oh, *nee*! Not me," she said quickly.

Addie laughed. "I'm just teasing you, Fanny. You take things too seriously." Peering into the box, Addie nodded her head approvingly. "Girl! This is right *gut*. Just before the weekend!" She looked up at Fanny. "Why, no sooner do I stock my shelves than your goods just disappear."

Fanny lowered her eyes.

"So modest!" Addie clucked her tongue and set the box on the counter. "And we all know that the nice even weave of these baskets comes from your hand. I've been around long enough! I can certainly spot the difference between your baskets and the other Bontragers!"

"Oh, I don't think so," Fanny retorted, trying to deflect Addie's compliments. Baskets were baskets, but it was true that Fanny took special care when making them and, on occasion, remade the ones that Miriam threw together without any regard for quality. Still, Fanny didn't want Addie to think she was proud. "Mine are no better than anyone else's, I'm sure."

But the older woman seemed intent on praising her. With a nudge at Fanny's arm, Addie gave a long, slow wink as she said, "I'm almost seventy years old, Fanny. I know a superior weave when I see one, even if I need my glasses to double check!"

The back door opened and Addie's grandson, Benjamin, walked in, his black pants covered with a fine dust, most likely from stocking the back shelves. Like everyone else in Mount Hope, Benjamin was related to most of the other Amish families, and the bishop was his uncle on his father's side. Yet with his straight blond hair cut haphazardly over his ears, he looked like a younger version of his maternal grandmother.

"Is that Fanny?" He grinned when he saw her and set down a book that he had been carrying before he walked across the room to greet her.

Through his friendship with Elijah, Benjamin had always been kind to Fanny, almost like another big brother. Lately, however, when he stopped by the Bontragers' farm, he lingered in the kitchen visiting with the women, and Fanny suspected that he had eyes for Julia.

"What brings you over this way, Fanny Price?" Benjamin asked.

She gestured toward the box filled with basket, but Addie answered for her. "Benji! As if you need to ask! You know Fanny brings us baskets each week!"

Benjamin peeked into the box. "Oh, *gut*. I needed to restock those. The tourists buy them right away, you know!"

Fanny couldn't hide her embarrassed smile as Addie turned and give her an I-told-you-so look.

The large wall clock chimed and Fanny glanced up at it. "Oh, help! I best get going. Need to stop at the food store on my way back."

"*Ach*, that reminds me!" Addie turned to Benjamin. "Go fetch me some of that applesauce we canned weekend last, Benji! Send some home with Fanny."

Fanny raised her hand, politely holding it up as if to stop Addie from saying anything else. Her generosity was notorious in the church district, but Fanny didn't want to trouble the kind-hearted woman. "*Nee*, Addie, but *danke*. I only have the bicycle with the small basket."

But Addie would not hear of an objection. "Nonsense!" In a flash, she hurried around Benjamin, not waiting for him to fetch the applesauce.

Alone with Fanny, Benjamin scratched at the bridge of his nose and shrugged his shoulder. "She's a piece of work, ain't so?"

"For sure and certain," Fanny replied.

Benjamin leaned against the counter and hooked his thumbs under his suspender straps. "Heard that Timothy went to Pinecraft. Thomas go with him?"

Fanny nodded her head. "*Ja*, he did. Elijah's in charge of the farming now."

Benjamin pressed his lips together. "That's a lot. You let him know I could help in the early mornings. Not much to do here at the store before eight o'clock."

She promised that she would. She suspected his offer had just as much to do with being a good neighbor as it was to share a cup of coffee in the morning so that he could spend more time in Julia's presence. Fanny wondered if Julia knew about his interest in her. If she did, she made no indication. Unlike Miriam, who liked to flaunt her suitors, Julia took a subtler approach to courting, one that left Fanny guessing.

As Addie returned, her arms laden with a tall, rectangular box, Benjamin hurried over to help her. From the jiggling noise of glass that came from within the box, it was clearly filled with jars of applesauce.

"Oh, Addie!" Fanny knew that she couldn't accept such generosity. Clearly Addie had put a lot of work into making the applesauce and not compensating her for her efforts wasn't fair. "That's too much!"

But Addie insisted.

"I won't take so much for my work then," Fanny finally said as she took the box from Addie. "That's only fair."

Addie squinted one eye and looked at Fanny. "As I said already, nonsense. What on earth would I do with all that applesauce?"

Peeking into the box, Fanny quickly calculated that it contained at least six jars. "You could sell them, for starters."

At this comment, both Addie and Benjamin laughed. Their store shelves were already lined with so many canned goods that one box of applesauce would not make a difference.

"Now, off with you, girl. Your *aendi* will be wondering 'bout you if you linger much longer," Addie said, guiding Fanny to the door so that she could open it for her. "And I put some new linen at the bottom of the box...need my supply replenished as soon as you get 'round to it."

Benjamin walked outside with her. He helped her by holding the bicycle steady while she placed the box into the basket. "You heard about the Yoders then?"

Ah, Fanny thought. *That explains his help.* She shook her head, knowing full well that whatever came next from Benjamin's mouth certainly had to do with someone's health or gossip.

The box secured in the basket, Fanny took ahold of the handlebars while Benjamin shared his news. "Seems like my uncle has some visitors for a while."

"Oh, *ja?*"

He nodded his head. "His wife's younger sister and brother, Henry and Mary Coblentz. Visiting from Lancaster."

With the sun suddenly brightening, Fanny squinted as she looked at Benjamin. She wasn't certain why he was sharing this new with her. "That's *gut*" was all she managed to say.

"Heard tell that they might be moving out here," he continued. "*Mayhaps* looking for someone to court." He gave her a look that she couldn't interpret as he said, "You be sure to let Elijah know."

Startled, Fanny stared at him, her mouth agape. "Now why would I do that, Ben?" She had never been prone to gossip, and while she would not necessarily classify this news as earth-shattering or even sinful, the fact that family was visiting Bishop Yoder was of no particular significance, at least as far as Fanny could tell. As far as Benjamin's comment that the two visitors might be looking for spouses— well, *that* was none of her business, that was for sure and certain.

With a sheepish smile, Benjamin shrugged his shoulders as he slipped his hands into the front pockets of his black pants. "*Ja, vell,* they'll be at the Sunday service anyway. Reckon he'll find out then." He paused. "Would be right *gut* to invite them to the singing, don't you think?"

"I imagine they'll go, whether or not Elijah or you invite them," Fanny replied, still wondering what she was missing in this unusual conversation. Besides, she didn't usually attend the singings so she wasn't concerned with who attended or not. "But I'll be sure to pass along the message that visitors are coming."

Benjamin gave her a quick grin and stepped back from the bicycle. She tried not to frown at his strange behavior as she rode out of the small parking lot. Since long before she arrived, Benjamin had been a good friend to Elijah and Thomas. His father and Timothy were distant cousins, as were most people in that area of Holmes County—or so it seemed.

During her first years at the Bontragers, there had been more than one afternoon when the three young men were caught racing their horse and buggies down the long dirt road behind the farm. Timothy scowled and struggled to hold his tongue. They were, after all, on *rumschpringe*. But after the third time he caught them, Naomi reported it to her husband, who preached about the matter at the next Sunday service. The buggy races miraculously stopped on that dirt road, although Fanny later learned that they had simply relocated them to another, more remote, location.

Through the Amish grapevine everyone knew, somehow, that these races were still going on and probably would never stop. After all, *rumschpringe* or not, the races were a young man's favorite way of expressing his independence and his ability to excel amongst his peers. It was not even who would *win* the race. Pride over winning would be construed as a violation of the *Ordnung*, the unwritten code of behavior that every church member was bound to obey.

No, it was definitely something else. Perhaps the races were a rite of passage—a way to prove one had reached manhood and was now able to make his own decisions.

Besides, what could be more exhilarating than the swooshing of the wind on the driver's face, the intense rattling of the buggy's wheels over the hard ground, the obedient and submissive eagerness of an animal that was more than happy to show his master how well it could perform under his prompting! Very few young men in the community were immune to the appeal. The question was not who would partake in the races but when. If the races were kept a secret, they had become a very conspicuous one.

In the past year, however, the only time Fanny saw Benjamin was at the worship service or at the store. She didn't think that Elijah spent much time with him at all. Of course, Fanny knew little of what young men did to socialize. Miriam and Julia were often busy with their friends at quilting parties or canning bees. Sometimes they even had cookie frolics to attend, baking and donating hundreds of cookies to charities. That too had become something of an opportunity for the women to express themselves: their own version of the buggy race. Who would bake the most? Which cookies were more visually appealing or sweeter to the tongue? Which batch would come out as the most fragrant and delectable? The result was a mountain of sugar drop cookies, thimble cookies, molasses nut cookies, ginger cookies, and chocolate chip cookies—all testimonials to the skills and proficiency of their makers. But before adding cookies to the pile, it was common practice for each woman to display her own creations just in front of her at the kitchen table for everyone to catch sight of.

Recently Fanny was invited more and more to these events, but she always declined. She felt uncomfortable around the young women who talked with such ease to each other. It was easier for Fanny to avoid the gatherings, using the excuse that Martha needed her at home.

Thankfully neither Miriam nor Julia ever pressed her to attend.

She was still bicycling toward the farm, so engulfed in her thoughts that she didn't hear the sound of an approaching horse and buggy until it was pulling past her.

"Want a ride?"

Fanny almost swerved off the road and into the ditch as her cousin overtook her.

"Elijah!" She pressed her hand to her chest and tried to slow down her breath. "You keep scaring me!" she said, shaking her head at him. "I should be used to it, I reckon, after all of these years!"

He laughed as he brought the horse to a standstill and waited for her to move the bicycle closer to the carriage.

"Where you coming from, Fanny?"

Fanny glanced over her shoulder, even though the Yoders' store was down the road and around the bend. "On my way to Hostetler's store for some sugar and such. I promised Naomi I'd go there after I dropped some baskets off at Addie's store."

"Oh, *ja*?"

She nodded. "I ran into Benjamin at the store."

Elijah smiled to himself. "He was working there, was he? Haven't seen him in a while. What's he up to? Did he say?"

"Just helping his *grossmammi*, from the looks of it." She paused, shifting her weight on her feet as she balanced the bicycle beneath her. "Gave me a message for you. Says you should know that the Yoders have visitors. Bishop Yoder," she clarified. "His wife's family. Her *schwester* and *bruder* from Pennsylvania."

But there was a change in Elijah's eyes; a glazed-over look appeared. "The Coblentzes, eh?" He didn't wait for her to answer before he nodded his head.

"They should be going to the singing after church service." There, she thought. I did as Benjamin requested. "You know them then?"

He nodded. "Met them a long time ago, before you came here. When the bishop got married again, I think." He paused before adding, "He wasn't the bishop then."

"I didn't know she had younger siblings." Of course, she was much younger than the bishop, his first wife having passed away from cancer. Like most widowers with children, he remarried within a few months. After all, children needed to have a mother and a man needed to have a wife. And when they had married, he hadn't been the bishop, just a preacher. It was only after Naomi's husband died that a new bishop had been selected. As luck had it—or misfortune, as some thought—the lot fell to Bishop Yoder when he selected the *Ausbund* with the little white piece of paper in it.

Being selected as the new bishop for his *g'may* was not a small affair. The candidates for bishop were nominated by the people, but the ultimate selection was of God's choosing. Whoever selected the marked hymnal would have to put aside the greater part of his obligations to his own family and replace these with the even higher calling of the obligations to his *g'may*. He would have to provide comfort, spiritual counsel, and practical guidance to the members of his church district. He would have to make decisions that would impact people's lives. Some popular ones and some, less popular. He would have to prove worthy of the responsibilities bestowed unto him by the Creator Himself. This was a lifetime commitment that could not be broken. It was no small matter to have been chosen. Some feared it secretly. Others more openly. All were humbled by it. At least on the day that they discovered that slip of paper between the pages of the book.

"It'll be nice to meet new people," Fanny said, although she wasn't certain she meant it. She always shied away from strangers, especially the *Englischers* that came to their farm to look at the handmade baskets.

But Elijah wasn't paying attention. He seemed to have wandered away mentally, his mind now elsewhere. And there was a look in his eyes that bothered Fanny.

"Everything all right?" she asked.

He blinked and shook the daydream from his mind. "Oh, *ja*, for sure. Just thinking, that's all." He noticed the large box in her bicycle's basket. "Let me take that for you, Fanny." In one swift motion, he reached down to grab the top of the box, lifting it as if it weighed nothing. "Applesauce, eh? That Addie! She's something else." Settling the box onto the floor of the carriage, he made certain it wouldn't jiggle too much by wrapping the edge of a dirty blanket around it. "Early for making applesauce, *ja*? Well, *Maem* will be pleased anyway."

Fanny nodded. They usually waited until autumn to make applesauce, but with the extra early spring and unusually fine summer, many of the apple orchards had produced an early crop. With Martha feeling so tired and weak, her cough often keeping her awake well into the night, she didn't seem motivated to do much of anything anymore. It made Fanny wonder if they would make any applesauce this autumn.

Elijah held up the leather reins and motioned toward the road. "Alright then, Fanny. See you at home." He released the foot brake and, with a quick clicking of his tongue, slapped the reins onto the horse's back. The open buggy lurched forward, the wheels grinding and the horse's hooves beating against the macadam. He lifted his hand over his head, not looking back as he drove the horse down the road and toward the family farm.

For a long moment Fanny stared after him until the buggy disappeared around the bend. Behind her, she heard an approaching car and waited until it passed her. Then, balancing herself on the bicycle, she began to pedal. When she turned onto the road that led to the health food store, she was still wondering about Elijah's reaction to the news about the upcoming visit by the Coblentz siblings.

Despite her curiosity, she knew time would eventually reveal the answer. With Sunday just a few days away, she wouldn't have long to wait to meet the newcomers and, hopefully, find out what appeared to be so distracting to Elijah.

❦ *Chapter 3* ❦

O H, HELP!" MIRIAM whispered far too loudly as she reached out to touch Julia's arm.

Fanny couldn't help but look up and see Miriam stare at the back door of the house where the members of the *g'may* gathered for worship. The older women, all dressed in black dresses, stood nearby, softly talking before the church leaders and men entered the room, the signal that worship was about to start.

Most families arrived early for the service, using that time to catch up on the latest news or, in the case of the young women, gossip. While Fanny wasn't certain, she suspected that outside in the barn the young men were engaged in the same. After all, it was one of the few times that the church district gathered together, presenting the perfect opportunity for socializing before the three-hour-long service began.

Fanny stood just beyond her two cousins and their friends, not quite a part of their inner circle, but not entirely removed from it either. She was, after all, a baptized member of their Amish church and as such she was part of the church district, even though her family remained in Colorado. However, Fanny much preferred to stay on the periphery, not wanting to get wrapped up in the drama that sometimes accompanied the female clique that Miriam seemed to lead.

"What's wrong, Miriam?" one of the young women asked.

"Who is *that*?" At Miriam's overly exaggerated question, five heads wearing stiff black prayer *kapps* turned simultaneously to look in the direction of Miriam's gaze.

On the other side of the room, just outside the open doors, a young man and woman were standing. The young man, probably no more than twenty-five, seemed to look around the room as if inspecting the people. A soft smile played on his lips. With dark curly hair, he was quite the handsome man, that was for sure and certain. His clean-shaven face with sharply defined cheekbones and almond-shaped eyes seemed to have caught the attention of several unmarried Amish women. And he clearly knew it.

By his side, the woman waited for him to guide her to the group of women. She was as equally beautiful as he was handsome, her dark hair framing her heart-shaped face and her pretty heart-shaped prayer cap accentuating her facial features. Her dress was a bright pink, a variation of the standard colors and one that wasn't normally worn in Holmes County. It made Fanny's dress look dowdy and pale in comparison. Fanny glanced around and noticed that she was not the only person watching the woman and she knew that, if the men were admiring her beauty, the women were admiring her fabric.

As for Fanny, she could only wonder at the gleam in the woman's eye. She seemed to tilt her chin just a little too high, something that gave her somewhat of a haughty look. A look that made Fanny uncertain if she would like this newcomer.

"Yes, who are they?" Julia echoed, clearly as taken with the young man as Miriam was.

Remembering her discussion with Elijah, Fanny suspected that she knew exactly who they were. What surprised her, however, was that her cousins did not. While it wasn't like Elijah to gossip, she had thought he would have shared her news from the other day with the rest of the family. From both Miriam and Julia's remarks, Fanny realized he hadn't. And she couldn't imagine why.

"They're the Coblentzes," said Barbara, one of Miriam and Julia's friends who stood in the circle of young women. Her eyes brightened, clearly elated to provide an answer to the question on everyone's mind. "They're staying with Bishop Yoder."

Miriam raised her eyebrows. "Whatever for, then?"

"I heard he's their *onkle*," another woman responded.

"*Nee*," Barbara countered. "Bishop is their brother-in-law."

It was Julia's turn to express her incredulity. "I hadn't realized the bishop's *fraa* had siblings. They're awfully young, don't you think?"

"She's their half-sister." Barbara lowered her voice. "We met them when the bishop remarried. Don't you remember?" Neither sister did, as a matter of fact. "Anyway, they're from Lancaster County. Gordonville, I reckon."

"Lancaster County?" Miriam stared at the two newcomers with even more interest. "I've never heard of Gordonville."

Fanny, however, perked up. Not only was Lancaster County where her brother, William, had been sent to live with her father's older brother Aaron, but Gordonville was also the very town!

"That's a long way to visit."

"Five hours or so, I reckon," Barbara said.

"It's a wonder that they are here!" Miriam straightened her shoulders and reached up her hand to ensure her hair was neatly tucked under her *kapp*. "What could possibly be of interest to them in Mount Hope?"

The group of young women continued to whisper back and forth, speculating why the brother and sister were visiting their half-sister in a town so far away from their home.

Fanny did not join the discussion, not wanting to be a part of their gossip, but she couldn't deny that she was more than curious about the newcomers, at least as far as Elijah was concerned. If Elijah was acquainted with the Coblentz siblings, why weren't Miriam and Julia? But it wasn't a question that she felt comfortable asking, just as she didn't want to contribute to their circle of hearsay and speculation.

Fanny never could quite find her voice around Miriam and Julia's group of friends. It wasn't that they were unkind; truly the opposite was true. However, Fanny never felt that she was considered an equal in their eyes. Over the years Fanny never had been very talkative with any of them, preferring to remain in observant silence rather than participate in inconsequential conversation. She found their discussions irrelevant, anyway—talking about who might be courting, who might be getting married, and who was misbehaving.

One of their favorite discussions—and the one that most irritated Fanny—was whispering about the latest person to be reprimanded by the bishop. Whether it was a young man caught keeping a cell phone under the seat of his buggy or a young woman found with makeup in her bedroom, the young women loved to chatter amongst each other about the details. The worse the infraction, the more they talked, especially Miriam, who always acted horrified—a fact that amused Fanny, since gossip was also a sin.

But Fanny knew better than to laugh or say anything that might possibly draw attention away from Miriam.

Her thoughts were interrupted when a hush fell over the gathering, and Fanny knew that the bishop and preachers had entered the house, a signal that the service was about to begin. One by one, the bishop and his preachers greeted each of the women, shaking their hands and saying "Good morning" before they continued down the line. Miriam and her friends quickly found their place at the end of where the older women were already waiting. Worship could not begin unless everyone greeted each other. Fanny quietly stood at the very spot, knowing that, as usual, the greeting would be quick and usually without the bishop even looking at her. His attention, undoubtedly, was on the service, not the greetings.

After the church leaders took their seats, the women found theirs before the men would enter the room.

Since the worshippers were separated by gender and sat in order of their age, Fanny sat on the hard bench between Katie Troyer and Anna Mast, the former two months older than Fanny and the latter just one week younger. Despite her feeling shy around nonfamily members—something that she just couldn't seem to overcome, no matter how much Elijah tried to coax her out of it—she sometimes enjoyed the three-hour respite from Miriam and Julia's company.

In fact, most Sundays when Elijah, Miriam, and Julia went to the evening youth singings, Fanny remained at home. It wasn't that she didn't *want* to go with them; it was merely that she *preferred* to stay by herself. Besides, when everyone was home and she tried to find time to write her correspondence or to read the Bible, Naomi would interrupt her. Since Naomi's husband had been the bishop, she had felt qualified to offer her own interpretation of a particular passage. Without complaint, Fanny would quietly shut the Bible so that she could appear respectful as Naomi continued her long-winded discourse.

But when Elijah, Miriam, and Julia went to the youth gatherings, Martha often retired early—Fanny was always on hand to willingly assist her aunt, who seemed to grow weaker and less capable with each passing day. With Martha in bed, Naomi had no reason to come over from the *grossdawdihaus* unless she was visiting with Timothy. Fortunately he too often retired early for a long night's sleep, especially since he awoke early for the morning milking.

Now today in church Fanny sat between Katie and Anna, listening to Bishop Yoder as he gave the first sermon. As he preached about the sins of worldliness, Fanny felt a bit of relief. With Timothy having left for Pinecraft, there would be no one to scowl at conversational chatter or scold anyone who laughed while he read Scripture before supper.

She felt someone nudge her arm. Startled from her thoughts, Fanny refocused her attention on the worship service and realized that the congregation had begun to sing the second hymn, *Das Loblied*. Without referencing the black chunky hymn book in her hands, she let her voice join the other members as they sang the hymn of praise to God:

> Oh God, Father, we praise thee
>   And thy kindness glorify.
> Which though, oh Lord, so mercifully
>   To us anew has shown.
> And hast us, Lord, together led
>   Us to admonish through thy word,
> Give us grace to this.

The short hymn usually took over twenty minutes to sing, each syllable of every word sung in harmony to its own tune—a tune that had been passed down from generation to generation. The result was a chant-like song, so reminiscent of the stories that Fanny read in the *Martyrs Mirror*, a book that chronicled the persecution of the Anabaptists from the early 1500s to the late 1600s. The same songs had been sung back then, a lifting of voices to sing the glory of God during their time of worship.

As the congregation sang the last line, Fanny glanced across the heads of the older women seated before her and scanned the faces of the men who sat on the opposite side of the room. She noticed Elijah way in the back of the room, and for just those last few minutes, she watched him as he sang. She almost imagined that she heard his voice over all of the other men singing. His attention was focused on the place in the front of the room where Bishop Yoder had stood preaching just twenty minutes earlier.

Then, as they sang the last word, breaking it down into syllables, she saw something that surprised her: Elijah was glancing toward the women. She started to smile, knowing that he would catch her gaze, and even though his face would remain serious, his eyes would sparkle when he saw her.

They usually did. He was, after all, her best friend and greatest champion.

Over the years, since she had arrived at the Bontragers, Fanny had become quite adept at reading faces. Perhaps because of her inherent shyness and frugality with words. Perhaps because of her own genetic makeup. Among some of the more conservative Amish families, vocal outbursts and conversations involving anything beyond simple community matters or the impact of the weather on a family's God-given stewardship of their plot of land were still considered superfluous and inappropriate. So reading faces had become second nature to her, a skill stemming from the force of habit.

Today Elijah's eyes sparkled, but Fanny quickly realized that they sparkled at someone else, for he was not looking at her. Instead, his gaze fell upon someone else, a someone who was seated on a bench in the row before Fanny's and whose prayer *kapp* was heart shaped. Fanny's smile quickly faded and she leaned forward, just enough to see Mary Coblentz, her back straight and proper with her face turned toward the spot where the second preacher began the longer sermon of the worship service. If she knew that Elijah was sparkling at her, however, she did not let on.

Still, Fanny's heart quickened against her chest as she realized, without any second thought, that Elijah's interest was awakened by the mere presence of Mary Coblentz.

Fanny realized that, over the years, Elijah must have asked his share of young women to ride home in his buggy. He was, after all, twenty-four years of age. But young men often took women home without becoming serious. They merely offered a friend a ride or just wanted to get to know someone a little bit better. The idea of Elijah becoming serious with someone, of taking courtship to the next level, was an eventuality that Fanny had never really considered, at least until now. He was blatantly *not* listening to the preacher and shamelessly sparkling at a young woman.

Fanny felt her shoulders slump, and suddenly the pine bench felt harder under her backside, causing her to fidget. If Elijah married, surely their special friendship would come to an end. After all, any godly husband would take care of his wife before others; a wife was second only to God, and that meant Fanny would lose the very person she considered her best friend in Mount Hope. The idea of that made her feel just as melancholic as Martha always acted.

Almost ninety minutes later, when the worship service came to an end, Fanny tried to slip away. She didn't want to see any more of Elijah's face riveted upon pretty Mary Coblentz, especially since he did it with such blatant interest and curiosity. His attention to this newcomer to the community was not welcomed by Fanny.

However, as usual, Naomi caught sight of Fanny standing alone, and never one to miss an opportunity to assign some task to her, called her name aloud: "Fanny! Fanny Price!" as she waved her hand and beckoned for her niece to join her.

Obediently Fanny did as Naomi instructed.

"You should help your cousins setting the tables, Fanny," Naomi said, her voice carrying a sharp tone as if reprimanding her for not having thought to do so without being told. With Naomi everything she said sounded like a reprimand, at least when it was directed at Fanny and especially when it had to do with Miriam.

Fanny glanced over her shoulder. The men were assembling the tables, slipping the legs of the benches into wooden trestles and converting them into long tables for the fellowship meal. Already there were eight young women hurrying to put plates, utensils, and glasses along both sides of the makeshift tables.

"I think there are enough people helping, *Aendi*," Fanny said softly.

"But Miriam complained of a headache just after service," Naomi quickly replied. "It's best if you help her, Fanny. You know how she gets when she has headaches. She needs to rest so she's better in time for the singing tonight."

Headaches. It was always headaches with Miriam, and while no one else seemed to notice, Fanny observed that Miriam's headaches conveniently happened when she was not getting enough attention. Fanny glanced around the room and noticed a small group of young women who, because there were more hands than work, were not busy with the food preparation or setup of the tables. At the center of that group stood Mary Coblentz.

Standing closer to her, Fanny could see the true extent of Mary's beauty: flawless skin, sparkling blue eyes, and a heart-shaped face framed with her dark brown hair, which she kept tucked under her pretty, heart-shaped prayer *kapp*. She certainly wasn't one to work outdoors, that was for sure and certain.

Naomi glanced over her shoulder to see what had caught her niece's attention. "*Ah, ja!* The bishop told me that they were expecting guests."

Fanny looked away, a faint blush covering her cheeks at having been caught in her not-so-secret observation of Mary.

"It's so delightful to have new young people to share their experiences with our own youth," Naomi said, more to herself than to Fanny. "And such *wunderbarr gut* people as the Coblentz children. Their parents were here not so long ago." She paused as if trying to remember just how much time had passed between now and then. "Five years? Mayhaps it was six. That Mary was well behaved and mannerly even back then. A fine and righteous woman, for sure and certain."

Fanny refused to look back at the young woman, knowing that it was wrong to automatically dislike her based on her conflicting feelings for Elijah. Perhaps it was the level of compliments or, even more likely, the source of them, but Fanny knew she did not care for that woman one iota.

Naomi noticed that Fanny was not paying adequate attention to the newcomer, or, perhaps even more irritating, to her ramblings about her. "Have you met her, then? Mary Coblentz?" she asked in a sharp tone.

Fanny shook her head.

"Hmm," Naomi said, the noise coming from deep within her throat. "She's pleasant enough, I reckon, but clearly not suited for farm life. Bit too white in the cheeks for my taste. And I'd wager that her hands have not one callus on them!" She glanced at Fanny and quickly added, "If betting weren't a sin, of course."

Of course.

Without another word, Naomi turned her back to Fanny. Seeking to distract herself, Fanny hurried to help Miriam, who was helping to set the tables.

"Oh, Fanny," Miriam said, a hint of relief in her eyes but with a dearth of sincerity in her voice. "*Danke* for relieving me. I have *such* a headache."

Fanny did not respond. Instead, she simply shook her head and took the silverware tray from Miriam, holding it so that Julia could place the knives and spoons beside the plates.

"It is so warm, don't you think?" Miriam said, fanning herself with her hand. She glanced around the room as if looking for something. "I reckon I could use a glass of cool water."

Fanny didn't have to look; she sensed that Miriam had walked away. Curiosity got the best of her so she glanced over her shoulder, not entirely surprised to see Miriam walking right past the group of women—a route that conveniently took her near the place where Henry stood with the bishop—as she headed into the kitchen.

"You should come to the singing tonight, Fanny," Barbara said. "I heard that those two new people, that Henry and Mary Coblentz, are going to be there."

"*Ja*, Fanny, you should," Julia added.

There was something light about Julia's tone that caused Fanny to turn around and look at her. She too seemed to be more interested in what was happening in the direction of Henry Coblentz than setting the table.

"*Nee*, Julia," Fanny replied, jiggling the utensil tray just enough to let her know that she was waiting for her cousin to continue setting the table.

"*Kum*, Fanny," Katie added, nudging her arm. "You haven't been since early summer!"

With the three of them staring at her, Fanny had little choice but to smile and nod her head. Besides, with Timothy not home as of late and Naomi busy elsewhere, Fanny could write her letters anytime, with no fear of any intrusion. "*Mayhaps*," she finally answered. "I'll speak to Elijah. See if he takes me..." She left the sentence unfinished, knowing that Elijah would be more than happy to take her. It was who would bring her home that actually had her worried.

It was, indeed, typical of the young men to bring along siblings or friends to these singings. This was a special occasion for them to harness their carefully groomed horse to the family buggy—or in some cases and if they were of marrying age, their open-top courting buggy. These singings had been an accepted tradition amongst the Amish since generations long gone. Even the most conservative members of the *g'may* approved of these activities as a necessary yet proper way for young people to interact and socialize with the ultimate goal: to create a matrimonial bond.

Raising families was both their God-given right and their obligation. To bring home a particular young woman was, to some, a declaration of intent on the part of a particular suitor. Should she turn down the offer, the matter was considered settled once and for all without additional complications, pleas, or unnecessary overtures. That did not mean, however, that the young lady's acceptance of the trip back home was tantamount to giving her absolute consent, but that she would favor the opportunity of considering a particular young man as her future lifelong partner.

Over a period of several of these repeated invitations, conversations would ensue, often made longer by the propensity of the driver to take the longest possible route, during which affinities and feelings were shared, hopes and dreams expressed, ultimately resulting in a common pledge. In such a close-knit community, many young people already had their sights on a possible life partner, but these rides would help make their hopes and aspirations a reality. Banns were announced a few months later at a church service. Or it was the short route home.

Back in July Elijah had convinced Fanny to attend the youth singing. When Miriam and Julia chimed in that she should join them, Fanny had finally acquiesced, but only after Timothy and Martha agreed. With the four of them crowded into the open-top buggy, it had been a fun ride over to the Yoders' home. But at the end of the singing, Elijah had been nowhere in sight. When she realized that he was gone, most likely off with Benjamin and some other young men, Fanny walked home by herself along the dark roads. She much preferred the solitude of her own thoughts to the giddy chatter of her two cousins.

She hadn't gone back to a singing again.

———◆◇◆———

After the Sunday fellowship meal Fanny found herself in between her aunts and her cousins as they walked home. Up ahead, she could hear Miriam and Julia whispering and thought she heard the name Coblentz uttered several times. Behind her, Naomi rattled on about the way several of the young women, Katie Troyer included, had not tied the strings of their prayer *kapps*.

"Can you imagine, Martha? Why, I even think that Troyer girl's dress was soiled!"

Martha clicked her tongue, giving the usual disapproving *tsk tsk*, although Fanny wondered whether she truly cared. Since Timothy's departure, Martha had remained unusually quiet. Fanny did what she could to take care of her, making certain that she was never alone. But she noticed that Martha didn't seem to mind whether Fanny was there or not.

"And the Millers' son—that...Jake?—I saw him fall asleep! Not once, not twice, but three times!"

"Oh, help," Martha mumbled without any real emotion.

Fanny sighed, knowing full well that Naomi sometimes nodded off during the longer sermons, especially during the hot summer months. With close to two hundred people sitting in one large room, it was almost impossible to not give into waves of somnolence. But Naomi always found something, or someone, to grumble about. If Timothy had attended, he too would have complained. In his eyes no one could ever be righteous enough to follow the *Ordnung* properly.

"When my husband was bishop," Naomi started as, despite herself, Fanny pressed her lips together, "he never would have permitted such inappropriate behavior!"

For the rest of the walk, Naomi continued to talk about the superiority of her husband's leadership for the *g'may* and how everything seemed to be falling apart since his death. Fanny didn't have to listen, for she had heard this lecture many times since her uncle's death just three years after she arrived in Ohio.

When they walked down the driveway to the farm, Fanny felt a sense of comfort. She felt that it was home, even if she always knew that it was not *her* home. The windmill blew in the light summer breeze, the rotor making a loud clacking noise. Overhead, the clear blue sky almost appeared more like autumn than summer. She knew that the rest of the afternoon would be quiet, everyone sitting in the kitchen and talking, or, if someone felt moved, reading the Bible. Fanny hoped that she could find a way to stay outside, to sit in the sun and feel the breeze on her face. Soon it would be autumn, and with the change of season, more days would be rainy and cold. Most of the days would be spent indoors, sitting around the wood-burning stove and making baskets in the dim light of the kerosene lanterns.

"Did you hear me, Fanny?"

She looked up, surprised to be addressed by Naomi. "*Nee, Aendi*, I did not."

"Go fetch that blanket for Martha, I said. We're going to sit out here on the porch for a spell and I don't want her catching a chill."

"Of course," she mumbled and hurried past Naomi and Martha to enter the house.

Leaving the front door open behind her, she ran over to the sofa where the old, faded quilt was tossed, unfolded. As she grabbed it, her eyes fell upon an envelope, already torn open, which had fallen to the floor. She recognized the handwriting as being Timothy's. For a moment she hesitated and almost picked it up to read. But she knew that it was not addressed to her and reading it would be almost as bad as lying or stealing. Still, she couldn't help but wonder why no one had mentioned that he wrote to the family.

Because I'm not their family, she thought with a heaviness forming inside her chest.

She held the quilt against her chest as she walked back toward the door.

"...and Fanny's to go to the singing too," Julia was saying when Fanny approached the chair-swing.

"Oh, I don't know if I can do without Fanny," Martha said nervously as Fanny covered her aunt's legs with the quilt. "What would I do if she weren't here?"

Miriam frowned. "It's only for a few hours, *Maem*."

Naomi shot her a look that did not go unnoticed by Fanny.

"It's fine," Fanny said. "I'd be too worried to go anyway."

Martha gave her a soft smile.

"Oh, Fanny!" Miriam sounded exasperated. "How will you ever get married and have babies if you don't go to the singings?"

The question caught her off guard. She never gave much thought to getting married. While all of the other young women talked about courtships and marriage, their dreams of having child after child, Fanny had always presumed that she would just stay on the Bontrager farm. And she certainly did not envision herself taking care of *kinner*. She had her hands full taking care of Martha and, when necessary, Naomi.

"Speaking of which..." Naomi changed the subject. "I heard too much noise last Sunday evening. That rocking chair squeaks against the floorboards, and I'd like a decent night's sleep tonight."

Miriam flushed and Julia looked away.

Martha reached over to touch her sister's arm. "That's to be expected, Naomi. It's the way it's always been done."

"Doesn't mean it can't change, Martha!" Naomi replied harshly, and Martha withdrew her hand as if she had been slapped. "Nor that it shouldn't. A woman my age needs her sleep!"

Fanny coughed into her hand. "It *is* getting chilly out," she said, hoping to divert Naomi to a safer topic. "Maybe Martha should go inside."

Courtship was a strange time in any Amish house where daughters resided. While it wasn't normally discussed, the ritual of bedside courtship remained a fact among even the most conservative church districts. Most courtships were limited to the kitchen where the couple sat together on a single rocking chair to talk—and sometimes kiss!—in the darkness. It was not unheard of for the talking to also take place in the girl's bedroom on the second floor of the house, especially since the parents often kept their bedroom just off to the side of the kitchen.

Yes, bedside courtship was something most people did not discuss, but it was a known practice. Just one more reason Fanny didn't want to court a young man.

❦ *Chapter 4* ❦

"HURRY THEN, FANNY!"
From her small bedroom at the back of the second floor Fanny could hear Miriam impatiently tapping her foot on the hardwood floor as she waited in the kitchen. Fanny could only imagine Miriam standing there, arms crossed and a scowl on her face, at the terrible and horrible inconvenience of having to wait for Fanny. *For once*, Fanny thought. Usually it was the other way around.

With a big sigh Fanny left her bedroom, and after shutting the door behind herself, she walked toward the staircase.

Oh, how she didn't want to go to that singing! Her reluctance to socialize before and after the worship service was only magnified at the youth gatherings. As usual, the other women talked about silly things, simply more gossip and most of it of little importance. Her lack of enthusiasm for sharing her own comments meant that her opinion was infrequently sought. Apparently she had offered her true thoughts, that gossip was irrelevant and sinful, just once too often. The only person who ever seemed to care about her opinion was Elijah, and that certainly wasn't at youth gatherings, where he spent most of his time with his own peers.

But Fanny didn't mind. She often felt fortunate to spend so much time with the finest of company: her own thoughts.

"Are you coming yet?" Miriam yelled.

"*Ja, ja*! I'm coming," Fanny said, holding onto the handrail as she began to descend.

Elijah stood at the bottom of the stairs, peering up the stairwell at her. He gave her an encouraging smile, most likely because he knew of her discomfort. He always seemed so attuned to her unspoken emotions, one of the very reasons she felt her nerves begin to settle. At least Elijah would be there, she thought, hurrying down the steps. She would ride over to the singing in his buggy, and if all things went in her favor, she might even ride home with him too.

"Now calm yourself, Miriam. Here comes our Fanny!" he said cheerfully.

Just as Fanny reached the second to bottom step, her shoe slipped and she stumbled forward. She cried out as she fell, her hand leaving the banister as she tried to break her fall. But she never hit the wall or the floor. Instead, she felt strong arms grab her by the waist and hold her tight.

"Gotcha!"

It took her a second to realize what had just happened. Her hand was pressed against his chest and he held her in a tight, if not awkward, embrace. She looked up at him, her eyes meeting his. For a moment she felt as if her heart might stop beating, for he gazed down at her with a look that words simply couldn't describe.

Just as soon as she saw it, it was gone. Blinking, Elijah helped her stand upright, his hands still around her waist but his eyes averted from hers.

"Now what?" Miriam snapped. When she saw that Fanny had fallen, she clucked her tongue and mumbled under her breath.

Fanny, however, ignored her cousin. She placed her hands on Elijah's shoulders, too aware of his chest pressed against hers as he held her. Her heart beat rapidly and she felt tingles racing up the back of her arms. His hands on her waist felt strong and protective. For what felt like an eternity, she couldn't tear her eyes off his. Finally, when he didn't release her, she forced herself to look away.

"I'm so sorry," she mumbled and started to press away from him. But his hold remained firm. "Elijah?" she asked, wondering why his arms still held her so tight.

"Are you alright? Did you hurt your ankle, Fanny?"

Impatiently Miriam sighed from the doorway. "Oh, she's just fine! Making us late, but fine! *Kum* now! Let's get going."

Fanny relaxed, just a little, under Elijah's concerned stare. "*Nee*, Elijah, nothing hurts," she said. She felt as though butterflies fluttered inside of her chest. This time, when she pushed away from him, he let go, one hand still on her waist as he made certain she was steady on her feet. "Miriam's right," she mumbled, looking down at the floor. "I am making everyone late. I'm so sorry."

He leaned over. "Stop apologizing," he whispered in a lighthearted tone. When she looked at him again, surprised by his sweet demand, he winked at her and finally removed his hand.

Fanny could hardly breathe. She stood there, stunned back into silence. Had that really happened? Had Elijah held her in his arms far longer than he should have? She felt a distinct warmth spread across her cheeks, thankful that Miriam and Julia were already heading out the door with Elijah slowly following.

He paused at the door and waited for Fanny.

Somehow she managed to cross the kitchen floor and pass him as he held the door open for her. As she climbed into the back seat of his buggy, she was still thinking about how she felt, pressed against Elijah's body, when he safely caught her from what could have been a terrible accident. She wondered if she had imagined the intimacy of the moment. After all, Elijah was like a big brother to her. To Fanny, he was also her best friend, and despite what she truly felt about him, she had never imagined anything more could develop between them.

But he had looked at her and not necessarily, she sensed, in a brotherly way.

For the entire ride to the singing, as the buggy's metal wheels rumbled along the road's hard surface, Fanny was barely able to focus on anything other than budding feeling of hope that was growing within her.

That evening the singing was being held in a barn. When they arrived, the men were outside, having taken the time to unharness their horses and lead them to a small paddock adjacent to the barn. Fanny followed Miriam and Julia inside, walking two paces behind her cousins. She could not help but wonder whether or not Elijah might be watching her, but she knew it would be improper to turn around to find out. Instead, she enjoyed thinking *mayhaps* it was exactly what he was doing.

Thirty minutes later, however, her momentary happiness took flight.

The men were gathered on one side of the barn and the women on the other. The singing hadn't begun yet, the youth were taking their time to converse with each other before the actual singing of hymns began. That was precisely when Henry Coblentz walked into the barn, his sister Mary walking right beside him.

A moment of silence befell the gathering. It was hardly noticeable at first, as just a few people stopped talking. But the crowd, though small in nature, was large enough for the quieting to be noticeable, if not to the newcomers then certainly to Fanny.

She too looked up from where she sat on a hay bale, a plastic cup of lemonade in her hand, as she followed everyone's eyes toward the door.

Admittedly Henry was a very handsome man. Tall with broad shoulders, well-defined facial features, piercing eyes, and a straight posture, he looked strong and sure of himself, which indicated that he probably had a work ethic to match. But Fanny knew that looks could be deceiving; the handsome Thomas had shown her that. As Henry Coblentz removed his straw hat, clearly new for the narrow brim had nary a straw out of place or a single tear in the black band, he ran his fingers through a thick shock of brown curls and smiled, for whose pleasure Fanny could not presume.

Fanny knew that beauty on the outside did not mean it carried through to the inside. She had never paid much attention to those who carried the trappings of good looks or the privilege of wealth. The former was apparent from one simple look, but the fine material of his shirt indicated the latter. Clearly it was not made from the same practical bolt that Martha and every other Amish woman purchased to make their sons' clothing.

No, Fanny was not one to be impressed by this Henry fellow. Pride in appearances often indicated a lack of motivation to develop true character and humility, while an exterior display of wealth often meant there was no reason to develop a deep relationship with hard work. How such a person could ever be righteous and walk right with God was a mystery to Fanny. Even more mystifying was how any Amish woman would be attracted to such a man. Surely a commitment to God gave a stronger impression than simply presenting a handsome face and wearing fancy clothing!

However, Fanny quickly realized that she held that thought in isolation; the way that the other young women stared at Henry with obvious interest etched into their faces clearly showed that they saw the superficial exterior with no consideration of what lay beneath. When Henry continued smiling, his eyes traveling across the room and in the direction of where Fanny sat with her cousins and their friends, Fanny watched with amusement as Miriam accepted the smile as if it were for her and her alone.

It took only a few minutes for Mary to make her way over to the small group of women. Her confidence was as bold as her beauty. Fanny glanced over at Elijah, not surprised to see that Mary's brother had joined him. What did surprise her was that Elijah's eyes seemed fixated on the young woman who now stood before her.

"Wilkum!" Miriam said with genuine eagerness and extended her hand toward Mary as she introduced herself.

The young woman who looked no older than twenty-five years of age shook Miriam's hand, a thin yet confident smile on her face. Clearly she was not intimidated about being in a new place and meeting new people.

"Mount Hope is so different from Lancaster County," Mary remarked after the introductions were made. "Much more...rural." Spoken from anyone else's lips, the comment might have been taken as a slight. Mary, however, let the words roll from her tongue in such a way that *rural* did not sound quaint and backward. Instead, she spoke with such esteem that it could only be meant as an observation steeped in admiration.

Miriam, however, raised her eyebrows. Fanny wasn't surprised. The favorite of Naomi, Miriam seemed to mirror her aunt's habit of finding something—anything!—to dispute in any opinion that did not reflect hers. In fact, oftentimes even if it *did* reflect hers. "Really?" she said in a tone that masked any indication of faultfinding. "My *daed* always comments that it's becoming far too commercialized as of late. And too many tourists."

It was, indeed, a sign of the times that tourists were becoming increasingly attracted by anything Amish-made. The abundance of cheaply designed and poorly manufactured goods that had invaded the world of the *Englischers* made many people long for solid, handmade items carefully crafted the old-fashioned way.

And the tourists loved Amish food as well. Tired of prepackaged, overly processed food, more and more tourists were now shopping at local Amish grocery stores. This trend had not gone unnoticed by the community, prompting the more enterprising amongst its members to travel as much as four hours away to sell produce at local farmer's markets. It made good business sense, and the community, organizing itself as a cooperative, thrived as goods were gathered and purchased from the families in each district, providing a great sales outlet for those who canned, cooked, rendered, baked, stitched, or handcrafted the old-fashioned way.

"Is that so? Your community has become too commercialized as well, then?" Mary remarked with genuine surprise.

Fanny wanted to point out that the tourists helped them by buying their baskets. The small shed on the dairy barn where they sold baskets during the summer months often brought in three hundred-plus dollars a day, money that was used to help pay for things on the farm. If it weren't for the tourists who strayed down the back roads off of Route 241, they would have had to economize or find another income stream.

"I suppose your *daed* would not care very much for Lancaster County, then," Mary added. "Although I must confess that I did not see the town proper yet."

"*Daed*'s old fashioned," Julia replied. "His parents were raised Swartzentruber, but neither one of them joined."

"Oh?"

This time, however, there was the slightest hint of disapproval in Mary's voice. Neither Julia nor Miriam seemed to notice. But Fanny picked up on it right away, especially when Mary lifted an eyebrow at the word *Swartzentruber*. Some of the Old Order Amish communities did not always think highly of the overly strict Swartzentruber Amish way of life, finding them backward and far too conservative. Clearly Mary fell into that category.

Unaware of the undercurrent of Mary's comment, Julia explained further. "They joined the Danners, instead. I think it had something to do with the plumbing."

"Well! Can you blame them?" Mary laughed. "Imagine! No running water! Why, that sounds so…primitive."

This time, it was Miriam who joined the conversation and dragged Fanny into it as well. "Even Fanny had running water when she lived in Colorado!"

With renewed interest, Mary turned her attention to Fanny. "Colorado? Is that where you are from?"

Fanny stumbled over her words. Colorado wasn't something that she frequently thought about. Let alone mentioned. Her communication with her parents was limited to a few letters each year. She had no relationship with her siblings, save William. To Fanny, her life in Colorado was from such a distant past that she no longer associated herself with the child that spent her early years there, way back when.

"It was a long time ago," she finally said.

"And you came here because…?"

Fanny wasn't used to having such inquisitive questions asked of her. She felt awkward and uncomfortable at being the center of attention. "The community in Colorado," she managed to say. "It struggles."

The simplicity of her response said enough and Mary nodded, indicating her understanding of the matter. "How fortunate for you to have family here, then."

It was a kind remark, a way for Fanny to avoid answering any more questions regarding her past. For that, Fanny was grateful. Had she misread her first impressions of Mary

Coblentz? Could Mary have more compassionate insight into others than she originally thought?

Oblivious to Fanny's reconstruction of her character, Mary returned her attention to Miriam and Julia. "It's been a while since Henry and I have been here." Fanny thought she saw Mary look over Miriam's shoulder in the direction where Henry stood with Jeb and Elijah. "So much has changed, I reckon."

"I hadn't known you'd been here before," Julia remarked. "When was that?"

"Oh, when our *schwester* was married. When was that? Ten years or so? There were so many people there, I'm not surprised we didn't meet."

But she *had* met Elijah, a fact that Mary neglected to mention. From the way her eyes lingered on the small group of men, Fanny began to wonder if there was a particular reason for Mary's silence on the matter.

"My *bruder* William lives in Lancaster County," Fanny offered. "Mayhaps you know him? William Price?"

Miriam scoffed. "Oh, Fanny. How provincial! As if she would know everyone in Lancaster County!"

Mary, however, looked upward, her eyes searching the ceiling as if the answer resided there.

Ignoring Miriam, Fanny added, "He's a carpenter," as if that might help narrow it down.

"I'm not certain that I have met him," Mary admitted but without a lot of conviction. "As Miriam stated, Lancaster County is quite spread out, you see."

But Fanny picked up on an undercurrent of falsehood in Mary's words. If she was from Gordonville, surely she would know a young, unmarried man that lived in the same town!

She didn't have time to respond to Mary, offering this bit of information, for Miriam stepped forward and turned her body to slightly block Fanny from the conversation.

"Our little town is not as large as where you are from, I'm sure. But you will find Mount Hope most welcoming," Miriam said as she smiled at Mary. "For both you and your *bruder.*" Her eyes flickered in the direction of Henry Coblentz. "Will you be visiting us for long?"

"Until Council," Mary replied. "We'll have to return for that and Communion."

Miriam brightened at this comment. "Why, Council isn't until October! You'll be here an entire month!"

Mary graced her with a charming smile. "I reckon so, Miriam. Although our Council is a week before yours, or so we've been told."

Fanny noticed Julia remained silent throughout this exchange, her eyes lingering on Henry as he stood talking with Elijah and Jeb near the refreshment table.

"We wouldn't leave at all," Mary continued, "but we aren't members of your church district. Yet."

Her last word caught Fanny's attention. Were Mary and Henry considering moving to Mount Hope? And, if so, why wouldn't they simply have their bishop write to their own brother-in-law rather than return to Pennsylvania to attend the Council Meeting and take communion?

Every year, right after the autumn baptism service, the members of the church district gathered after Sunday worship to discuss everything that was happening in their community. Any new rules or changes to existing ones were discussed, debated, and decided upon at that meeting. Any grievances with others were openly aired and resolved.

Baptized members of the *g'may* attended this meeting so that the entire church district could be right with God before accepting communion at their next worship service. It was the one time of year when most Amish people did not travel, unless it was to return from elsewhere to attend this meeting.

"Are you thinking about moving here, then?" Fanny asked.

Mary nodded. "It just depends on Henry."

At this comment, Miriam lit up. "Well, now my curiosity is piqued!"

"Henry is considering moving out here," Mary explained. "Our older *bruders* are working the family business in Gordonville, so *Daed* wishes to expand out here." She gave a soft laugh. "Plus, it's become far too congested in Lancaster County."

Fanny frowned. First Mary had described Lancaster as spread out and then as congested. Her words seemed rather contradictory. "If it is so congested, I would think that would be the *best* place for new business, unless his business is farming, wouldn't you say?" Fanny offered, surprisingly out of turn.

Miriam gave a frustrated sigh. "Oh, Fanny, don't be so argumentative." She shook her head and looked at Mary as if to gain her sympathies in having to put up with Fanny. "Always giving opinions when no one asked!"

But Mary looked at Fanny, seeming to study her with a new sense of piqued curiosity as if noticing her for the very first time. Finally she gave her a soft smile, but directed her statement back to Miriam. "Her statement is actually quite correct. And my *bruder* does, indeed, wish to become a farmer. Land in our county is far too dear for him to purchase outright. However, the bishop has land that could be worked and farmed. His own children are already settled in their lives and not one of his boys is a farmer." Mary turned to look at Miriam. "If Fanny's opinions are not frequently sought, perhaps they should be. She seems more astute than she is given credit for." And then, without waiting for a response, Mary turned and waved for her brother to join the small group. "I would like to introduce my *bruder* Henry..."

None of the women spoke as Henry, along with Elijah and Jeb, joined their group. Fanny watched as Elijah nodded his head in Mary's direction. He seemed to stand straighter and with a more formal expression on his face. Mary's response was a wistful smile, but her eyes traveled to her brother.

"Henry, I wanted to introduce you to the Bontrager sisters and their cousin, Fanny Price."

Neither Miriam nor Julia seemed to notice that Mary had not offered their first names. He looked at Fanny, his eyes taking her in before he reached out to shake her hand. She felt uncomfortable under his steady gaze and withdrew her hand as quickly as she could. He seemed amused by her reaction, but his attention was soon diverted.

"I'm Miriam. It's so nice to meet you!"

The honey sweet tone that her cousin used to greet Henry Coblentz caused more than one head to turn. Fanny looked up in surprise while Jeb blinked in concern. Unfazed, Miriam shook Henry's hand, her touch lingering more than a few seconds too long.

"How very…" Henry paused as he held Miriam's gaze and hand. "…welcoming."

"Everyone's been so friendly," Mary said, glancing at her brother. "Wouldn't you say, Henry?"

"Hmm, *ja*." The words came from deep within his throat as if he barely heard his sister.

From behind Henry, Jeb cleared his throat. "And you should meet Julia," Jeb offered, casually forcing his way to stand next to Miriam, his arm brushing hers in a subtle way that was clearly intended to send a loud signal. He positioned his body so that he blocked Miriam from Henry's view.

Fanny noticed that Henry greeted Julia in much the same way and with much the same reaction from her cousin. She had never met someone like Henry Coblentz and she knew, without a doubt, she didn't like him even if both of her cousins clearly did. Wiping her hand on her dress, Fanny hoped she could rid her skin of the itch she felt from his touch.

"And Elijah," Mary said at last. The way she rolled her head to look at him reminded Fanny of a sleek barn cat, lazy yet purposeful at the same time. "How good to see you again."

"Your journey was uneventful, I presume?"

She laughed, a light and airy sound. "As uneventful as one could hope for!"

Elijah smiled. "Indeed."

Fanny watched this unexpected interplay between Mary and Elijah, confused at first by their reaction to each other. They were comfortably uncomfortable with each other in a way that said far more than their words indicated. In the eight years she had known Elijah she had never witnessed him act so *ferhoodled*.

"I suppose the question everyone is wanting to ask," Miriam said, pushing against Jeb so that she was no longer hidden, "is how long you will be staying in Mount Hope. A good long time, or will you be returning soon?"

Fanny frowned. Hadn't Miriam already asked Mary that very question? Only this time, she directed the question to Henry.

"Until Council," he responded, his eyes staring directly into Miriam's in a much too forward way to suit Fanny. "Our district will have that the second Sunday in October."

"Well," Miriam responded. "That's long enough anyway, I reckon."

Fanny wasn't certain if she meant that it was long enough or too long. Since their own Council meeting would be held on October 16 after their regular worship service, the Coblentzes would be in Mount Hope for almost five weeks.

"*Ach*, Miriam," Jeb said, turning so that he, once again, blocked her from Henry's view. "You'll be plenty busy with preparations for our own celebrations, I imagine. Not too much time for visiting with our own wedding on November first!" He gave an insincere laugh as her eyes flashed angrily at him. "Well now, I think I see Benjamin over there. *Kum*, Henry. Let me introduce you before the singing starts, *ja*?"

Before Miriam knew what happened, Jeb had led Henry away, guiding him toward another group of young men near a folding table with pitchers of lemonade and meadow tea, leaving Miriam standing before Mary and, as such, with the sole responsibility of now introducing her to the other women.

Fanny smiled to herself as she saw Miriam struggle with the not-so-obvious slight from Jeb. Anyone else watching probably would not have noticed. His behavior toward Miriam was so casual, and the men so often separated from the women, that he appeared no more interested in her than he was in a bale of hay. Only every so often he might glance in her direction, as if checking up on what she was doing and whom she stood by. It was such a slight indication that most people would never see it. Fanny, however, found that by observing in silence she could often discern what so many people often missed.

❧ *Chapter 5* ❧

THE SUN FELT warm on Fanny's back as she knelt in the garden. She plucked a few unwelcome weeds from between the rows of tomatoes and tossed them into the black bucket by her side. Soon the garden would produce the last of its vegetables for the season. In the meantime she was happy to enjoy the time away from basket weaving and house cleaning, the two things that Naomi demanded she do. However, the garden had been neglected of late, especially with Fanny helping Elijah with the animals in the early morning hours. Finally Naomi had consented that she could tend to the weeds instead of sitting in the house weaving baskets.

Pausing, she sat back on her heels and wiped the sweat from her forehead.

Somehow she had managed to be assigned the task of gardening by herself. While she didn't particularly mind, for it meant she didn't have to listen to Naomi bossing everyone around inside the house, she resented the fact that, once again, Miriam had claimed to have a headache. The heat and humidity of the late summer day was apparently too much for her cousin...as was the windy chill of autumn days, the biting cold of winter mornings, and the dampness of spring rain. In reality, however, Fanny knew that Miriam had snuck out the previous evening, presumably to meet up with Jeb. She had heard the stairs creak at eleven o'clock at night as someone descended the stairs in the darkness.

To Julia's credit, she was stuck inside on a gorgeous day, catching up on some orders for baskets. More often than not, Julia seemed to quietly contribute just the right amount of work so that she did not fall prey to Naomi's criticism. However, not once did she offer to assist Fanny, instead choosing to disappear in the early afternoon to visit with two of her girlfriends who lived on a neighboring farm.

Fanny returned her attention to the weeding, taking her time to pluck each weed so that she didn't have to return to the house anytime soon.

"Fanny!" Elijah whispered in a loud voice.

She smiled when she heard his voice and started to look around, trying to see where he was. "Elijah? Where are you?"

"*Nee*! Keep pretending to weed!" he instructed, a playful tone to his loud whisper.

Obediently she did as he asked, trying not to smile. She knew this game. He played it with her frequently. When she had first arrived at the Bontragers, Elijah began sneaking up behind her and, out of sight of Naomi or Timothy, he'd beckon her away on some little adventure so that they could talk, or as was often the case, just get away from the farm. It was a great game that he continued to play with her, claiming that he liked to see her laugh at him. But in reality she suspected that he noticed the unjust distribution of labor among the women, and since he was not inclined to speak up, he rebelled in a less vocal manner.

"Come now, Fanny. I've tacked up the pony! Let's go for a ride!"

Ah, she thought, risking a glance in the direction of the garden shed. "I can't, Elijah. I'm weeding," she whispered back but loud enough so that he could hear.

"That garden has no more weeds than Naomi has tact!"

Fanny laughed, covering her mouth with her soiled hand, and, once again, looked over her shoulder toward the shed. "*Ach*, Elijah! You're impossible!"

He poked his head around the corner of the shed and gave her a brotherly grin. "You've been working all day, Fanny. You're entitled to some fun. Just don't let Naomi see you!" he teased.

"See me have fun?" Fanny questioned teasingly.

"See you not working," he corrected and made a face at her. "Just hurry to the side of the barn so she doesn't see you leaving. Otherwise, she'll be out here to investigate why you stopped working!"

"And report me to your *daed*, no doubt!"

The longer Timothy remained away, the more Naomi browbeat everyone, especially Fanny, although no one was immune from being a target. Naomi's knack for noticing even the slightest hint of laziness seemed to increase with every passing day, although she often seemed to excuse Miriam with her frequent headaches or need to lie down in the afternoon.

Unfortunately the more Naomi complained, the less Martha talked at all. And that created an even larger problem for Fanny. Her worry about her one aunt was trumped only by her dislike for the other. While she'd never voice her concerns, she did go out of her way to avoid Naomi. Still, Martha's melancholy worried Fanny, who sat by her side to ensure that her aunt ate properly and didn't catch a chill when the sun went down. While Martha seemed to appreciate her efforts, sometimes even talking with her when they were alone, Naomi saw Fanny's concern and fussing as more reason to criticize her niece. After all, she claimed, Fanny was paying more attention to Martha than to her chores.

"I'm afraid I can't go, Elijah," she said when she realized that as much as she wanted to ride the grey pony she simply could not. Besides the fact that she was almost finished weeding, she wanted to check on Martha. "What if your *Aendi* Martha needs me? She was feeling fatigued this morning."

"You worry too much." His words, though critical, were spoken kindly. "She'll be fine for a short while. Besides, you're outside anyway."

"I promised to make that bassinet for the *Englischer*'s order."

He frowned. "Miriam was supposed to make that yesterday. Has she tricked you into doing that too?"

How well he knew her, she thought. "I don't mind," she said. "Not much anyway." And she didn't, really. Making baskets was much better than washing clothing anyway.

Elijah, however, did not seem to agree. "*Nee*, Fanny. Besides worrying too much, you work too hard while the others find ways to play. Now, I insist, and *Daed* put me in charge, ain't so?"

While she could have argued that Naomi, not Elijah, was assigned the role of "in charge," she decided against it.

"We can ride for just half an hour," he said. "*Maem* won't be any less fatigued whether or not *you* ride. And any other chores…well, you can do them later." He gestured for her to leave the garden, pointing toward the barn. "Now you go and fetch that pony, Fanny. I'll meet you at the oak tree by the pond in five minutes," he added. "That gives me enough time to divert Naomi's attention, to tell her that I have sent you on an errand."

"But you haven't sent me on an errand!" she replied, alarmed that Elijah might tell a lie on her behalf.

"*Ach*, Fanny. But I have indeed, and a quick one!" He gave her a friendly smile and winked "Your errand is to meet me there so we can race through the paddock by the tree line!"

This time she stifled her laugh as she couldn't help feeling pleased. She could always count on him to cheer her up when she was feeling poorly or, in this case, realized that she needed a break from the tedium of constantly working. "Oh, Elijah! You are so very clever, aren't you!"

He tilted his head in response and motioned toward the barn, putting his finger to his lips for her to remain silent. Then, with great fanfare, he pretended to tiptoe toward the house even though it was clear that Naomi could neither see nor hear him approach her section of the house. Fanny covered her mouth with her hand, delighted with both his antics and his attention. Under the circumstances, she could not have asked for a better cousin-brother, a term she had made up to describe their relationship. To call him just *cousin* felt insulting, as it hinted that he was no different from the other Bontrager children—he clearly was superior in *her* eyes, anyway!—and to call him *brother* felt disrespectful to William, her own dear sibling.

Fanny wiped her hands on her apron as she stood up. Lifting the black bucket, she carried it in the direction where she knew the pony would be waiting. If Naomi saw her, she would just say that she was dumping out the weeds. But, as luck had it, Naomi was not near a window and did not see her leave the garden.

Once she was behind the shed, she set down the bucket and turned to Penny, the medium-sized chestnut pony. It was Elijah's, but he had made it clear that he had purchased it for her. That only made the pony dearer to her.

True to his word, he had already saddled it. She double-checked the cinch on the Western saddle before she unhitched the pony from the post. Grabbing its mane, she swung herself upon its back.

"Let's go, Penny," she said in a soft voice, moving the reins so that the pony headed away from the farm in a direction that was safe from view of any prying eyes.

Fanny had barely arrived at the oak tree by the pond when she heard the thunderous sound of a horse's hooves pounding against the earth. He was galloping his horse and the noise sent a thrill through her. She perched atop the pony and waited until she could see him approach over the slight rise in the hill.

The pony lifted its head and spooked, dancing to the side as Elijah neared. With gentle hands, Fanny held the reins and calmed the pony.

"What did Naomi say?" she asked.

"Nothing out of the ordinary." He grinned. "Only that she should have approved the errand since *Daed* put her in charge."

Yes, that was indeed a typical Naomi response. For her aunt, it was always about being the oldest and, therefore, the wisest among them. The decision maker in the absence of the head of the household. While Naomi would never challenge Timothy's authority, she certainly made it clear that, ever since her husband died, her brother-in-law was the only one who held more authority on the farm than she did.

Together they rode through the field, Elijah insisting that she keep the pony at a walk. The fresh air and freedom from the farm lightened her mood. Slowly she felt herself relax. Only with Elijah could she feel as if she had no worries. She did not need to fret over his needs the way she agonized over others.

"I wonder how *Daed* and Thomas are doing in Pinecraft," Elijah said at last.

"I was wondering just the same," Fanny admitted. She didn't dare to mention to Elijah that she had spotted a letter from Timothy. Since he hadn't mentioned hearing from his father, her aunts hadn't shared any news with Elijah and that most likely meant that there was trouble brewing. She could only imagine that it was with Thomas, not their grandfather. But all she said to Elijah was, "I've been praying that your *grossdawdi* gets better."

Elijah sighed and shook his head. "If only they hadn't moved to Florida."

Fanny wanted to point out that *if onlys* were as pointless as *what ifs*. She had learned that lesson a long time ago, starting from the day she had been sent away from Colorado. But she had never met his grandfather. Like many older Amish couples in the community, Elijah's *grossdawdi* and his second wife had moved to the Amish community in Florida where the warmer weather suited their golden years and accommodated his arthritis.

"I do wonder how long they will be there," Fanny offered, gently guiding the conversation into another direction. "Council and Communion are rapidly approaching." She didn't want to remind him that, before both of those worship services took place, Elijah would take his kneeling vow. Unlike his sisters and Fanny, Elijah hadn't accepted his baptism yet. This year, however, he had decided that it was time.

A solemn expression crossed his face and Fanny realized that he was thinking the very thing that she did not say. Baptism was the most important day in the life of any Amish man or woman, representing a decision to commit his or her life to the Amish church. Once taken, it was a vow that could not be broken without serious consequences. Committing to live by the *Ordnung* was not a decision that was made without years of contemplation and reflection.

"And then, wedding season," Fanny added in a soft voice, as if to divert his thoughts. Most young women took their kneeling vow when they were ready to leave their *rumschpringe* behind and begin courting young men with the intention of settling down. The young men, however, usually became baptized members right after they had decided which young woman they wanted to be their wife. Fanny often wondered why Elijah had decided that this was the year for him to officially join the church since he wasn't courting anyone. At least not that she was aware, anyway.

"Ah yes, the wedding season." He laughed. "The announcements will be on the thirtieth of October. That's Communion, *ja*? I sure hope *Daed* is back for that service. Miriam will not be happy if her wedding isn't announced right away." He gave a soft smile. "She's not one to take too kindly to being forced to wait."

Fanny remained silent. Ever since Timothy had acknowledged Miriam's upcoming wedding to Jeb, Fanny had dreaded the event, not only because it would be a very long day with a lot of people to feed, but especially because of the tradition of the bride and groom pairing up couples. Fanny did not want to be paired up with any young man, especially one not of her choosing.

At the last wedding the bride had matched Fanny with John Troyer, a sixteen-year-old boy who looked as if he were fourteen. Fanny had eaten the fellowship meal in silence, her eyes occasionally wandering over to where Elijah sat next to John's older sister, Katie. While they didn't seem to engage in too much conversation, Elijah hadn't looked as miserable as Fanny felt. In fact, a few times she saw Elijah speaking to Katie and she responded with a smile.

While there was usually one or two of the matched couples who eventually married, Fanny had breathed a sigh of relief when, a few weeks later, she overheard Miriam and Julia talking about Katie riding home from a singing in the buggy of another man.

"Well, your *daed* needs to get home in time for Council, anyway," Fanny said. "Otherwise he can't take communion."

Off in the distance, the sound of a bell ringing caught both of their attention.

Fanny looked at Elijah, the color draining from her cheeks. In the middle of the morning or afternoon, there were usually only two reasons that anyone would ever ring the bell, and they both involved the unexpected: a medical emergency or a death.

"What do you think it might be?" Fanny asked, her eyes wide with fright. "Your *maem* was doing well when I went outside to garden. Oh! I hope nothing has happened! I knew I should have checked on her!"

Elijah's reaction was much more relaxed. "Now, Fanny! Must you always jump to a conclusion that involves your worry?" He shortened the left rein, gently guiding the horse's head back toward the farm. "We'll find out when we get back to the farm, eh?"

Although short, the ride back seemed to take a lifetime. Fanny's mind whirled with far too many thoughts about what could possibly have motivated someone at the farm to ring that bell. She couldn't even remember how long it had been since she had heard the rich sounds of the bell tolling across the fields. Years for certain, and most likely when Naomi's husband had passed away.

The recollection caused her a moment of panic and she quickly redirected Penny to catch up with Elijah and his horse.

No sooner had they rounded the side of the barn, however, than Fanny saw exactly why the bell had been rung. A car was pulling out of the driveway and there was a tall, lean man standing by the porch, talking with Julia and

Naomi. There was a visitor and Julia had pulled the bell string to alert Elijah and Fanny to return to the house.

"William!"

Fanny barely pulled the reins hard enough for Penny to stop before she leapt from the pony's back and ran across the driveway. She didn't care that Naomi watched, scowling from the doorway of the *grossdawdihaus*—whether from Fanny's outburst or from the realization that Elijah had not sent Fanny on an errand as he had told her earlier. Eight years had elapsed since she had last seen her brother. Fanny laughed and wept at the same time as she hugged him, feeling her hands pressing against his back, a back that was no longer that of a child but that of a man.

"Oh, William!" she cried out, not embarrassed that tears of joy fell from her eyes. "How *wunderbarr gut* to see you at last!"

He waited until she pulled away from him before he responded jokingly, "Why, you've barely changed at all, *Schwester!*"

Fanny's smile faded, Timothy's words echoing in her head.

"Let me look at you!" he said, taking a step backward and assessing the young woman who stood before him. "I always knew you'd be a beauty, Fanny!" He grinned. "And probably still smart as a whip, eh?"

Flattery? Fanny didn't know if she was ready for flattery. It was something she certainly wasn't used to receiving. Instead of responding, she glanced over his shoulder at the women standing on the porch: Miriam, Julia, Martha, and, of course, from the other porch, Naomi. She could see Miriam suppress a smile while Naomi flaunted a scowl.

"I reckon you met everyone then?" Fanny managed to ask.

"Oh, *ja!*" A flicker of his eyes indicated that Elijah had approached from behind. "Except for...?" He paused as he reached out his hand to greet Elijah.

"This is Elijah," Fanny said, introducing the two men.

"Ah! Elijah!" William grinned and shook his head. "The other big *bruder* in my dear Fanny's life!"

Fanny blushed. Not only was she not used to such attention, she certainly did not want Elijah thinking that she wrote letters to her family calling him her "big *bruder.*" With her discomfort so apparent, she could barely find the words to invite her brother into the house. Fortunately Martha managed to take over and find her voice.

"*Kum*, William. Visit in the sitting room while Julia makes some fresh meadow tea from the last of the summer mint."

Inside the house William stood in the center of the room and looked around, his eyes wide as he took in the spacious room and windows. He whistled, just a little, under his breath. Fanny noticed Miriam smirk at his apparent admiration for the Bontrager home.

"*Vell* now," William said, "this is a far cry from Colorado, don't you think, Fanny?"

She felt small and timid under his steady eyes. No one really asked her for her opinion. For a moment she thought of Mary Coblentz and her comment from the singing. It felt awkward to have someone, besides Elijah, place a value on her thoughts. "I—I don't really recall Colorado."

"Best forgotten, I'd say!" he replied with a quick smile, despite the harsh undercurrent of his words. "But I reckon you don't have to share a room, do you now? You'd have to if you were still there, Fanny. Although you and Susan always got on well, so I don't suppose it would be unpleasant for you."

He crossed the room and took a seat on the sofa. After pushing aside a worn decorative pillow, he leaned back and crossed one leg over the other. "The boys though. Why, they are all in one room, just full of bunk beds and babies!"

He laughed and Fanny blushed.

Naomi slipped through the door that led from her small house to the Bontragers' kitchen. She must have overheard his words for she immediately jumped into the conversation. "Have you been back there, then? To your parents?" Naomi asked.

"Oh, *ja*, twice now. Once to help *Daed* and the other time, I was just passin' through."

"Like now?" Miriam asked. "Passin' through?"

If, moments ago, William's comment about her parents' having so many babies had brought color to Fanny's face, Miriam's question drained it. Fanny didn't need to look at her cousin to know what Miriam was implying. William was her dearest blood relative, but Miriam knew enough to infer that in Miriam's eyes he was uneducated and unsophisticated, even by Amish standards. That meant Miriam only had scorn for him. He was of no use to her and, therefore, should continue "passin' through."

Fortunately William didn't notice the insinuation or, if he did, ignored it. "*Ja*, heading to Indiana."

"Oh?" Fanny had not heard any news from her family and, despite William's best attempts to correspond with her, his letters had been few and far between and not always full of details. "What's in Indiana, William?"

"A job. Aaron sent me to oversee a job out there since he can't travel so far from home for so long." William explained. He turned to Elijah. "I've been interning with my *onkle* Aaron since I left Colorado."

Elijah, who had been leaning against the kitchen counter, moved over to take a seat in the rocking chair and motioned for Fanny to join her brother on the sofa. "Interning? Doing what trade?"

"Carpentry. Building sheds and the like."

Miriam clicked her tongue.

"Aaron only had two sons. One passed away quite a while ago and the other didn't join the church. He wants me to buy his business when he's ready to retire," William explained.

Sitting beside her brother, Fanny tried to relax. It had been so long that she had seen any of her family that she felt as though she might be dreaming. Her head felt fuzzy as she tried to make sense of the man sitting next to her. Was he truly the grown-up version of the young brother she had left behind in Westcliffe?

"So now you're headed to Indiana. You'll return to Pennsylvania then?" Elijah asked.

"Oh, *ja*. There's so much new construction in Lancaster County and everyone wants sheds, it seems. Even in Gordonville!"

This time, Miriam looked up, her interest suddenly piqued. "Gordonville?" she asked. "Is that where you live?"

Fanny bit her lip, watching with curiosity as Miriam began to listen more intently to William talk about Gordonville, Pennsylvania, and how the farms were so far apart compared to Ohio. His description of the area was far different from how Mary described it. No one else seemed to notice or, if they did, no one interrupted William for clarification. Fanny didn't care. She was simply content to sit there and listen to her brother: his cheerful voice and bright expressions soothed her. He hadn't written much, and from what she could gather, he hadn't focused on studying at school when he was sent away. But he seemed happy, and that was all that she could ask for.

"*Mayhaps* you know the Coblentzes," Miriam said, interrupting his story.

Immediately William stopped talking.

"Mary and Henry Coblentz?" she added inquisitively. "I'm sure you know them. Everyone knows them."

"A fine family," Naomi said with conviction. "Righteous and good-natured young people."

Slowly William nodded his head. "Mary and Henry Coblentz. Uh, *ja*, I'm familiar with them indeed." From his reaction, Fanny wondered if he didn't know them well or if he merely was unimpressed with having met them at all.

"Such a shame you won't be here tomorrow," Miriam continued, oblivious. "They're coming for a picnic. What fun it would be to have you meet with them, being old friends and all."

Fanny pressed her lips together and narrowed her eyes at her cousin. She was mocking William and for what gain, Fanny didn't know. Perhaps she found him far too provincial for her liking.

William made a noise, acknowledging what she said without stating what he thought. Apparently William knew enough to keep his mouth shut, a trait that Miriam clearly lacked. It wasn't until an uncomfortable silence fell over the small group that Miriam finally realized what his lack of words meant: confirmation that he knew the Coblentzes and was, indeed, not dazzled by the acquaintance. Abruptly Miriam ceased her monologue about Henry and Mary, scowling at her cousin as if his dislike for the Coblentzes was a personal affront to herself.

Oh, Fanny thought, *if only I could sit with William alone!* She would have asked him why he didn't seem to care for Henry or Mary or perhaps both of them. But, when Miriam finally excused herself, her headache conveniently reappearing, William and Elijah began talking as if they had known each other for a lifetime.

She watched her brother as he talked with Elijah, realizing that he had become a stranger. The closeness they had shared as children had developed into nothing more than a remote familial bond. Time and distance had a way of doing that. Even more so, his situation upon leaving Colorado had turned out far different from hers. From his letters, infrequent as they were, she understood that he lived a happy life with Aaron, learning his trade. Despite having other children, Aaron treated William like one of his own, fully welcomed and wanted.

Fanny, although well provided for, lived under the burden of never feeling fully wanted. As a result, she could never face the world with the cheery nonchalance that her dear brother William had achieved.

Sadly his visit was only a short one. The driver had merely let him off while he refueled the car and visited some of his own friends. When Fanny heard that William was not even staying for supper, she felt like a child on

Christmas morning awakening to gray skies pouring down rain instead of snow.

"Driver wants to get there tonight," William explained when he stood up to leave not even ninety minutes after he arrived. "'Sides, I have a full day of work tomorrow, I'm sure."

Fanny walked with him outside and toward the car.

"You seem to have done quite well," William said. "You know, it didn't seem right, what *Maem* and *Daed* did at the time, sending us away like that, but I've been back there. They did us a favor, Fanny."

"Is it that bad?"

He nodded his head. "*Ja*, it is. I feel for the others, especially Susan. What future does she face?"

Fanny stopped walking and stared at him. She had not thought of her siblings in a long time. "Oh, William! What a poor *schwester* I have been!"

He placed his hand on her arm. "*Nee*, Fanny. We were the lucky ones. Only they don't know that. They've known nothing but Westcliffe. What do they have to compare it to?"

He gave her a quick hug and kiss on the cheek. Then, without another word, he walked toward the car and got in on the passenger side. As the car pulled away, he gave her one last wave.

The lucky ones, she thought as she waved back. The disappointment she had felt just moments ago when she learned that William was leaving so soon was replaced with sorrow for her younger brothers and sisters whom she would never get to know at all.

To her surprise, as she turned back to the house she saw Elijah standing on the porch, leaning against the railing.

He had been watching them say good-bye and had a concerned look on his face.

"You okay?" he asked.

She tried to smile as she nodded her head. "*Ja*, Elijah. A short visit is better than no visit, right?"

"You amaze me, Fanny Price," he said with a warm smile. "I think *we* are the lucky ones."

Her heart lightened as she realized he had overheard their conversation and sought to console her. At least there was one person here who wanted her... for now.

❧ *Chapter 6* ❧

WHEN THE BLACK open-topped buggy pulled into the driveway, Fanny was already carrying a large tray of food to the picnic table: bowls of pretzels, sliced apples, plates of bread, and fresh homemade butter. She had already brought out the platter of sliced meats, cheese, and sour pickles. A tall oak tree shielded the picnic table from the midday sun, and despite the gentle breeze it was hot for late August.

Earlier Benjamin had arrived, eager to spend some time talking with Elijah. Almost an hour ago the two of them disappeared into the barn. Fanny set the tray onto the picnic table and tried to decide whether she should return to the house to alert Julia and Miriam that the Coblentzes had arrived or try to locate the other two men in the barn.

"They're here!" Miriam called out from the kitchen, her voice carrying through the open window. She sounded excited, too excited, and Fanny could only imagine her cousin running over to the small mirror that hung near the door. Certainly she was pinching her cheeks so they'd be rosy and making sure that her hair was not sticking out from under her prayer *kapp*.

Fanny heard Julia say something to her sister, but her voice was far too low for her to make out what she said. Undoubtedly it had something to do with Miriam's interest in her appearance, which was far too obviously for the benefit of one, and only one person: Henry.

It seemed that all Miriam talked about anymore was Henry Coblentz, to the point that even Julia shook her head at her sister's wanton attraction to him. After all, Miriam was engaged to another man! Whenever someone dared to remind her of this, Miriam would make a face and remain silent just long enough until she could excuse herself to take a brief rest, her headache miraculously having reappeared in time for her to disappear.

When the buggy stopped, Mary gave a short, quick wave in Fanny's direction, more of a dismissive reaction than a true greeting. Fanny didn't respond. Instead, she watched as Mary climbed down and reached into the back seat for a box while Henry climbed down and began to unharness the horse. He glanced over his shoulder at Fanny and gave her a hearty grin.

Her skin crawled. It was very infrequent that Fanny disliked someone. Henry had the honor of being the very kind of person who warranted her immediate disdain. Rather than greet either Mary or Henry, Fanny decided that fetching Elijah and Benjamin was a safer option. So while Miriam and Julia practically tripped over each other in order to greet their newly arrived guests, Fanny hurried toward the barn, her bare feet against the dry dirt driveway raising a small dust cloud behind her. She knew that she'd feel much more comfortable being in Henry's presence, with his roving eyes and leering smile, if Elijah was nearby.

The barn was dark and it took a moment for her eyes to adjust. The smell of manure hit her nostrils and she winced, just a little. Even though she was used to the pungent odor, she couldn't pretend it didn't exist. With the heat, the fumes within the barn were that much more overwhelming.

She hurried down the aisle that led past the holding pens and toward the back of the barn. "Elijah?" she called out. She avoided the area where the cows lined up when it was milking time and headed toward the hayloft. She had to climb a wooden ladder to get to it, and as she poked her head through the opening, she saw Benjamin and Elijah standing close together and looking through a book.

Fanny finished her ascent and quietly stole across the wooden floor that was covered with stray hay.

"Elijah? Henry and Mary just arrived," she said softly, not wanting to startle them.

But apparently she did just that.

Immediately Benjamin shut the thin book and quickly held it behind his back. Elijah took a step away from Benjamin as if distancing himself from whatever they had been studying with such grave intent. Fanny stared at both Elijah and Benjamin, her eyes drifting from one to the other. She didn't say anything, letting her silence speak for itself. Whatever it was, it was clearly something that was not permitted on the farm under the best of circumstances.

Elijah's face turned red and he avoided meeting her eyes. "*Ja. Vell.* Reckon I best go greet the Coblentzes, then," he mumbled.

Readily Benjamin agreed. With barely a glance, he brushed past Fanny and disappeared down the opening as he crawled down the ladder. But when Elijah tried to do the same, Fanny reached out and touched his arm.

"Elijah?" she asked. Her disappointment in his judgment was only matched by her dismay at his inability to face her.

He stopped walking and stood beside her, his shoulder almost touching hers even though they both faced opposite directions.

"It isn't what you think," he said in a flat voice.

"How would you know that since I'm not certain what I think?"

He glanced at her. "It's a hymnbook, Fanny."

"Hymns?" She repeated the word in disbelief. Their regular hymnbook, the *Ausbund*, was a small, black, chunky book. The book that Benjamin had whisked away was larger and the cover appeared burgundy, not black. "It didn't look like the *Ausbund* to me."

Elijah glanced away. "It...it's not the *Ausbund*."

"Elijah..." Her voice carried the disappointment that she felt. "Not the *Ausbund*?"

"They are religious songs, Fanny!" he said, far too quickly, which only added further to his shame. "Only they are in English, not German. Benjamin wanted to share it with everyone and he showed it to me for my advice."

Fanny shut her eyes and shook her head. "That's not a *gut* idea, Elijah. Your father doesn't want us singing anything except hymns in the *Ausbund*."

Elijah straightened his shoulders. "I didn't ask Benjamin to bring it." When she didn't respond, he took a short, quick breath. "I told him it wasn't a good idea. So he was showing me some of the hymns and we were discussing whether singing them is a sin."

"Sin or not, you shouldn't have been looking at them," Fanny said in a flat tone. "You know how Benjamin is. Just that little bit of attention will encourage him."

Elijah shut his eyes and nodded his head.

They said nothing further on the matter, but Fanny knew that Elijah felt guilt for even having looked at the English hymnbook. Timothy's rule about singing was one that no member of the household ever broke. In fact, there were only two other books that he allowed: the Bible and *Martyrs Mirror*. Even the newspaper and church-approved *Family Life* magazine had to pass through Timothy's approval. Only then was the family allowed to read. After all, Timothy had once explained, as the head of the household, it was his job to protect the spiritual well-being of his family.

She wondered how Timothy would react if he knew that the spiritual well-being of his son had just been soiled by a non-approved hymnbook.

Quietly Elijah walked beside her as they left the barn and joined the others at the picnic table. While Fanny had fetched Elijah and Benjamin, Jeb had arrived. He stood in between Benjamin and Henry, barely listening to them as they talked, for he was more interested in staring at Miriam. His eyes looked lost in thought, as if he were thinking of his upcoming wedding.

Fanny watched him with curiosity, trying to imagine how it felt to be near someone that, in just five weeks, one was to marry.

She certainly hoped that her fiancé would react in a far different manner than how Miriam responded to Jeb's *fer-hoodled* gaze. Whether Jeb realized it or not—and Fanny suspected that even a blind person could sense it!—Miriam avoided all of his glances as she focused her attention on Henry instead. When he spoke, she hung onto every word. When he laughed, she joined him. To Fanny, her behavior seemed disgraceful. But she knew that Miriam's business with Jeb was none of her business at all.

Thankfully Julia emerged from the house, carrying two plastic pitchers of water. For a brief moment, Miriam's attention was distracted by the appearance of her sister. Julia greeted Benjamin, Mary, and Jeb, but her soft smile was spared for Henry. Julia slid in between Miriam and Henry and set down the pitchers on the table. He barely paid her any attention and did not offer to assist her. Instead, he moved away from the picnic table and joined the other three men.

Discouraged, Julia flopped onto the bench next to Miriam and scowled at her.

"Well, you certainly invited us on a beautiful day," Mary observed. "It's not nearly as humid here as it would be in Pennsylvania this late in August."

At the sound of Mary's voice, Elijah stopped paying attention to Jeb and turned his face toward the picnic table. His eyes wandered to Mary's face, studying her with such intensity that Fanny felt uncomfortable. She forced herself to look the other way.

"Not as humid as here? Why, it's so warm out," Miriam responded, fanning herself with her hand. *"Mayhaps* I'll go stand under the shade of the tree where it's cooler."

Miriam slid out from the picnic table and practically pranced over to the tree. She leaned against the tree trunk and continued to fan her neck. Every so often she would sigh and lift her eyes up toward the heavens as if seeking solace there. But Fanny suspected that her cousin's intentions were not merely to cool off under the tree but to heat up the interest of another man.

Fanny realized that she was not the only one paying attention to Miriam. Quietly she observed the reactions of everyone: Julia's frustrated envy, Henry's too obvious interest, and Jeb's increasing irritation. There was no denying that Miriam's theatrical antics made her the center of attention. Again.

Sighing, Fanny looked over to where Elijah stood with Benjamin and Mary. Whatever they were talking about, Mary seemed animated and engaged. With Elijah being a farmer and Benjamin helping with the family store, Fanny couldn't imagine what they were discussing with Mary that would have captured her interest in such a lively manner.

Even more worrisome was the fact that Elijah looked enthralled by Mary's contribution to the discussion. He stood close to her, his body leaning forward and his eyes never leaving hers. Even Benjamin seemed to have more sense in masking his interest in the pretty, young Amish woman from Gordonville, Pennsylvania.

None of this would have happened if Timothy were there, Fanny told herself. He would have been there, seated on the porch in the rocking chair with the Bible on his lap, alternating between reading Scripture and monitoring the exchange between the young adults so that nothing inappropriate occurred. And he would have viewed Julia's visible anger, Miriam's flagrant flirtation, and Elijah's undeniable interest as clear violations of his unspoken rules for discretion and proper behavior.

It was Jeb who finally cleared his throat. "Reckon we might as well eat," he said. He gestured for Miriam to join him, but she ignored his attempt to have her stand by his side.

"Aw, I'm not quite ready for dinner yet. What say everyone? Perhaps a game of corn hole?" Elijah said. "I set it up behind the barn."

Miriam pooh-poohed that idea. "It's too hot in the sun, Elijah." She gave a little laugh and caught Henry's eye with a coquettish glance. "Almost makes me long for the colder weather!"

"Hmm, I reckon you'd sure like November to just hurry up," Julia said, her voice a little louder than she usually talked, "given that your wedding is the first Thursday of the month."

At the mention of a wedding, a silence fell over the group. Miriam's smile faded and Henry took a step backward, his attention suddenly diverted away from her. There was no sense playing with fire, for no one dare interfere in the courtship of an engaged couple. Julia, however, seemed more than satisfied with the rapid shift in attention away from Miriam.

Mary perked up, and her eyes sparkling, she smiled.

"A wedding?" She clasped her hands before herself. "Oh, that's *wunderbarr*! I so love weddings!"

Miriam pressed her lips together, and in great contradiction to her flirtatious behavior from just a few second earlier, avoided looking at anyone in particular, including Jeb. "Since it hasn't been announced yet, Julia, I'd remind you to not gossip."

This time Jeb spoke up. "Now, Miriam, it will be announced after the communion service." He puffed out his chest as he spoke and placed his hand upon her shoulder in a way that clearly indicated his relationship with her was more than friendship, just in case there remained any doubt among the others. "That's just one month from today!"

Henry looked from Jeb to Miriam. To Fanny, it appeared that he was making the connection at last. And, to further her surprise, she noticed that he did not appear discouraged by the news. Clearly he did not view Jeb as enough of an adversary to be worried. And Fanny decided at that very moment that her first impression of Henry Coblentz held true. If she had previously suspected she would not like him, she now knew it for a fact. Regardless of the fact that she had not interacted with him personally, simply put, she did not care for this brazen newcomer to their community.

Mary, however, sat on the picnic bench, the hint of an uncomfortable smile on her lips as she listened to the exchange. While Fanny wasn't certain what she thought about her, she did notice that someone else was quietly observing the scene: Elijah. Only his attention was focused more on Mary than Miriam or Jeb.

"If *Daed* gets back in time," Miriam replied.

Jeb narrowed his eyes, his wide-brimmed hat barely hiding the dark expression that crossed his face.

"Water, anyone?" Fanny asked, eager to break up the increasing tension that was building in the air. Without anyone replying, she reached for the closest pitcher and began to pour water into the assortment of glasses she had brought out earlier.

"*Danke*, Fanny," Elijah said as he took the glass from her. When she looked up at him, he gave her an appreciative nod and she knew it was not just for the water. She hid her smile and quickly served the others.

"Where is your *daed* anyway?" Mary asked, directing the question to both Julia and Miriam.

Still sulking, Miriam did not respond, so Julia took the rare opportunity to speak. "Pinecraft. Our *grossdawdi* fell and broke his hip."

Mary perked up. "Oh, *ja*? Pinecraft?"

To Fanny, that was a strange reply. She began to study Mary, especially when she continued speaking of Pinecraft and made no inquiry of their injured relative.

"I've heard that Pinecraft is *wunderbarr*! It's warm all year round and service is held in a church building with the Mennonites!" Her eyes took on a distant look. "Such a shame your *daed* couldn't go when it's colder here, *ja*?"

Elijah took the opportunity to speak up, but to Fanny's surprise, made no mention of Mary's omission of concern for his grandfather. "Not a fan of cold weather, then?"

Mary gave a little laugh. "*Nee*! Why, I can't imagine how a farmer does it, working all winter outside, his hands as chapped as his lips at the day's end and with little to warm himself but a small wood-burning fire when the sun sets!"

At this comment, Henry chuckled. "*Ja, vell*, I'm not so sure about that!"

Mary rolled her eyes at her brother's suggestive comment, but continued. "And a farmer certainly cannot travel to places like Pinecraft! They can hardly even take a day off!"

"Our *daed*'s a farmer," Elijah pointed out. "He managed to leave."

Turning her body so that she could look directly at Elijah, Mary paused before responding. Fanny didn't like the way that, in that short moment of hesitation, Mary's eyes opened as if seeing Elijah for the first time. "Ah, true! But he left the farm in such capable hands!"

If her former comment had seemed biting and critical, the latter was definitely softer and complimentary. While Fanny was increasingly certain that she did not care for either one of the Coblentzes, it was quite clear that the three Bontragers were oblivious to the flaws that were so painfully clear to her.

"So you take back your disparaging comment about farmers?" he asked, a semi-teasing tone to his voice softening his reprimand.

Mary must have noticed that she struck a nerve, for she straightened her back and returned to the slightly flirtatious tone. "*Nee*, I do not. Your *daed* is certainly an exception to the rule, but apparently so is his son."

Fanny almost blushed for Elijah. Such forwardness! Fanny could tell that Mary was used to charming people with her pretty face and far too familiar rapport. In Fanny's opinion playing coy was not becoming of any woman, especially one that was targeting that attention at Elijah.

To her further dismay, while Elijah did not respond to the comment, something warmed in his face. His eyes glowed as he stared at her. "Do you not like farmers, Mary?"

"Not like farmers? I wonder if you mean as people in general or as an occupation?" She gave him a forced smile as she answered her own question. "People, yes. Occupation, yes—but only if it's not mine."

"Not yours?" Elijah sounded like a mimicking bird.

"I do not shirk hard work or long days, but a farmer's wife works far too hard for that to be a role that I aspire to," she explained. "There is no joy for me in working before the sun rises and well after it sets. Why, a farmer's wife probably works even harder than her husband, especially when they have *kinner*." She paused, lifting her chin just a little, her forced smile slowly changing into one that reflected a softness. "*Nee*, I'd much prefer to spend those evenings in the company of my family, particularly my husband. Life is too short to be working so many hours of the day and then be tired for the rest!"

There was a moment of silence as everyone stared at Mary. If it were not for the lighthearted tone and semi-teasing expression on her pretty face, Mary's words might have offended more than just Fanny. After all, the Bontrager family came from a long line of farmers, and in all likelihood, Elijah, not Thomas, would inherit the farm one day.

"I see," Elijah said softly.

Miriam, however, wasted no time in pointing out the error of Mary's comment. "Elijah intends to farm, Mary," she said. "His heart is torn between honoring God and working the land, although we all suspect that he might have the opportunity to do both one day."

Mary's eyes opened wide and she stared at him with a new level of intrigue. "A possible preacher? Oh my!"

At this, the color rose to Elijah's cheeks as Fanny observed the exchange. She wished that she could jump into the conversation and defend her champion from the curious remarks that seemed to pour out of Mary's mouth. Her nerve, however, would never rise up enough to let her do such a thing.

"See how modest he is?" Miriam laughed, just a little too loud. "Why, he'll be chosen for preaching one day, mark my words!"

His discomfort became even more apparent at his sister's remark. "That lot falls to God," Elijah reminded her, "not man."

"We shall see," Miriam replied with a knowing look in her eyes. "Personally I'd be rather bored with playing the preacher's wife." Simultaneously Julia and Fanny looked at her, their mouths falling open. Even Jeb looked taken aback by that unusual confession. But Miriam only shrugged her shoulders. "Listening to everyone's problems. Dealing with strife in the *g'may*. *Nee*, I would not like that at all."

The strangeness of her comment made Fanny feel uncomfortable. She wanted to remind her cousin that Jeb could very well be chosen to become a preacher—or even a bishop!—in the future. All men who accepted the baptism were eligible to be nominated if the need arose for a preacher in the *g'may*.

No one commented, but Fanny noticed an odd look in Henry's eyes. He seemed to ignore the fact that Jeb stood nearby while he studied Miriam with even more interest than he had before he learned that she was to wed Jeb. Julia, however, appeared to make the same observation, for the wrinkles in her forehead deepened and the corner of her mouth turned down.

"There's a calf," Elijah said, clearing his throat as he spoke. "Born just two days ago."

The attention shifted from Miriam to Elijah, the suddenness of the change in topic surprising Fanny just as much as it appeared to startle the others. But it was so much like Elijah to try to smooth over the awkward moment that his sister had created with her thoughtless comments.

Fanny caught onto Elijah's intentions and spoke up. "Oh, *ja*, the calf!" She took a step toward the barn, pausing as she moved closer to Mary. "*Kum*, Mary. Let's go see the newborn calf!"

As she started toward the barn, Fanny paused long enough for Mary to realize that she had little choice but to accompany her. A grateful-looking Elijah joined them with Julia and Henry walking slowly behind the group. When Fanny glanced over her shoulder, she saw that Jeb remained with Miriam, a stern lecture being given from the former to the latter. Unfortunately it appeared to fall on deaf ears, for Miriam looked unfazed by his words as she tilted her chin in silent defiance.

It took a moment for Fanny's eyes to adjust to the darkness of the barn, even with the double doors open and light streaming inside the wide walkway between the individual stalls and the large area for the cows. She imagined that everyone else encountered the same problem so she slowed her pace, just for a moment, in the hopes that they would catch up to her.

"Fanny," Elijah said, "go fetch a bottle to feed it, *ja?*"

She nodded and hurried toward the back of the barn. There was a short step under a low doorway to get into the milk containment room. The containment system, powered by diesel fuel, kept the milk at 46 degrees Fahrenheit until the collection truck came to fetch it for pasteurization, packaging, and distribution. Fanny always wondered what happened to the milk after it left the farm, and on the several occasions that Elijah tried to explain it, she realized how fortunate they were to live on a farm and have fresh milk on a daily basis.

There was a bottle of milk already set aside for the calf. Fanny grabbed it along with the large nipple that someone, probably Elijah, had prepared from the morning feeding. It took her three tries to slip the nipple onto the mouth of the bottle, but once she was successful, she hurried back to rejoin the others.

Only half of them were missing.

Mary and Elijah stood by the wooden door to the calf's stall. Julia and Henry were conveniently missing. As Fanny approached, Elijah turned toward her and reached out to take the bottle from her. But as she neared, her foot stepped into a previously undetected pile of manure and she slid forward, the bottle almost slipping from her hand as she fell.

Elijah moved quickly, bending forward and grabbing her waist with his hand. He pulled her toward him, using his weight to balance both of them so that Fanny would not fall to the ground.

"Careful now!" he said in a soft voice.

Fanny's free hand fell to his shoulder, and for just a moment, she felt his chest pressed against hers as he held her. She forgot that Mary stood just three feet away, her eyes watching them with so much curiosity that, when Fanny realized they were being watched, she blushed and quickly pushed herself away from Elijah.

"*Danke*, cousin," she whispered. Without looking at him, she thrust the bottle into his hand and took a step away.

But Elijah did not seem to notice. He took the bottle and turned toward Mary. "Careful where you step, Mary," he cautioned. "Lots of manure in a barn." Without another word, he squeezed his way into the calf's pen, holding the gate open for Mary to follow. Fanny realized that while her heart still beat rapidly from the touch of his hands, Elijah had already forgotten about that moment of intimacy when he rescued Fanny from a potential fall. However, it was a moment *she* would not soon forget.

❧ Chapter 7 ❧

ON THE FIRST of September Thomas unexpectedly returned home from Florida. There had been no warning—no letter and certainly no phone call. He just walked into the kitchen and dropped his bag on the kitchen floor. At first the family rejoiced, believing that *Grossdawdi* must be largely recovered from his injuries and, therefore, Thomas was no longer needed to help his father. However, Thomas's silence on the topic indicated that his departure from Pinecraft might not have been under the best of circumstances. A letter that Timothy sent to Martha and Naomi was the center of a whispered conversation between the two sisters, a conversation Fanny overheard but did not quite comprehend. The only thing she learned was that Thomas's behavior was at the root of his dismissal and that Naomi's take on the situation confirmed there was no love lost between her and her nephew. Whenever he was around, his presence set Naomi's tongue clicking and head shaking, leaving Martha even more subdued than normal.

Fanny couldn't blame either one of them.

From the moment Thomas had returned, his father no longer there to rein him in, he had done nothing but cause trouble. On both Friday and Saturday, he woke late to help with chores. Just the previous night Fanny even heard him return one morning singing a song in a slurred voice. She hoped he hadn't been drinking, but in the morning his bleary, bloodshot eyes indicated the truth behind her suspicion.

If only Thomas would find God, Fanny told herself as she watched him nursing some coffee that morning.

But Thomas, surprisingly, was the least of her worries. Since the gathering the week before, Fanny had noticed a change in Elijah. He seemed more easily distracted, his attention often focused inward rather than on his surroundings. He spent less time reading the Bible in the post-supper hours and more time staring out the window, obviously deep in thought.

Even in the mornings, when Fanny helped him with the milking, she often had to call out to him that a cow was ready to be moved back into the holding pen because the milking machine had popped off her udders. Usually he was more attentive and didn't need reminders.

She didn't like this change in Elijah, and she suspected that the root cause had something to do with a certain Mary Coblentz.

The night before Thomas returned, Naomi had invited the newcomers to visit in the evening. With the bishop and his wife in tow, everyone had sat around the kitchen while Fanny and Martha served hot chocolate and popcorn. Mary sat with the other women, but Fanny was far too aware that Elijah continued to let his eyes wander to Mary, even though he was deep in discussion with Henry for most of the night.

That was the moment that Fanny knew. She watched Elijah, his gaze continually looking in the direction of

Mary Coblentz, even though she paid him nary a lick of attention. At first, Fanny thought he was staring at her, for she sat next to Mary on the straight-back chairs that were set up in a semi-circle near the sofa at the far end of the kitchen. But when she smiled at him and he did not respond, she realized that he was looking at Mary.

Fanny had stolen a glance at the pretty woman sitting next to her and saw that, even though she appeared focused on what Naomi was saying to the bishop, Mary was clearly aware that she was being watched. The soft upturn of her lips and the way that she occasionally touched her ear as if making sure her *kapp* was properly fastened made Fanny suspect that her appearance of inattention was deliberate.

Realizing that Elijah was, indeed, intrigued with Mary—if not outright interested!—caused Fanny to feel a tightening in her chest. She couldn't imagine what Elijah saw in Mary beyond a pretty face and a heavily masked flirtation with him. After all, she had made it quite clear that she did not want to marry a farmer, despite Elijah's future being solidly rooted in the fields of his parents' farm.

What type of wife would Mary make for Elijah? Fanny thought as she felt her heart beat and her head start to hurt. Elijah needed a wife who understood the meaning of hard work. A wife who didn't mind rising before dawn and going to bed shortly after dusk, especially during the spring and autumn seasons. Elijah needed a wife who respected his decision to follow in the footsteps of his ancestors, farming the land and milking the cows.

Would Mary roll up her sleeves to help with birthing a cow? Would she mind canning freshly butchered raw beef so that the family could eat during the winter? Could she wring the neck of a chicken and undress it for cooking just hours after it had run across the yard? Fanny highly doubted that Mary had any experience with the activities that contributed to the success of family life on a farm.

But the more she observed, the more she realized that Elijah was smitten with the pretty-faced Mary Coblentz. His infatuation was founded not in practicality but in her personal charm. And as Mary touched her ear for the sixth time in half an hour, she clearly enjoyed his attention.

"Excuse me," Fanny said as she stood up. She had to leave the room to catch her breath. For a few minutes she stood outside the front door and leaned against the porch railing. She gulped the air and fought the tears that threatened to expose her emotional distress. It would do her no good to cry. Elijah had to make his own decisions about his future, and if that future involved Mary Coblentz, then it surely would not include her.

When she had finally calmed down and returned to the room, she realized that no one had even noticed she had left. Quietly she stole upstairs to the solitude of her bedroom. Being alone in the company of others was worse than being alone in the company of herself.

Now it was Saturday evening. With worship service in the morning, the young group of friends had gathered in the Bontragers kitchen for some fellowship, for once free from the prying eyes of the adults in the family. Naomi and Martha had taken the buggy to visit a neighbor, but not before Naomi delivered a stinging lecture on how she expected them all to behave in their absence, and how she wanted everyone to leave by eight o'clock. Being too tired for church was not something Naomi tolerated.

As the newcomer this evening Thomas seemed to dominate the group. Being the oldest, he captured Mary's attention, an observation that seemed to drive Elijah to the brink of jealousy. He watched his older brother interact with Mary and shook his head from time to time. Fanny realized the irony of the parallels between them: as he pined for Mary, Fanny pined for him. From the looks of how attentive Mary was to Thomas, it was clear that Elijah felt the same way Fanny did upon realizing that another person captured the interest of their intended.

Ever since Thomas's return, Elijah had been unusually quiet. Fanny didn't know whether this was because Thomas promised to help Elijah but failed to follow through or whether it had do with Mary. When Thomas reappeared at the farm, Fanny had returned to her regular chores instead of helping Elijah in the barn, something that disappointed her tremendously, for she had enjoyed those quiet moments together, the silence occasionally interrupted by a short conversation about the cows or his plans for working later in the fields.

During that time, in Fanny's closed world, it was just the two of them. No Naomi barking orders. No Miriam trying to be the focus of everything and everyone. No Julia working hard to stand out from the shadows of her older sister. And no Martha, who seemed to do little more than sigh and declare how tired she was.

No. For Fanny, those early morning hours when she assisted Elijah were the best part of her day. And Thomas's return from Florida had stolen those cherished moments of peace from her.

Nor would this evening offer any respite from Thomas's antics, she soon realized. The nine of them had gathered around the kitchen table and were discussing what to do. Elijah again suggested a game of corn hole, but no one took up the idea. Instead Jeb suggested that everyone sing hymns.

"Oh Jeb!" Miriam said as she rolled her eyes.

Fanny noticed that Thomas quietly stole from the room while Miriam fussed over Jeb.

"Singing hymns! We'll have plenty of time to sing hymns tomorrow at the worship service. Honestly!"

Jeb started to respond to her, but Miriam had already walked away from him.

"I suggest we find something to do that is more creative..." she said as she positioned herself next to Mary and Henry. "...and fun!"

Thomas returned to the room. "I agree!" he said with great enthusiasm. "Instead of singing German hymns," he continued, waving a hymnbook that appeared similar to the one Benjamin had shown to Elijah at their previous gathering. "I propose that we sing some of these."

While Henry eagerly took the hymnbook to examine it, Elijah shook his head. "I think not, Thomas."

"Oh come, Elijah!" Thomas said, his voice loud and far too dramatic. "It's a hymn! What's wrong with singing a simple hymn?"

"It's not from the *Ausbund*," Elijah said, his chin jutting forward as he tried to maintain some semblance of decorum. But he and everyone else knew he fought a losing battle with his brother.

"Oh, Elijah!" Thomas waved his hand at him as if dismissing Elijah's concern. "How simple minded!" He laughed as he looked at Mary and Henry, shrugging his shoulders with his hands held out before him, palms up. "I give up with him."

Benjamin stepped forward, taking the hymnbook from Henry. "I tried telling him last week that the *Englische* hymns still glorify God. Where is the sin in that?"

All eyes turned in Elijah's direction as if they were not just expecting but waiting for an answer.

The color drained from Elijah's cheeks. It was one thing to have an older brother who strayed from the faith, but to have the same brother try to force him to stray and to have a friend defend Thomas was clearly more than he could manage.

Seeking to release Elijah from Thomas's badgering and Benjamin's betrayal, Fanny finally found the courage to speak up. She was proud of Elijah for taking such a strong position about obeying their father's rules, even when he was not physically there. She had been worried when Benjamin tried to lead him astray regarding the hymnbook. Now his own brother wanted to achieve that same goal.

"I...I think that singing *Englische* hymns isn't proper and..." she started to say, looking at Elijah while she spoke.

"Oh, nonsense, Fanny!" Thomas said, a harshness to his voice that startled even Mary. "There's nothing wrong with singing hymns."

"But your *daed*..."

"Oh, fiddle-faddle!" Miriam interrupted her this time. "*Daed*'s not even here, Fanny."

"Singing an *Englische* hymn is not a sin," Henry added to the conversation, pausing before he said the word *sin*. Fanny looked at him, surprised that he spoke up at all.

That was when she noticed that Henry's eyes were focused on Miriam, the corner of his mouth smiling. And while Henry watched her, Jeb watched him.

Oblivious to the energy passing between the others, Thomas shot Henry a quick grin and then turned back to address Fanny. "See? And he's related to the bishop."

"Ah, but by marriage only," Mary added, a light tone to her voice.

Miriam and Julia laughed too loud for Fanny's liking. And when both women looked at Henry, the kitchen suddenly felt unusually warm to Fanny. She sat on the hard bench by the table, her hands folded on her lap as she watched everyone else crowding around Thomas. Everyone else except Elijah and Fanny.

Fanny stole a glance at him. He stood to the side, leaning against the kitchen counter. It pleased her that they were united in their refusal to succumb to the pressure of the others. She had always known that he was a righteous man, and apparently his infatuation with Mary did not trump his faith.

Maybe now he would see the limits of Mary's character, for she had not spoken up in defense of Elijah like *she* had, Fanny thought.

Benjamin handed the book to Julia, who flipped through the pages, with Miriam quick to look over her shoulder.

"They're in English," Julia said, casually handing the book to Miriam. "I don't know the words to sing them."

"That's the point. We don't know them yet. But we will learn them."

"There's only one book," Julia said at last, handing the book to her sister.

"We'll share the book," Thomas declared.

Miriam glanced at the cover. "This is definitely not Amish." She didn't seem disturbed by that, especially when Henry raised his eyebrow at her. "Not that anything is wrong with that, I suppose."

Fanny stood her ground. "Your father would not approve."

Ignoring Fanny's objection, Benjamin moved so that he stood directly behind Julia. "Let's pick one out. We can learn the words together."

Julia watched as her sister turned a page, her eyes scanning the words of a hymn. Henry was far too close to Miriam and Julia scowled. As she turned away in disgust, she accidentally bumped into Benjamin. Smiling apologetically, she moved to the side, closer to Miriam so that she could position herself near Henry. "Where did you get this, Thomas?"

"Florida." He paused. "From a Mennonite friend."

Fanny raised an eyebrow. The way he said a Mennonite friend sounded suspiciously like it might be a woman. Perhaps that was why Timothy had sent Thomas home.

Henry moved behind the two Bontrager sisters. "Seems harmless enough," he said as he reached over Julia's shoulder and pointed to a page. "How 'bout this one, Julia? 'Draw Us to Thee'?" When he withdrew his hand, his wrist brushed the side of her neck. From the way he smiled, Fanny was certain it wasn't by accident.

When Julia blushed, Fanny responded by fidgeting and waiting for someone—anyone!—to say something to him. Instead, Mary laughed softly and Miriam fumed.

"You start, Thomas," Mary said. "We can follow along if you sing it slowly."

"I don't like the idea one bit," Elijah said as he raised his hand to rub his forehead.

Fanny's silence was her dissent.

But Miriam and Julia eagerly agreed with Mary, and wanting to please his soon-to-be wife, Jeb joined along. Benjamin too showed no signs of disapproval, as his previous interest in singing *Englische* hymns had already been established when he showed a hymnbook to Elijah in the barn.

Elijah stood next to the kitchen table, watching with a look of disappointment on his face. Occasionally he would glance at Fanny, and for those moments, she felt connected to him.

That Elijah agreed with Fanny was not a surprise to her. Evidently he had thought long and hard about the hymnbook that Benjamin had presented to him in the barn. His resistance to the others meant that he agreed with Fanny, not them, that his father's rule overruled his own curiosity.

In the Amish church obedience was everything. Whether complying with the Bible, the *Ordnung*, or the head of the house, Amish were expected, above all else, to obey. In all of her life Fanny had never refused to follow an order or directive, starting with her own parents, and once she moved to the Bontragers' house, continuing with Timothy. If she disagreed with something, she would comply in silence. It was not her place to question the rules of those in charge, even if she did not like what they said.

Elijah was no different. It was the one thing about him that made everyone suspect that, one day, he might be nominated to become a preacher in the church. He rarely complained and always followed the rules. Even now, as he watched the rest of the gathering laugh and discuss how they would sing the *Englische* hymn, he appeared disheartened with their decision.

"*Kum* now, Elijah," Mary said softly. She had left the others in the sitting area and joined Elijah by the table.

Fanny looked over her shoulder as Mary stood next to Elijah, her hand placed upon his arm. With her dark coloring and her deep blue dress, she looked particularly pretty, a fact that made Fanny's heart begin to beat rapidly and her palms sweat.

"It's just fun. Join us."

Elijah lifted his chin and did not meet Mary's eyes. "*Nee*, Mary. Not in my father's house," he said. "I will not do what I know my father would forbid."

Henry laughed in a mocking sort of way. Miriam, overhearing what Elijah said, remarked, "*Daed*'s not here, now, is he?" Miriam smiled when Henry rewarded her mischievous comment with a wink.

Fanny grimaced at Miriam's words as well as Henry's flirtatious actions.

The more she saw of Henry, the more reasons she found to dislike him. Neither Julia nor Miriam seemed to realize that Henry was toying with them, and they often made fools of themselves in their attempts to vie for his attention. Henry in fact seemed to delight in their flirtatious antics, which grew so overt that even the normally clueless Jeb began to notice. Now with her back turned toward Jeb and her smile reserved for Henry alone, Miriam made no secret of her favor for the young man, a fact that Jeb seemed helpless to thwart.

After all, how could a young man control his fiancée?

With everyone crowded around Thomas so that they could try to see the words, they began to sing:

> Draw us to Thee,
>   For then shall we
> Walk in Thy steps forever
>   And hasten on
> Where Thou art gone
>   To be with Thee, dear Savior.
>
> Draw us to Thee,
>   Lord, lovingly;
> Let us depart with gladness
>   That we may be
> Forever free
>   From sorrow, grief, and sadness.
>
> Draw us to Thee;
>   O grant that we
> May walk the road to heaven!
>   Direct our way
> Lest we should stray
>   And from Thy paths be driven.
>
> Draw us to Thee
>   That also we
> Thy heav'nly bliss inherit
>   And ever dwell
> Where sin and hell
>   No more can vex our spirit.
>
> Draw us to Thee
>   Unceasingly,
> Into Thy kingdom take us;

Let us fore'er
Thy glory share,
Thy saints and joint heirs make us.

When they were finished, Mary tried one more time to coax Elijah. "See, Elijah? Everyone else is singing." Once again she reached out to touch his arm. "Surely your *daed* would not be upset with singing praise to God."

The way that she looked at him, her dark eyes so large and bright, seemed to melt away his determination to remain true to his moral compass. And Mary's hand. It remained on his arm, just above his wrist, where his bare skin was exposed. Fanny bit the bottom corner of her lip, watching in disbelief as Elijah shifted his weight, moving ever so slightly in the direction of Mary.

"Elijah!" Fanny whispered. "You're to be baptized in four weeks!"

For the first time in speaking to Elijah, Fanny's words fell on deaf ears. He avoided looking at her. Instead, he maintained eye contact with Mary and gave the slightest nod of his head.

Unable to hold back, Fanny gasped.

Miriam shook her head. "Such a spoilsport, Fanny. Honestly!" she said, her tone light but cutting. She turned to Henry. "Isn't she now?"

Henry did not respond, saving his scrutiny for Miriam at that moment. He let his eyes travel the course of her body and gave a wicked smile when she blushed. Fanny's mouth opened in surprise and disgust, especially when Miriam did not move away from him.

With his decision made, Elijah moved away from the counter and joined the others who were already picking out the next hymn. Mary stood beside him, her hand still upon his wrist. When he looked at her before taking the hymnal from his brother, she rewarded him with a broad smile. "*Wunderbarr!*"

Fanny spun around on the bench, placing her elbows on the table and letting her head rest upon her hands. Her disappointment in Elijah's choice caused her heart to ache. She had thought she knew Elijah, that he was her big "brother" and protector. Now, however, she couldn't help but think that she barely knew him at all.

When the others began to sing, laughing when they missed a word or sang out of chorus, she stood up and quietly left the room. She wanted no part of their mischief. It was against the rules, and she refused to be coerced into disobeying the *Ordnung*—or Timothy—in order to please other people.

Outside, she wandered to the basket shed and lit a kerosene lantern. Rather than frolic in such a manner, Fanny decided she would put her time to better use. She could weave a few baskets, one of her favorite things to do anyway, and keep herself company by reciting Scripture in her head. Usually she enjoyed the peace of being alone. But this time the peace was broken by her disappointment in Elijah—of all people!—for not only had he sacrificed his values and beliefs, but he had done so for a woman like Mary Coblentz.

❧ *Chapter 8* ❧

OVER THE NEXT several weeks Thomas continued his antics, staying out late and failing to awake on time to help Elijah with the morning chores. When Fanny realized this, she began to slip downstairs at four in the morning to make a fresh pot of coffee before Elijah came downstairs.

"You're up again, Fanny?" he said when he sat at the table one Thursday morning. She was preparing some coffee for them to drink before heading outside. "You really don't have to keep helping me. It's Thomas who should be up so early."

Fanny shrugged. "I don't mind. Honest, Elijah."

He gave her a weary smile. "He's been home several weeks now, *ja?*"

She didn't answer, although she knew that it had been exactly two weeks. Two very long weeks.

"What does he do all day?" Elijah asked, more to himself than to her. "How can a man live with himself if he is not contributing to the well-being of the family? What sort of woman will ever want to marry a man with no constitution for work?"

Fanny bit her lower lip and turned away from Elijah. She wanted to reply that the same could be said for a woman who only wanted a husband who worked so that she would not have to. "Black, *ja*?" Fanny poured some coffee into a mug and walked over to set it before Elijah.

"You know it. But only in the morning, *ja*?" He wrapped his hand around the mug and lifted it to his lips. "Cream and sugar after chores."

She smiled at him. "Black for the bitterness of waking before the sun and sweetened for the day after morning chores are done."

"Ah, Fanny!" He smiled at her. "How well you know me! If only one day I could have a wife who is half as attentive as you are to my needs!"

If he noticed her smile fade, he didn't say anything. Instead, he focused on putting on his boots so that, once he finished the coffee, he could head outside to begin preparing for the milking. Fanny, however, stood there in the kitchen for several minutes after he finally left the house.

The blind eye that he turned to her affection for him continued to surprise her. And while she initially wondered if he noticed at all, now she began to believe that he never would.

Outside, in the cool morning of mid-September, the birds were beginning to sing as the sky shifted from darkness to the tawny shades of dawn. Fanny walked to the dairy barn, already hearing Elijah talking to the cows, his voice barely audible over their soft moos as they waited for the morning routine to begin.

"Everything ready then?" she asked as she climbed through the gate to the pen.

"*Ja*, just need to ring them on down to me like usual. Hay's out in the field for when they're done."

She nodded and, without needing to be told what to do, carefully made her way toward the back of the barn. She would herd the cows into the milking area, two on each side of the pit where Elijah would be waiting. Once the cows could not move further, Fanny would shut the gate behind them. With nowhere to move, the cows were ready for milking.

Fanny leaned against the gate and watched as Elijah sterilized their udders before placing the milking cups on them. The machine made a rhythmic clicking noise as the pump slowly pulled the milk from the cows' udders. She could watch Elijah in peace while he worked. His focus was on the cows and not what she was doing. As he tended to each cow, he talked to it in a soft voice, occasionally running his hand across its stomach as he placed the milking cups onto its udder.

And, despite his inability to recognize her feelings for him, as she watched him Fanny still thought he was the best of men.

◆◈◆

With the harvest brought in and last field of hay cut, there was more time for visiting in the afternoons. While Fanny didn't mind spending time with Elijah, she did mind the fact that the Coblentzes made their way over to the Bontragers' farm too frequently in her opinion. The way that Henry continued to trifle with both of her cousins did not go unnoticed by Fanny, and while she wasn't one to speak her thoughts out loud, she made her displeasure known by remaining silent in his company. She could barely watch as

Henry flirted with Julia one minute and then engaged in teasing discourse with Miriam the next.

On three separate occasions Jeb arrived to come calling on Miriam only to find himself displaced by Henry. The scowl on his face clearly expressed his disapproval of seeing Henry engaged in conversation with Miriam. But once Jeb arrived, Henry would immediately shift his attention to Julia, which seemed to suit her well enough.

Benjamin often joined the group too, seemingly eager to steal Julia's attention when Henry was engrossed with Miriam. As Fanny watched the awkward dynamics of the group, she could only thank the good Lord that she usually had reason to stay away from the gatherings. Naomi often gave her so much work to do that she could easily escape to the shed or the garden.

Of course, the worst part was observing as Mary continued to exploit Elijah's affections.

If she felt any thirst, Elijah would fetch her some water. If she wanted to stretch her legs, he was the first to offer to accompany her. While Thomas sometimes joined the young visitors, he did not seem to take any particular interest in Mary. Instead, he much preferred to leave in the early evening hours to visit with his own friends, rather than court a young woman.

And that left Mary with only one other person's attention to misuse for her own gain: Elijah.

"Come sit with us, Fanny," Mary said to Fanny.

It was early evening on a Saturday. They were all seated around the picnic table, a small open fire burning in a makeshift fire pit that Elijah and Benjamin had made from river rocks. Henry had not offered to help, claiming that he wore a new shirt that he preferred not to soil, and Jeb remained by Miriam's side, not trusting either one of them if he were to leave to cart back the rocks.

"*Nee*, I cannot," Fanny said as she walked from the barn, a bucket full of fresh milk in each hand. "Naomi wants me to make cheese this afternoon."

"Cheese?" Mary laughed and looked at Elijah. "Why, Fanny, that's such a long process to make cheese. It's so much easier to simply go purchase it at the store."

She stumbled over one of the rocks that had been carelessly left on the path. Henry stepped forward to grab her arm so that she neither fell nor dropped one of the buckets.

"Careful there, Fanny," he said, his lips so close to her ear that she could feel his warm breath on the back of her neck.

She pulled away from him, eager to escape his touch, but her manners prevailed so she thanked him. "*Danke*. I'm fine," she said, refusing to look at his face.

"I see that," he mumbled under his breath. The hidden intonation of his words made her suddenly look up, startled to see him staring at her with the slightest hint of amusement in his eyes.

Quickly she left the group and hurried into the house.

"Fanny!"

She stiffened at the sound of Naomi's voice, always full of disapproval for whatever she was or wasn't doing. "*Ja, Aendi?*"

"You need to get that cheese started. It should have already been in the press! What's taking you so long today?"

Fanny glanced over at Naomi, who sat in the rocking chair knitting a small washcloth that they would sell to the stores for the tourists. Martha sat on the sofa, listlessly leafing through an old *Family Life* magazine. From the way she turned the pages, Martha was clearly not reading anything, just shuffling through the pages.

"I had to help Elijah with the afternoon milking, and then I brought in the laundry from the line before their friends arrived," Fanny said as she poured the milk from both buckets into two large pots that already sat on the stove.

"Now careful there! Don't spill anything!" Naomi shook her head and clicked her tongue. "Honestly, girl. Julia just washed the floor this morning!"

No, Fanny wanted to say. *I washed the floor while Julia ran over to the neighbor's farm to visit her two friends.* But she said nothing and returned her attention to the milk in the pots.

Naomi set down her knitting and sighed. "The sun must be starting to set. My eyes can hardly see my own stitches."

Martha looked up from the magazine she wasn't reading. "Shall I turn on the light for you?"

"*Nee*, I might as well retire to my side of the *haus*." She stood up and pressed her hand against the small of her back. "Oh, the aches of aging!" She collected her knitting basket and started to walk toward the door but paused to look back at Fanny. "I reckon that can set overnight, Fanny. You should join the others."

Fanny looked up. "The others?"

Waving her hand toward the door that led to the porch, Naomi frowned at her. "Be social! With the Coblentzes and others. The way you disappear whenever they arrive, it's almost as if you are avoiding them."

Fanny said nothing to refute her aunt's accusation.

"Hmmph," Naomi gave a disapproving shake of her head. "That's what I thought. And for what reason, I can hardly begin to imagine. Why, that Henry and Mary! They are just the finest of folks. I fail to see why you hide when they visit. It's rather bad-mannered." As she slowly walked toward the back door that led to the *grossdawdihaus*, Naomi mumbled under her breath.

From the safety of the far side of the kitchen, Fanny rolled her eyes. If only her aunt could see how Henry flirted with both Miriam and Julia while Mary enticed Elijah, perhaps Naomi would change her opinion of just how fine they truly were.

"You know, Fanny Price," Naomi said as she opened the door, "it would do you some good to make yourself agreeable to Henry. There aren't too many young men hanging around our *haus* now, are there? A wise young woman would try to attract Henry's attention rather than hide from it!"

Frustrated, Fanny pressed her lips together and gripped the edge of the counter with her hands, her fingers pressing against it until her knuckles turned white.

By the time she had the milk at the right temperature, the sun had disappeared behind the barn. The noise of Henry's laughter caused her to look up. They were coming inside, for the fire had died and the air turned too chilly to continue sitting outside.

"Come now!" Henry said as he burst through the door. "You know this song."

The way his voice was soft and playful made Fanny presume he was talking to Julia. With Jeb around, Henry paid far less attention to Miriam, which seemed to suit Julia quite well.

Earlier in the week, during one of the Coblentzes' visits when Jeb was there, Miriam had openly pouted over Henry's attention being spent on Julia. To Fanny's surprise, Jeb had taken Miriam by the elbow, insisting that they speak privately. When they returned, Miriam acted more subdued and proper. Certainly she must realize that an unhandsome man with 160 acres was far better than a handsome man with nothing.

The others followed Henry into the kitchen and sat down in the now vacant sitting area. Thomas laughed as he pulled a chair over from the kitchen table. "*Ja*, you know the words, Miriam. Sing it with us and the louder the better, I say! After all, we want *Aendi* Naomi to hear us next door so that she knows we're behaving ourselves."

Fanny rolled her eyes, even though no one could see her. Thomas had crept up the stairs at four in the morning, just about the time Elijah had to arise and tend to the cows. When Fanny had heard the door to Thomas's room shut and the creaking noise of his bed, she had sighed and once again forced herself to leave her warm, cozy bed.

In good conscience she couldn't leave Elijah alone to milk the cows and feed the animals. That just wasn't fair, and she knew he'd never complain or ask for help. Besides, she missed her special mornings alone with Elijah. It wasn't even work, in her mind. It was more like a little gift of time that she treasured more than words could say.

But when Fanny returned with Elijah, Naomi was in the kitchen, scowling at her. In all likelihood, her aunt had known the reason Fanny was awake: Thomas had behaved irresponsibly once again. But rather than praise Fanny, she had scolded her for being late to help prepare breakfast. The only satisfying moment of the morning was Naomi reprimanding Thomas when he finally awoke at ten o'clock, asking him if he could find it in his power to behave for just a few days to give the rest of the family a break from his antics.

Clearly his comment about singing loudly was in retaliation for Naomi's complaints.

Fanny was the only one who didn't participate in the singing. Instead, she sat at the table and traced circles on the tabletop with her finger. The smudge marks left behind made interesting patterns that she knew she'd have to clean later.

"Fanny," Martha called from the other room.

Eager for a distraction, Fanny hurried into the dark bedroom to see what her aunt needed.

"I'm feeling rather chilled. Might you fetch me a blanket?" Martha asked.

"Going to bed so soon, then?" Fanny hurried to the large hope chest that was pressed against the wall near the dresser. It was heavy to open and Fanny struggled to pull out the quilt. "Shall I tell the others to leave?"

Martha shook her head. "*Nee*, Fanny," she said, smiling her appreciation as Fanny covered her with the blanket. "I'm sure that I'll fall asleep quickly. I simply cannot shake this weary feeling that makes me feel tired all the time."

Tired and depressed, Fanny wanted to add. And it had been many years coming.

She couldn't blame Martha. Even before Naomi's husband had died, Naomi had exerted control over her sister.

Once the bishop died and Naomi moved into the *grossdaw-dihaus*, Martha lost any remaining say in her own household. In the days before the bishop died, Fanny remembered that Naomi visited far too frequently. However, there had been stretches of time when she wasn't there. On those days Martha appeared so much happier and more cheerful. Now, with Naomi constantly barging through the door that separated the main house from the *grossdawdihaus*, Martha had shriveled up within herself, each day becoming less of a person and more of an object.

Fanny wondered why she was the only one who noticed the drastic change in Martha, for surely if anyone else had marked her decline, they would have insisted upon taking her to see a doctor. But Martha's children were either too self-obsessed or too busy keeping up with the farm to note any changes in their mother.

"Won't their singing wake you?" Fanny asked.

Martha shook her head. "*Nee*, it will not. Besides I like hearing those hymns. They are easier to understand than the German ones."

Her answer surprised Fanny. After all, Timothy was her husband and the head of the household. Surely she knew his rules as well as anyone else. In all of the years that Fanny had been living there, not once had Martha questioned or countered any of Timothy's rules, no matter if she agreed or disagreed with them.

After she finished helping Martha, Fanny quietly stole back out to the kitchen, avoiding the rowdy group singing from the sitting area. She peeked into the pot to check the curds, taking a knife to cut through to see if the pot was ready for draining. If she could only finish the cheese, or at least, get it to the point of being able to drain in a cheese-cloth overnight, she would disappear to the safety of her bedroom.

"What. Is. This?"

At the sound of the booming voice that addressed the gathering from the door, Fanny dropped the knife, and it fell with a clatter to the floor. When she looked up, she was just as surprised as the rest of them to see Timothy standing there, his hands on his hips and a scowl upon his face.

"*Daed*!" Elijah moved away from Mary, as if trying to put a safe distance between them. "You're back?"

Timothy ignored the rhetorical question and entered the room, staring at Benjamin, who held the forbidden book in his hands. He crossed the room and, with a fast move-ment, snatched the book from Benjamin. His eyes glanced at the cover.

"Mennonite hymns? In English?" First Timothy stared at Benjamin and then at his oldest son. "This is not the *Ausbund*!" He shoved the book back at Benjamin, pushing it against his chest as he turned to face Thomas. "Was it not bad enough that you misbehaved in Pinecraft? Must you bring your poor judgment and penchant for trouble to my own home?"

"*Daed*, I..."

Timothy silenced him by raising his hand and holding it in the air. He took his time, assessing the situation and looking at each one of the participants. When his gaze fell upon Fanny, standing by the stove, he paused. Fanny wished that she could shrink away, feeling uncomfortable under the scrutiny of her uncle. When he stepped closer to

151

her, the air escaped her lungs and her shoulders slumped forward. His eyes glanced into the pots and realized that she was in the midst of finishing her chores.

"I don't know if I am more surprised by *your* lack of involvement," he said to her in a kind voice before returning his attention to the others and continuing harshly, "or my own *kinner*'s participation!" He glared at Jeb. "And you! Dishonoring me when you are to wed my *dochder*?"

Jeb stammered over his words. "I—I beg your forgiveness."

But Timothy appeared less than impressed with the apology. He turned toward the only two people in the room that he did not recognize. "And who are these two?" He glowered at Henry and Mary. "Let me guess. The Coblentzes? I imagine your *onkle*, the bishop, will not take kindly to hearing that you introduced Mennonite hymns to my family!"

For some reason it did not surprise Fanny that Henry did not shirk from the wrath of Timothy's anger. Whether his nonchalance was because he felt no intimidation or because he simply didn't care, Fanny couldn't determine. "It was not I who introduced the hymns," Henry stated. The shifting of his gaze toward Thomas gave away the true culprit. To Fanny, the betrayal spoke more of Henry's inferior character than Thomas's poor decision.

Timothy took two steps and stood before his oldest son. The look upon his face was intense and spoke of years of disappointment. This was not the first time that Thomas had stepped well outside of the boundaries that Timothy set for his family. Fanny could not help but suspect that it would also not be the last.

"I would say that I am surprised, but I am not." That was all that Timothy said in recognition of Thomas's role. Fanny suspected that he too was unimpressed with the deftness at which Henry so willingly threw another man under the buggy.

The bedroom door opened and Martha appeared, her robe covering her nightgown. For a moment her face lit up when she saw Timothy and she paused in the doorway. "You've returned! Oh, how *wunderbarr* to have you home! You were gone for far too long, Timothy!"

Her voice gave away the true emotion she felt: relief. With Timothy back at home, Naomi would no longer be in charge. Fanny wondered if his return and Naomi's demotion might help Martha snap out of her depression.

"*Ja*, I have returned and none too soon!" he snapped. "Are you privy to this"—he gestured toward the gathering—"singing of Mennonite songs?"

Martha's smile immediately faded from her face, her excitement at seeing her husband quickly replaced by reality. Despite his return signifying the end of Naomi's reign, she was now reminded that it would be replaced by his own. She didn't look at anyone else in the room. "*Nee*, Timothy. I have no idea what you are talking about," she said. "I only just came out from the bedroom. My head, you see. And I've been so tired…"

Her answer did not please Timothy, and Fanny suspected that no answer would have. Had Martha known about the hymns, he would have berated her for disobeying his rules in his absence. However, by stating that she was unaware, she was admitting that she had not properly managed the household. Timothy always said that a good parent knows exactly what his or her children are doing.

"Why, I am in shock. The only one of you with any sense," he said, "is Fanny!" He pointed at her while glaring at his own children.

Fanny stared at the floor. His compliment—the first in all the years that she had lived there—made her feel uncomfortable and self-conscious. She did not like the attention from Timothy and worried that the others would feel that she was proud. However, he gave her no more compliments and said no more on the subject.

Soon enough the quiet that had greeted Timothy's declaration was quickly replaced by the scrape of chairs and the shuffle of feet as one by one the guests left the house under Timothy's stern glare. Only the family remained, Thomas smirking defiantly, Miriam and Julia squirming uneasily in their chairs, and Elijah steadfastly averting his eyes from the one person who had warned him about the inevitable wrath of their father: Fanny.

❧ *Chapter 9* ❧

O N THE FIRST Sunday in October the Millers hosted the baptism ceremony for the Bontragers' *g'may*. Like many of the church districts, theirs only baptized new members once a year and always before the other two important church meetings: Council and Communion. For most families with a son or daughter who were taking the kneeling vow, a lifelong commitment to shun the world and live according to the *Ordnung*, it was an emotional, even special, time of year.

Having children join the church was often viewed as a sign of good parenting. While gossip was frowned upon, a direct violation of Jesus's command to love thy neighbor, the joy with which families shared the news of their children's upcoming baptism was the subject of much discussion and carried more than a whisper of judgment against those who had still not committed to join the church.

When a young adult made that decision to accept their baptism, the parents could breathe a sigh of relief. Too often stories circulated of a youth who started a *rumschpringe* and decided not to join the church. And always, when those stories circulated, there were whispers among the Amish grapevine that the parents had been far too permissive in raising their children.

This year, with Elijah finally committing to the church, Timothy appeared hard pressed to balance his pride in his younger son with his disappointment in his older one.

His daughters and Fanny had accepted their baptism two years earlier, a sign that they had finished their running-around years and were ready to settle down. Sons, however, tended to wait longer to make that commitment.

The large shop over the Millers' barn was large enough to accommodate all of the families and invited relatives who came to the baptism service. After all, baptism was a day of celebration as well as reflection. Often times family members came from other districts to share in the glory of the day.

Just like the regular Sunday services, the congregation gathered for worship, the men on one side of the room and the women on the other. For the first forty minutes, the congregation engaged in singing one of the German hymns from the *Ausbund*, the *vorsinger* starting the song by singing the first syllable of each line with the rest of the congregation joining him to complete the different verses. Each verse was long and drawn out, the a cappella song eerily comforting on such a gray day. But after the song, the bishop stood up and motioned to the baptismal candidates to follow him as he left the shop.

Fanny sat on the hard bench, listening to the preacher while watching the door at the side of the large room. From her own experience, she knew that the bishop was giving them their final instructions and making certain that each candidate fully understood the commitment that they were about to make. And she also knew that Elijah was most certainly nervous. This was a serious decision—perhaps the most important one in the life of any Amish man or woman.

It was not a decision to be made lightly, and Fanny knew that Elijah had prayed many nights over the past year regarding his commitment to the church. He never had doubted that he would join the church, and Fanny often wondered why it had taken him so long to do so. She suspected that he had waited in the hopes that Thomas would be baptized alongside him. But, after so many years waiting in vain, Elijah had finally decided that he could wait no longer.

If Timothy was upset with Elijah about the *Englische* hymns, it was long forgotten. And the disappointment in Thomas's ongoing *rumschpringe* was far from his mind today. Instead, he sat upright on the other side of the room, his face all but glowing with pride that his now-favored son was joining the church.

Fanny looked away from the men's side of the gathering, her eyes trailing over the white-capped heads of the women seated in front of her. On the bench in front of her sat Mary. Fanny couldn't help let her gaze linger on Mary, whose body was turned just enough that Fanny knew she was staring attentively at the preacher. It was what Fanny should be doing, and when she realized that she hadn't listened to any of his sermon, she bit her lip and forced herself to follow Mary's example.

For the past week Fanny hadn't seen either Mary or Henry. Timothy's displeasure over the hymn singing was enough of a deterrent for the Coblentzes to stay away from the Bontrager farm. While fortuitous for Fanny on several fronts, neither of her cousins felt the same. With Henry's absence, Miriam returned her attention to Jeb, and Julia faced the cold reality that Henry did not fancy courting her. Fanny, however, was relieved to not have him visiting in the afternoons. His trifling with the hearts of her cousins had won him no favors with Fanny.

Meanwhile Elijah was just as distracted as ever. While the rest of the family commented out of his hearing that he was struggling with the seriousness of his upcoming baptism, Fanny had her doubts. Of all the Bontragers' children, Elijah was the most righteous and devoted follower of God's word and the *Ordnung*. She suspected that his pensiveness had less to do with the seriousness of his upcoming commitment to the church and more to do with the severity of his intense attraction to Mary.

Just two nights ago, on Friday evening, shortly after supper, Fanny had thought she heard the sound of a horse and buggy leaving their farm. Her heart felt heavy when she realized that Thomas had left earlier with his friends and Timothy had retired to bed. That left only one person who would have harnessed up the horse and gone visiting: Elijah. And she knew exactly where he had gone.

Now, as Fanny and the rest of the congregation waited for the bishop to lead the three baptismal candidates out of the back room and to the front of the congregation, Fanny felt a mixture of emotions. While she was happy that Elijah was officially joining the church, something that she never really doubted he would do, she had a new worry. Young men who joined the church usually had marriage on their minds. And even though Elijah had planned to take his kneeling vow long before the Coblentzes arrived in Mount

Hope, Fanny wondered if his piqued interest in Mary had nudged him more strongly in that direction.

Whenever she thought about this—and it was something she was increasingly prone to do—she felt her chest tighten and her heart race. Sometimes she found herself catching her breath as if she could no longer breathe properly. After a few minutes the wave of panic would pass. But it took longer for her to feel back to her normal self. Even now, as she tried to focus on the preacher's sermon, she could feel that familiar agitation begin to surface. It didn't help that, despite the cool autumn weather, the crowded gathering room grew increasingly warm.

The door opened just as the preacher sat down, his sermon over. The congregation stirred as the bishop led the candidates to the front of the room, where they knelt down. The congregation then began to sing the *Das Loblied* hymn, and Fanny peeked at Elijah, wondering if he was singing or praying.

He was singing.

Feeling the hint of a proud smile on her lips, she couldn't keep herself from watching him. For the moment she put all thoughts of Mary Coblentz out of her mind and focused on the only important thing: Elijah's commitment to God.

When the people finished singing *Das Loblied*, the bishop cleared his throat, an indication that he was about to begin the baptism sermon. Elijah bowed his head, raising one hand to cover his face in a sign of humility. Fanny sensed the magnitude of the ceremony and felt an unfamiliar burning in the corner of her eyes.

She fought the urge to cry as she listened to the bishop speak to the congregation. He talked about John the Baptist baptizing Jesus and then about Philip baptizing an Ethiopian. Fanny listened intently, appreciating that it was the same sermon that had been given to generations before and would most likely be the same one that future bishops would give, long after these three people were baptized. Yet, to Fanny, the words felt especially poignant and powerful on this dreary, gray day.

"In Matthew 6, the Savior says that no man is able to serve two masters," the bishop said in a loud voice. "For if a man tries to serve two masters, he will certainly hate the one and love the other! Man cannot choose to honor God's Word if he chooses to live in sin. A life of obedience and humility versus worldliness and vanity. That is the battle that faces these young people today. Which will they choose?"

Fanny noticed someone fidgeting further down the bench where she sat. Glancing in that direction, she saw Miriam, who was not only ignoring what the bishop was saying but blatantly gazing across the room at Henry.

The bishop paced in front of Elijah and the other two people kneeling before him. "I ask you now if you are willing to renounce Satan and all of his followers, for the dark kingdom is filled with deceitful and worldly riches!" He paused as he paced. "Will you renounce your own carnal and selfish will, lusts, and affections? Do you pledge yourself to be faithful to God, to receive the Savior Jesus Christ, and to allow yourself to live a life that is led by the Holy Spirit in all obedience to the truth and to remain in this unto death?" Once again, he paused, this time standing still for a long, drawn-out moment. He looked at each one of the people kneeling before him, even though they could not see him, their hands still covering their eyes. Finally the bishop asked a simple question, "Can you acknowledge this with a yes?"

After the bishop continued with the rest of the questions concerning baptism, he paused again, his eyes carefully scanning the bowed heads before him. "If you are still intent on taking this baptism," he began, his voice serious and deliberate, "then I ask you to stay kneeling before me and the congregation. If, however, you have any doubts, this is the time to speak up."

Silence.

When enough time had passed, it was time for each of the candidates to profess their confession of faith.

"Elijah Bontrager, do you renounce the devil, the world, and your own flesh and blood?"

He nodded his head. "*Ja.*"

"Can you commit yourself to Christ and his church, to abide by it and therein to live and to die?"

Fanny thought she saw Elijah swallow before he responded with another simple, "*Ja.*"

The bishop took a deep breath before he asked the third and final question, "And in the *Ordnung* of the church, according to the Word of the Lord, to be obedient and submissive to it and to help therein?"

This was the one that Fanny worried about the most. She knew that if she broke one of the church district's rules, she risked being shunned, and she fretted constantly that she might inadvertently say or do something against the *Ordnung*, those unwritten rules that governed their Amish community.

But Elijah seemed more confident than Fanny had felt when she took her vows. He was always more confident.

That was one of his traits that she admired so much. While Fanny worried and prayed that God would help her keep that vow, she knew that Elijah would never stray. Once Elijah made a commitment, he would not break it.

"Please speak your confession of faith, Elijah Bontrager," the bishop said.

"*Ich glaub dab Jesus Christus Gottes Sohn ift*," Elijah said.

Fanny's heart pounded as she heard him profess his steadfast belief that Jesus Christ was, indeed, the Son of God. Once the words left his lips, the bishop placed his hands upon Elijah's head.

"Elijah Bontrager," the bishop said as the deacon poured water on his bare head. "Upon your confessed faith, you are baptized in the name of the Father and the Son and the Holy Spirit, amen. Whoever believes and is baptized shall be saved." He removed Elijah's hands from covering his face and helped him stand before the congregation. The bishop kissed the back of Elijah's hand, the indication of the completion of Elijah's baptism.

When Elijah turned to rejoin the rest of the congregation, Fanny sat straighter and craned her neck in the hopes that he would see her. She wanted him to know the extent of her joy at this moment, her joy that he had accepted his baptism. But the joy quickly faded and the feeling of pressure in her chest returned when, upon walking back to his seat, Elijah's eyes sought out and paused on Mary Coblentz. His kneeling vow over, Elijah was now a true Amish man. Clearly his thoughts were already on the next ceremony of importance to an Amish man: his wedding.

❧ *Chapter 10* ❧

THE FOLLOWING SATURDAY Elijah found Fanny sitting outside in the sun, the weather being unseasonably warm for autumn. With her chores finished and the sun beginning to set, she had taken some time to sit on the porch swing to think. Ever since Timothy had returned to Ohio, Fanny had noticed a tension in the air, especially in the evenings. Miriam and Julia both seemed pouty, although no one else seemed to notice. Elijah remained distracted, and Thomas was rarely home at all. Naomi tended to visit less frequently, and Martha's lethargy was increasingly obvious to all. She had even heard Elijah speaking with his father about the need to take Martha to a doctor for some medicine for her melancholy and constant fatigue.

Timothy had responded with a curt "Let me think about it."

As far as Fanny knew, the discussion had not resurfaced. Timothy was not a proponent of modern medicine and felt that Martha's depression would eventually resolve itself in due course. Fanny wondered if it would resolve itself quicker if Naomi spent less time trying to run the household, an opinion she never spoke aloud.

Fanny watched all of these changes from the sidelines of the family, knowing that her opinion was neither sought nor welcomed. But she couldn't keep herself from worrying in silence.

Upon leaving the barn, Elijah crossed the yard and climbed the porch steps where she had been praying with her eyes closed. But as she heard him approach, she ended her prayer, opened her eyes, and greeted him with a warm smile.

"Fanny," he said, making a gesture that he wanted to sit beside her on the porch swing. "How fortuitous that I found you!"

She laughed as she moved over to make room for him. "Fortuitous? I doubt that there is anything 'fortuitous' about finding me. I'm never far from the house. Just look and you will always find me, Elijah."

He nudged her arm with his shoulder. "*Ach*, Fanny! You know what I mean," he said. "I never see you anymore."

"You've been rather..." She paused. "...preoccupied, Elijah, since your baptism." Most evenings, he excused himself from the supper table and retreated outside. No one seemed to question his comings and goings, not the way that they frowned upon Thomas's. But Timothy seemed to have an extra spring to his step, often looking as if he knew a great secret that pleased him tremendously.

Fanny feared what that secret might actually be.

Elijah returned her smile, but there was a distant look in his eyes. "*Ja*, I have, I reckon."

He looked away, his eyes scanning the horizon and admiring the fields. She followed his gaze but saw nothing of interest there. The cornfields were bare, the stalks having been cut and ground for feed. Beyond the incline of the field stood a scattering of trees, the leaves just beginning to fall, the highlight of their rich autumn colors having faded to an orangey-brown. *Autumn*, she thought. *A time of change for everyone.*

In one week, on the following Sunday, their church district would hold the Council meeting after worship service. In order for the Amish to take communion, every member of the church needed to attend the Council meeting where the *Ordnung* would be discussed and new rules added. Last year, the members of the *g'may* had voted that the use of cell phones, even for business, would not be permitted. They felt it was giving the youth too much accessibility to the outside world and that could lead to temptation and sin. Fanny suspected that the same issue would be raised this year, since so many young men especially needed access to phones to coordinate drivers to their non-farm jobs.

The other objective of the Council meeting was to right any wrongs that had been done throughout the year. Fanny remembered a mild feud between two neighbors when a cow broke through the fencing and trampled some of the corn crops. While the owner of the cow fixed the fence right away, he had not recompensed his neighbor for the damaged corn. It was a sore subject among the farmers in the church district.

Only after everyone was in agreement and outstanding issues made right would the *g'may* be permitted to take communion at the following worship service.

All of this made Fanny happy. After all, Mary and Henry were not members of the Mount Hope church, so, just the previous day, they had returned to Gordonville in order to attend their own Council meeting and to participate in the communion service. Miriam had been quietly pouting since their departure, which made Fanny wonder about her sincerity regarding marrying Jeb. Why would she marry a man just because he had a large farm if her affections rested with another?

As for Julia, she too was unusually quiet. Fanny noticed that Benjamin seemed to come around more often under the false pretense of visiting with Elijah, but Fanny caught him on more than one occasion making an excuse to enter the kitchen where Julia was working on a basket. She welcomed the distraction, shoving the unfinished basket in Fanny's direction so that she could visit with Benjamin. Whether Julia's joy was due to seeing Benjamin or merely getting out of work, Fanny couldn't tell. But she did know that Julia fancied Henry much more than Benjamin. He was merely a distraction while she pined for another.

Of all the Bontrager family, Fanny appeared to be the only one relieved that Mary and Henry had departed. She simply was not a fan of Elijah's attention to Mary Coblentz. He doted on her every word, laughed at her little comments—some of which Fanny felt were a touch too sarcastic!—and seemed to focus just on her when she was around. The more Mary visited the Bontrager farm, the more Elijah became *ferhoodled* in love.

Now that they were gone, Fanny thought, life could return to normal. Or, at least, whatever normal meant considering so much would change in the upcoming weeks.

After the communion service, the bishop would begin announcing upcoming weddings. Jeb and Miriam would be among the first named. Fanny wondered how it would feel when Jeb began spending the nights at their farm, another person to add to the Bontrager family until spring came and Miriam moved to his parents' 160-acre farm that she kept talking about whenever the opportunity arose.

And then Fanny wondered about Julia. Would she be the next to marry? With her sights once set on Henry, Julia certainly had held high hopes that she would. But now that he had left Holmes County, those hopes were dashed. Perhaps in Henry's absence, Benjamin would finally have some success in gaining her interest and attention.

Once her cousins married, most of the domestic work would fall upon Fanny's shoulders. Naomi complained that her arthritis hurt too much to do laundry or scrub floors, while Martha's "condition" continued to worsen, her tendency to sit and silently stare out the window confirming to Fanny that the melancholy her aunt felt was more serious than anyone would admit.

"I have something I wanted to speak to you about," Elijah said at last.

She looked at him, surprised. "Oh?"

"I have a question to ask you."

Fanny stared at him, unable to respond right away. "I imagine that anything you would ask I would respond to with great favor," she managed to say.

He laughed at her response. "Oh, *ja*, that's our sweet Fanny! Always eager to do anything anyone asks."

She felt the color flood to her cheeks. She wondered if that was how he saw her. Eager to please all? If only he knew her constant acquiescing to additional chores was not from eagerness to please but to avoid a browbeating by Naomi and to be left alone by the others in the family. The only caveat to that was Elijah. *He* was the one person that she was always eager to please.

"But it's a different type of question, Fanny. And I'm not quite sure how to ask it." He began to tap his fingers against his knee as if nervous. "I've been thinking about it for quite some time and..." He stole a peek at her. "...well, you are really the only person I'd ever dream of asking."

Fanny caught her breath. "Oh."

He nodded. "*Ja*, it's true." Another pause and then he cleared his throat. "It's silly, really. Well, maybe not so silly, but I feel silly asking you. I'm sure I know what your response will be..." The way he rambled on made her heart feel light and happy. Was it truly possible that, at last, he might ask her the one question she so longed to hear?

"Go on, Elijah," she heard herself coax.

"All right then." He seemed determined, even though he was clearly uncomfortable. "So what I wanted to ask you, Fanny, is about Mary."

If the color had just risen to her cheeks, now she felt as if it drained from them. "Mary?"

He nodded his head, a sheepish look on his face. "*Ja*, Mary. What I wanted to know is...well, what you think of Mary."

Fanny caught her breath. If she suspected that, after the baptism ceremony, Elijah might try to intensify his relationship with Mary, Fanny now knew that she had guessed correctly. However, she was taken aback to realize that, not only was Elijah interested in Mary Coblentz, but he hoped Fanny would approve of his choice.

"I—I hadn't given it much thought," Fanny managed to say. "She appears godly, I reckon. Righteous for the most part."

He made a noise as if agreeing with her and then seemed lost in his thoughts.

"Why did you ask, Elijah?" She didn't want to know the answer to that question, but suspected that he wanted her to ask it.

"Oh, it's nothing," he said, his modest words not masking his smitten tone.

"Must be something..."

He shrugged and kept staring into the distance. His fingers continued tapping against his knee and she had the distinct impression that he was avoiding looking at her. "I believe she is a righteous woman. She appears godly, as you say. However, I've noticed that she has some notions that are unusual, don't you think?"

Fanny took a short, quick breath. So that's what was weighing heavily on his mind, she thought. She couldn't deny that Mary had some different ideas than most of the women in their church district. If anything, she seemed to be much more vocal about her expectations and opinions. While most women were eager to please a possible suitor, it was clear that Mary preferred a suitor who displayed an eagerness to please *her*. And Mary showed no qualms about speaking her mind, sometimes speaking long before thinking.

"You mean about farming, Elijah?"

He hesitated, just for a short second, before he nodded his head. "*Ja*, farming in particular."

"Elijah," Fanny said, her voice giving away her trepidation at what Elijah was certainly thinking. "Your *daed* will not turn the farm over to your *bruder*. He has not proven himself to be reliable or even remotely capable of being responsible for much of anything. Your future is here in Mount Hope on this farm—the farm that has been in your family for generations, Elijah."

"Fanny..."

When his voice trailed off, Fanny immediately panicked that her choice of words—and the manner in which she spoke them—offended him. She looked at the ground. Had she misread him? Taken his comment and assigned it an unintended meaning? The color started to drain from her face. "*Mayhaps* I spoke out of turn."

"*Nee*, that's not it." He waited for her to look at him and then he forced a nervous smile at her. "I reckon my real question is whether women really consider that when thinking of a husband?"

Fanny's mouth opened, just slightly, in surprise at his question. She couldn't begin to wonder why he would think she'd have an answer. After all, she rarely attended singings and certainly wasn't courting anyone.

"I mean, look at Miriam and Jeb—" he stammered. "She's quite impressed with his 160 acres."

"Oh, *ja*," Fanny managed to admit. "She is, isn't she? More and more every day as her wedding approaches too."

He scratched at the side of his head. "I wonder that she cares more for the appearance of wealth than the man she is committing to spend the rest of her life with."

Fanny had no response. While she silently agreed with Elijah's observation, she was not about to speak poorly of anyone, even to Elijah.

He turned to her, his face drawn and pale. "Fanny, are all women like that?"

For a moment she felt a wave of disappointment. If he truly believed that enough to question it, surely he included her in that classification. Clearly he was torn and conflicted, but she took no comfort in the fact that he respected her good opinion enough to seek her input, especially if it meant he wanted her to exonerate Mary of having a shallow nature.

"I'm—I'm sure I wouldn't know," she whispered at last. "I can only speak for myself, Elijah."

He stared at her, his eyes searching her face. His concern lacked the adoration that she so often saw in his expression when he looked upon Mary. "I don't even think I can ask whether *you* think that way, Fanny Price. I doubt that such thoughts would even cross your mind."

She wasn't certain whether that was a compliment. Once again, she looked down at the ground, her shoulders slumping forward.

"I reckon Mary's a fine enough Amish woman," Elijah continued, unaware that he might have hurt Fanny's feelings. "Attentive during services and helpful at fellowship."

Fanny wanted to add that Mary had a sharp eye and witty tongue that had cajoled him into doing something he knew was wrong. How could he still consider Mary as a potential life mate if he already suspected her of being superficial and foolish?

"And she seems to come from a fine enough family," Elijah said.

"A family she has returned to," Fanny managed to say.

Elijah nodded his head and sighed. "*Ja*, this is true." He reached up and removed his hat from his head. He fiddled with it for a few seconds before he arose to his feet and began to pace the length of the porch. "This is all too much, Fanny."

"What is too much?"

He gestured toward the road with his hand. "Decisions. Life." He exhaled loudly. "Mary."

Fanny felt a chill and shivered, although she wasn't certain if it was the air or his words that made her do so. "Oh."

"It's just…" He stopped pacing and ran his fingers through his hair. "How does a person know?"

Fanny watched him, her heart hurting for the turmoil that he felt. *How does a person know?* she wondered.

With a sigh, Elijah looked at her and forced a small smile. "I guess that's something you can't answer for me, can you now?"

She shook her head. "*Nee*, Elijah, I cannot."

He reached over and touched her shoulder, a gesture of appreciation but without any suggestion of intimacy. "*Danke*, Fanny," he said. "You always have been there to listen to me, especially when I cannot speak to anyone else."

Sliding his hat back on his head, he moved away from the porch, his hands thrust into the front pockets of his pants as he walked back toward the barn.

"*Ja*," she whispered as she watched him. "I have."

The silent sound of her heart breaking was louder than anything she had ever imagined.

❧ *Chapter 11* ❧

OVER THE NEXT few weeks the level of stress in the Bontrager household increased. First they endured the long Council meeting that followed the next worship service, and then Naomi took over the preparations for Miriam's upcoming wedding. The wedding season didn't begin until after Communion which, this year, was the last Sunday in October. Since Miriam had insisted that her wedding be the first one of the season, all of the wedding preparation had to be completed in advance.

With Martha not in any shape for managing the planning required of such an important event, Naomi happily volunteered herself for the job, taking over the responsibilities of cleaning the house, organizing the food, and inviting the people. Fanny watched as Naomi went into high gear with her lengthy lists scribbled on yellow pads of paper.

And, of course, the communion service would be two days before Miriam's wedding and that too was an important day that required extra baking for the fellowship meal which, for once, was more than just light fare after worship.

With so much happening at once, it was good to have Naomi in charge and, in Fanny's mind, preoccupied with something that kept her from complaining about other things. Unfortunately that did not mean that she was any less bossy. In fact Naomi wasted no time as she barked orders left and right, having Thomas and Elijah begin removing unnecessary furniture from the first floor so that Fanny and Julia could properly clean the floors, woodwork, and windows. When that did not prove enough to satisfy Naomi, she insisted that Elijah purchase fresh paint.

"Does nobody in this family any good if the walls look grungy for our first wedding since your *maem* married Timothy!" Digging through an overstuffed drawer in the kitchen, she searched for paint chips. "*Mayhaps* the bathroom needs a fresh coat too."

Elijah frowned, not appreciating the extra work. Even with Timothy home and helping with the chores, Elijah still worked from before sunrise to well after sunset most days. Fanny watched him, wishing that someone would speak up and make Thomas finally become a responsible and contributing member of the household. But no one did, and as always, Elijah did Naomi's bidding, leaving the house to harness the horse to the buggy so that he could fetch the fresh paint.

"Come with me, Fanny," he whispered when he returned to the house to retrieve money from his father. "It's no fun riding alone."

Fanny smiled, pleased that he had thought to ask her. Since their talk two weeks ago, Elijah had seemed less despondent and distracted. Even more importantly he began to return to his former self and often sought out her company.

"I can't," she whispered back to him, glancing over her shoulder at Naomi, who sat at the kitchen table, her head bent over her yellow notepad. "You know she wants me to make more cheese this afternoon so it's ready for the wedding. Plus, I think an order for several baskets came in."

"Let Julia and Miriam do them," he said.

But they both knew that would never happen.

Miriam spent her days fretting more about her wedding dress and what food would be served than about the upcoming marriage and the dramatic change it would bring to her life. When tough tasks needed to be tackled, Miriam always appeared by Naomi's side, suddenly interested in the details of her ever-growing list or asking Naomi for advice on a matter of sudden and very grave importance. That meant that most tasks fell to Fanny and Julia to handle.

Later in the afternoon hours Jeb often visited his soon-to-be bride. With Henry no longer in Mount Hope, Miriam's attention focused on him. So when his horse and buggy pulled down the lane toward their house, in the rare case where she was actually working, Miriam would drop everything and hurry to fuss over Jeb as she served him coffee and supper.

The smile on Jeb's face indicated his pleasure in Miriam's attentiveness. On some evenings he sat at the table next to Timothy, sipping decaffeinated coffee as they discussed their plans for planting crops the following spring.

One night, the sky already dark even though it was barely after seven o'clock, Fanny sat at the table working on a small basket. For once, Miriam and Julia were tending to the cleanup of the kitchen, probably preferring that chore to working on the basket. Fanny listened to Naomi prattle off her list of to-dos and glanced over at Elijah, who barely paid attention to his aunt. He looked at her and made a face, almost causing her to laugh. Hiding her smile, she dipped her head so that no one could see her amusement at Elijah's mockery of Naomi.

"And you've spoken to the bishop?" Naomi sat next to Timothy at the table, her steely gray eyes piercing as she stared at Jeb. "We need to make certain it's announced right away."

Jeb nodded. "*Ja*, he knows. Spoke with him just Sunday last. And we've already alerted our family so they are certain to come. Everyone knows already, since the wedding is right after Communion Sunday."

With a bored look on his face—for details of such a feminine nature were of no interest to him—Timothy spoke up. "Speaking of Bishop Yoder, I ran into him today when I stopped at the Millers. He's selling that old draft horse of his." Timothy toyed with his coffee cup, spinning it around on the table and not caring that some of it splashed onto the table. After all, someone else would clean up after him.

Martha looked up, a moment of clarity in her face as she asked her husband, "You need another draft horse?"

Naomi scowled. "You don't need another draft horse!" she repeated as if she hadn't heard Martha.

"*Nee*, I don't, but I sure could use a new collar. Thought Miller might be selling that too. That draft horse is far too old for pulling plows and mowers anymore."

Naomi clicked her tongue and returned her attention to sewing the hem of a new dress that she wanted to wear to the wedding. "Irrelevant if the horse is too old, Timothy. Waste of money to think about buying it."

"I said I'm not buying it, Naomi."

Fanny glanced up from the basket she was working on, raising an eyebrow at the sharpness of Timothy's tone. She thought she saw Martha suppress a hint of a smile, especially when Naomi pressed her lips together and began furiously focusing on her sewing.

"Anyway, Bishop told me that Henry and Mary are returning to Mount Hope after their Communion Sunday," Timothy said, oblivious to the sudden silence that fell over the kitchen. Miriam stopped in mid-action as she was removing the plates and Julia, who stood at the sink, dropped a dish into the soapy water. Suds splashed onto her dress and, embarrassed, she quickly began to wipe them with a dry cloth.

Elijah, however, suddenly looked more alive than he had in days. There was no more teasing in his expression as he sat up straighter and leaned toward his father. "Oh, *ja?*"

"I extended an invitation for them to attend the wedding."

Fanny glanced from Elijah to Julia and then from Miriam to Jeb. Each one's reaction differed. While Elijah seemed overjoyed and Julia hopeful, Miriam tried to hide her shock and Jeb his concern.

"I—I hadn't known they were returning," Miriam said at last. She glanced at her sister. "Did *you?*"

Julia shook her head, a smug look of hope remaining on her face. "But what perfect timing! They'll be here for your wedding, Miriam. You'll need to add them to your list and figure who they should sit with during the meals." She smiled. With Miriam's marrying Jeb now a certainty, Julia clearly felt that her sister posed no further threat in regards to her pursuit of Henry Coblentz.

Miriam narrowed her eyes and glared at her sister.

In response, Julia's triumphant smile broadened.

Unaware of the unspoken exchange between his two daughters, Timothy wiped his mouth and pushed his coffee cup to the side. "Unfinished business, I reckon. Heard tell that they wanted to move here."

Not just a visit, but a possible move as well? Fanny could feel the added charge in the room's atmosphere, and she observed Miriam, Julia, and Jeb's reactions with mild curiosity. While amused by the expressions on her cousins' faces, she suspected that her own showed more than a little concern. With Henry came Mary, for sure and certain.

This was clearly on Elijah's mind, for when she looked at him, he too was lost in thought. With Mary's return, surely Elijah would renew his pursuit, perhaps courting her in earnest, especially if she was considering moving out to Ohio with her brother. And, of course, now that Elijah had become a baptized member of the community, he would most likely ask her to marry him.

Fanny felt the tightness return to her chest when she realized that it was not too late for Elijah to ask Mary to marry him in the upcoming wedding season. Stranger things had happened, especially when courtships were quick and short.

She raised her hand and pressed it against her neck, forcing herself to take deep breaths. If Elijah did marry Mary, she would move to the farm. After all, Thomas had demonstrated no interest in farming and it was generally accepted that Elijah would be the heir. Timothy would hand it down to Elijah, and that meant whoever he married would live with the rest of the family. When Fanny made breakfast or helped with the laundry, it would be

Elijah's wife who worked alongside her. And Fanny couldn't imagine that at all.

No, the thought of welcoming Mary Coblentz into the Bontrager home was not a joyous one to Fanny.

"And speaking of unfinished business," Timothy said as he stood up from the table. He stretched and belched. "*Ja*, Elijah, I need you to help with the bench wagon tomorrow. Needs to be moved to the Yoders' house for Communion. And they need some furniture moved out. Told them that you'd help with that too on Saturday." He glanced at his other son. "You too, Thomas."

Elijah didn't react but Thomas made a face.

"Best not be first thing in the morning," Thomas stated. He tossed his napkin onto his plate. "I've got plans on Friday night and won't be back until late."

Fanny shrank into herself, watching as Timothy stared down his oldest son. Ever since their return from Florida, an increasing tension had mounted between the two of them. No one had spoken of what happened in Pinecraft that caused Timothy to send his son home early and alone. In fact, Timothy rarely spoke to Thomas at all. Whatever had happened in Florida, the already fragile relationship between father and son seemed to have cracked just a little bit more.

"For once," Timothy said in a clipped fashion, "you will do what is right and help this community, if not this family." He did not wait for his son's response when he directed his attention toward Fanny and, with a softened expression, added, "And, by the way, the bishop personally requested that you, Fanny, accompany them so that you might help his wife prepare the house for Sunday worship."

Nothing could have surprised Fanny more. Had he misspoken? Did he intend that request for another person and accidentally said *her* name? She glanced to either side of herself as if looking for someone to be standing there. No one was. When she realized that Timothy was speaking directly to her, she all but squeaked out, "Me?"

"*Ja*, Fanny." For the first time in recent memory Timothy graced her with a kind look.

"Why me?"

"Perhaps the bishop knows that Julia is busy helping her *schwester* prepare for the wedding?" And then, to her further amazement, Timothy smiled. "Or perhaps your good nature has been reported to them by Mary and Henry."

At the mention of Henry, Miriam raised an eyebrow and Julia tried to hide her disappointment that it was Fanny, and not her, requested to help the Yoders.

"*Mayhaps* we should all go, *Daed*?" Miriam ventured.

"*Nee, Dochder*, you need to help your *aendi* and *maem*. It is," he said, leveling a stern look in her direction, "after all, *your* wedding that we are preparing for."

Long after the rest of the family retired, the supper dishes put away, and the kitchen quiet and dark, Fanny sat in her regular chair and stared out the window. Thomas had snuck away after his parents retired for the evening, and Miriam had gone for a ride with Jeb. Fanny didn't know where Julia and Elijah were, but she welcomed the silence and isolation. It was a rare treat.

Her thoughts drifted to Mary Coblentz and the way that Elijah's face had changed upon hearing the news that Mary would return to Holmes County. His tendency to appear deep in thought was replaced with something new that

Fanny had never before seen, an alertness and eagerness to act. There was a quickness to his step for the rest of the evening until he excused himself to go outside.

If he married Mary, Elijah would no longer confide in Fanny. Of that she was sure and certain. A husband needed to rely on his wife for advice and support, not his younger cousin. Of course she was his cousin only by marriage, she told herself. Yet they had been raised as siblings, and that was exactly what he thought of her: a little sister.

But she, however, no longer viewed him as just her cousin, nor as her big brother.

The realization that she felt differently about him, especially now that she knew Elijah was smitten with Mary, did little to lift Fanny's spirits. So she sat alone, in the dark, praying to God to help her be strong enough to face the upcoming weeks when Elijah would undoubtedly pursue a relationship with Mary. Despite her faith in God to know what was best for all of his children, Fanny could not take comfort in his plans for Elijah and Mary, and for that she also prayed for forgiveness.

❦ *Chapter 12* ❦

O N SATURDAY MORNING Fanny walked into the Yoders' house, her arms laden with a box of cleaning supplies as she followed Elijah while Thomas unharnessed the horse from the buggy. Fanny hadn't wanted to come help the bishop and his wife prepare for the communion service. But she knew that it was better than being at home listening to Miriam sigh all day long. Since Timothy's big news of the Coblentzes' return, she had grown as melancholy as Martha.

Suddenly Fanny bumped into Elijah. He had stopped walking, and with the box blocking her view, she hadn't seen him standing there in the doorway.

"Oh, Elijah," she cried out. "Are you alright?"

But Elijah hadn't even noticed that Fanny ran into him. "Mary!"

Fanny peered over his shoulder, just as surprised as Elijah to see pretty Mary kneeling on the kitchen floor, a scrub brush in her hand. Upon hearing Elijah's voice, Mary sat back on her heels and raised one hand to brush back any stray hairs that had fallen from beneath the simple white scarf she wore over her hair. When she saw Elijah, she smiled and lowered her eyes in a way that seemed far too coy to be natural, at least to Fanny.

If Elijah had been surprised to see Mary working along-side the bishop's wife, Fanny felt as if she had been knocked speechless. Hadn't it been only the previous evening that Timothy had mentioned that Mary and Henry planned to return? If they were already in Mount Hope, why hadn't he stated as much? Instead, with no further warning than Timothy's one comment, Fanny stood behind Elijah, looking over his shoulder at the one person she truly did not want to see in the Yoders' kitchen.

What Fanny had thought would be a nice day, spending time with Elijah while helping the Yoders, would certainly now be a day spent in the company of not just Mary, but her impudent brother as well—the only *other* person she did not want to see.

"Ah, Elijah!" Henry, carrying a box of canned food, emerged from the door that led to the basement. "Bishop told us you were coming today, didn't he, Mary?" He glanced at his sister who did not speak but merely nodded her head.

"I hadn't known you were returning so soon," Elijah said, the statement directed at Henry but his eyes clearly focused on Mary. "I trust all is well back in Gordonville?"

"*Ja*, of course. Why wouldn't it be?"

Fanny's eyebrows twitched as she fought the urge to frown. Henry's answer harbored a hint of hostility, as if Elijah's question was offensive. Elijah, however, failed to notice.

"And Fanny!" Henry set down the box and crossed the room, greeting Fanny as if they were old friends, warmly shaking her hand and smiling as he did so. "It was so good of you to come help us!"

Fanny withdrew her hand as quickly as she could and looked away. Just the way he stared at her made her feel uncomfortable. Add to that feeling his warm and somewhat intimate welcome and Fanny knew, without a doubt, that she did not care for him any more than she had when he had flirted with Miriam and Julia.

The bishop, however, seemed pleased with Henry's greeting to Fanny and placed his hands on both of their shoulders.

"Ah, *gut*, you two are acquainted already," the bishop said in an overly friendly way.

Henry responded with a hint of a smile at the bishop as if the two of them shared a secret.

At that moment Fanny felt that all-too-familiar tightening in her chest. Something was wrong, terribly wrong, with how the bishop had just greeted her. In all the years that he had been bishop, he never paid much attention to Fanny, not even during her instructional before baptism and certainly not afterward. He had no reason to. Suddenly now he had specifically requested her presence to help his wife prepare their house for worship service? Her head felt dizzy as she realized that something was amiss.

The bishop paid no attention to her discomfort. "I'll leave the two of you to help inside. Mary and Elijah can help outside to clear the area for the horses. I already put your *bruder* to work."

Fanny swallowed the panic that welled inside of her throat, too aware that Henry stood just a little too close to her. With her personal space invaded, she took a side step, small enough that no one would notice.

Glancing over the bishop's shoulder, she noticed that Elijah and Mary talked with their heads bent together. Their personal space was clearly invaded by the other, but neither one made a move to correct it. Instead, there was something far too relaxed between them. In the past Mary acted coyly around Elijah. Now she was openly comfortable with interacting with him in a gentler manner.

The bishop shooed Mary and Henry outside, accompanying them to the barn. Meanwhile the bishop's wife didn't wait to begin listing the things that needed to be done. Furniture needed to be moved, woodwork needed to be cleaned, and floors needed to be scrubbed. To Fanny, it was no different from what she had been doing at the Bontragers, and without being instructed further, she started to walk to the kitchen sink where a bucket and pile of cleaning rags awaited.

"Oh, heavens!" The bishop's wife frowned. "I need to go fetch some cleaning oil from the basement. *Mayhaps* the two of you could start moving the sitting room furniture onto the porch, *ja*?" She didn't wait for an answer as she hurried out of the room, leaving Fanny alone with Henry Coblentz.

It was all she could do to avoid looking at him. The memory of his flirting with both Miriam and Julia was not far from her memory, as well as his swift betrayal (and subsequent retreat) at the Bontragers' house during the *Englische* hymn singing. He reminded her of the man who wanted to follow Jesus but, when instructed to give up the things he loved the most to do so, refused. Like that man Henry Coblentz thought only of what added to his own prosperity and not how to walk with God. She just wished that more people could see that about him.

"Fanny," he said. "Let's start with the sofa, *ja*?"

She didn't like being alone with him and found that it was difficult to speak in his presence. Where Miriam and Julia all but fought for his attention, Fanny did all she could to avoid it.

"You got that end, Fan?" he asked as Fanny easily lifted the piece of furniture.

She cringed at being called 'Fan.' No one ever called her that and it spoke of an intimacy that did not—and would not!—exist between them. "*Ja*, I got it," she said.

Just like the preparation at the Bontragers' house for the wedding, everything in the Yoders' home would need to be removed from the first floor so that the rooms could be scrubbed clean.

"I'll walk backward," he said, another smile on his face. "It'll be easier for you to carry it forward, *ja*?"

Fanny tried to avoid looking at him as they carried the sofa through the kitchen and toward the main door of the house. All the time he gave over-the-top attention to her ability to complete this one simple task, asking several times if she needed to stop for a moment and take a break. Fanny shook her head, wanting to tell him that she could have shoved the sofa across the floor by herself if need be. While she would never be so bold or rude as to say such words out loud, she saw no harm in thinking them.

When they had finally managed to pass it through the doorway, Elijah and Mary on hand to take over from there, Henry paused and watched them carry the furniture to the barn.

"Everything's easier with two sets of hands, eh?"

Fanny didn't respond. She began wondering why, exactly, Timothy had insisted that she, not Julia, help the Yoders. And the bishop's reaction, inquiring about whether or not she had previously met Henry, seemed highly suspicious. Why this sudden interest in her? And why, exactly, had the Coblentzes returned from Pennsylvania so suddenly?

"Everything was well in Pennsylvania, I reckon?" she ventured to ask, curiosity getting the best of her.

Henry seemed delighted that she had, at last, spoken to him. "Why, indeed! As well as could be expected! How kind of you to ask, Fanny Price!"

At least this time he had not called her 'Fan.' "It was most surprising to learn of your return, especially so soon after your departure."

The way that he looked at her, clearly misinterpreting her questions for interest. He leaned against the edge of the sofa and grinned at her. "A joyful surprise, no doubt."

"Well, for some, I'm sure." It was the only response she could think of that did not require her to lie.

Henry, however, did not seem inclined to realize that Fanny was not part of the "some" that she referenced.

"Pennsylvania is rather nice," he began as they walked back into the kitchen.

Fanny didn't wait for instruction and headed over to the small stand full of devotionals and newspapers. That too would need to be moved outside. There wasn't a lot of furniture in the room, so removing everything would be over soon and then the real work would begin. With the help of Mary, she presumed, they would clean every nook and cranny of the walls, ceiling, and floor. They would wash the cabinets and also the windows. Perhaps then, she thought,

Henry would wander outside to help Elijah. Cleaning was typically a woman's job, not a man's.

Henry continued talking, oblivious to the fact that Fanny was focused on working, not socializing. "Such a small community, though. Both Mary and I found so many aspects of Mount Hope to be much more appealing," he said. "The quiet, understated aspects."

She handed him some newspapers to hold, ignoring the pointed look he directed her way.

"And it seems to be a much more thriving community, especially for young people with their whole lives ahead of them."

"I thought it was overly congested," Fanny said. "How can it be smaller and more congested at the same time?"

Henry gave a forced little laugh. He waved his finger at her. "Mary always tells me how very astute you are, Fan."

She cringed.

He did not take notice. "I reckon that it's just different. The town we live in...Gordonville..." He paused and looked at her.

"*Ja*, I recall," she replied.

"Gordonville has nice farms, but it is surrounded by *Englische* communities so the area where the church district's members live feels much smaller."

"Ah, I see."

He knelt down to help remove the papers and books from the stand. "Plus the people in Mount Hope definitely left a handprint on my heart."

His poetic words caught her off-guard. She looked up at him, surprised—and mildly uncomfortable—to see that his eyes remained on her face, even as he reached for more papers.

Surely he didn't mean her! Why, he had barely spoken to her at all prior to this day. All of his attention had been focused on another: Miriam. Or, rather, Miriam *and* Julia.

"I suppose there's a danger of that wherever you travel," Fanny finally responded. "People have a way of leaving the most indelible impressions upon us...wherever we go and whoever they are."

"And sometimes," Henry said as he stood up in such a way that he moved beside her, his foot lightly pressed against the heel of her shoe, "when you are away from that place, you have more time to realize how much a person has impacted you."

Fanny shifted her weight away from him. "Both positively and negatively, for sure."

"Ah, but even negative impressions can turn positive over time, wouldn't you agree?" he added. "And then there are times when positive impressions might turn negative. Those are always the most disappointing."

For some reason Fanny did not think he meant her own impression of him. Rather, he seemed to assume her steadfast good opinion of him with his former statement while she wondered if the latter may have been spoken in memory of Miriam.

His solicitousness toward her was a side of Henry that Fanny had not seen before, and she might have found it charming had she not seen the way that he had used those same attentions to trifle with Miriam and Julia's emotions. Yet the more that she tried to fend off his social advances, the harder he tried to force them on her. That alone made her realize that Henry Coblentz could try his hardest to be delightful and pleasing, but the real man underneath the sweet talk and smiles remained just as roguish as her initial first impression.

"I'm sure Pennsylvania suits the people just fine," she said as she began to pick up the small table. "It's not a new community, anyway."

"Hmm, no, it's not. But it's quite different from here where the community is so integrated with the *Englische*."

"You mean the tourists?" She noticed that he merely followed her, instead of asking to take the table from her hands. She wasn't surprised.

"Oh, *ja*, the tourists. I'm sure they bring quite an income to the Amish communities."

Fanny set down the table and stared at Henry. That familiar tightness returned to her chest, only this time it was from her immense dislike of the man that stood before her. "Some Amish would complain that the tourists corrupt our communities. I, for one, would much prefer to have less, not more, interaction with them." She gestured toward the door. "*Mayhaps* you would be so kind as to take this outside and see if either Elijah or Thomas need help." Before he could find a reason to argue, she added, "I'm sure the bishop could share numerous stories about how the worldliness of the tourists has enticed far too many of our youths to forget the vows of our ancestors."

She turned her back on him and hurried toward the kitchen, eager to begin cleaning the corners of the walls and floor so that she did not have to converse with Henry Coblentz anymore. He was a thorn that seemed to enjoy nothing more than to prick her finger and then, as she sucked at the wound, make his way to her other hand to cause the same damage, even if it was in a kinder fashion.

❧ *Chapter 13* ❧

FANNY KNELT BEFORE Miriam, who sat on a bench at the front of the room and, with the greatest of care, removed her shoes and stockings. The bowl of water, lukewarm and clear, was on the floor beside her. Once Miriam's feet were bare, Fanny placed first one and then the other into bowl. With a soft, white cloth, Fanny gently washed her cousin's feet. When she was finished, she removed Miriam's feet from the water and dried them on the awaiting white towel.

And then, Miriam's feet having been washed, they switched places, and with the same care, she took off Fanny's shoes and stockings so that she could reciprocate the act.

When she finished, Fanny turned to her cousin and whispered, "The Lord be with us. Amen, in peace."

Miriam repeated the same words and then they shared a holy kiss.

The men had already gone through the foot washing, and when the women were finished, it would end the special service and the families would retire to their homes. It was a solemn day, one that required self-evaluation and spiritual rebirth. However, after her long hours of added work recently—not to mention dealing with Henry yesterday—Fanny was ready for the end of communion.

While she understood the importance of the religious ritual, and she always welcomed reflection so that she could improve her relationship with God, she had never felt comfortable with the foot washing. That part of the service was, thankfully, over for another six months.

"Fanny," Elijah whispered to her when the service finally ended. "Shall we walk home together?"

Timothy was talking with one of the deacons, most likely slipping him some money to add to the emergency fund for the community. It would be better to leave beforehand. After all, once Timothy returned home, the rest of the day would be spent in silence, each person expected to sit and pray until it was time for chores. Only then would they break the fast that had started the previous day in preparation for communion.

Fanny nodded, and without waiting for the others, they slipped out the door and began walking down the driveway toward the road.

"It's startling to realize that, in just two days, Miriam will be married to Jeb," Elijah said.

Fanny had thought the same thing when she had been the one to wash Miriam's feet during the service. "There is so much work to do yet," Fanny said. She was tired already thinking of all the chores she would have to tackle in the morning.

"I'm sure it will be over before you know it," Elijah teased as they fell into step together. "And then we will be blessed with Jeb's presence at our *haus* during the weekends until she finally moves onto his farm."

Fanny tried to hide her smile. "All 160 acres of his farm?"

Elijah laughed. "*Ja*, Fanny. All 160 acres! She looked quite content when the bishop announced her banns, although everyone in the *g'may* has already been invited!"

"I don't fault her, I suppose," Fanny said cautiously. "A woman only gets married once in her life, after all. She should be content, don't you agree?"

Elijah leaned over and knocked her shoulder gently with his arm. "I do agree, Fanny. Although I secretly hold out hope for my future wife to regard me not with feelings of contentment but of love."

At the mention of his future wife, Fanny felt her good mood rapidly disappear. She had suspected his thoughts were on the future when he had taken his baptism earlier that month. Now she realized that, indeed, he was most likely actively pursuing it. From the way he had interacted with Mary at the Yoders' house yesterday, Fanny knew better than to pretend any more regarding the true object of his affection.

They walked the rest of the way home in silence, Fanny thinking about Elijah while she presumed that Elijah was thinking about Mary. For the remainder of the afternoon, while the rest of the family sat and reflected on the communion service, Fanny suspected that she and Elijah would continue pondering their futures: her over the loss of her one, true love and him over the possible wedding to his.

———◆◆◆◆———

After the long day at the Yoders' house and the even longer afternoon sitting in the Bontragers' company, deep in thought and prayer, Fanny hadn't wanted to go to the youth singing that evening. With its busy schedule of sermons, hymns, foot washing, and prayers, the entire day had exhausted her, both emotionally and physically. She wanted nothing more than to retire early in order to face the new week.

But Timothy and Naomi had insisted.

"You need to get out, Fanny," Naomi pressed, her attentiveness surprising her niece. In eight years Naomi had rarely noticed Fanny unless it was to criticize her or give her more work to do. "Be with other young people." She looked at Timothy. "She must go. It's unnatural for young people to not like being together!"

"*Ja*, you need to socialize."

That one word, *socialize*, spoken from Timothy's lips, gave Fanny even more reason to pause. Timothy never encouraged *any* of the women in his household to socialize, much less her. Most of his attention was on Elijah, and all of Naomi's was on Miriam.

Finally Fanny had given in to their wishes, and now, as she sat on a ladder-back chair in the Yoders' house, she eyeballed the battery-operated clock that hung on the wall over the stove and wondered how long she must sit there before she could sneak out the door and walk home. It was only a mile and a half walk. She could make it back to the farm in less than thirty minutes, and with any luck, Timothy and Martha would already be asleep. As for Naomi, she would have retired to the *grossdawdihaus* long before now.

When she looked away from the clock, she noticed that Elijah stood near Mary, their shoulders almost touching. Fanny didn't have to imagine that, for Elijah especially, the couple saw no one else in the room. Their attention to each other was more than obvious, even when Mary occasionally looked away from him in what Fanny thought was a coy and calculated manner. Oh! The sight of that made her feel the familiar tightness in her chest. How could it be that everything had changed, once again, after such a promising few weeks?

"Fanny," a deep voice said from her left.

Upon hearing her name, she turned her head away from Elijah and Mary. It was Henry, standing beside her with two cups in his hands. She stiffened her back and stared straight ahead.

He paid her no attention and sat on the vacant chair beside her. "I brought you some lemonade," he said, handing her a plastic cup. "You looked thirsty sitting over here by yourself."

"*Danke.*" She took the cup but did not raise it to her lips.

"I was surprised to see you come back for the singing tonight."

When his pause turned into an uncomfortable silence, she found herself embarrassed for not replying. As much as she didn't care for Henry, she didn't want to appear rude. So, despite her reluctance to engage with him, she managed to say, "I can't imagine why my actions would be of any interest to you, never mind surprise."

He laughed at her comment. "That is the very reason, Fanny Price! You expect no interest. And therefore you create interest!"

She didn't like the direction of this conversation.

"It was a compliment," Henry said when she did not react.

"I reckon I'd prefer to be ignored than to solicit untoward interest."

He laughed once again and Fanny took the opportunity to stand up, hoping to move away from him.

When she felt his hand on her arm, she stopped and turned to look at him.

"I was wondering..."

She felt her eyelids shut in a slow, heavy blink.

"...Elijah is to take Mary for a buggy ride later," he said.

"She is staying here," Fanny pointed out. "That's silly."

Henry shrugged. "*Mayhaps*, but I offered to take you home. I'm sure that is not something you'd say no to."

"*Danke*, Henry, but I'm more than happy to walk."

He glanced over his shoulder in the direction where Mary stood talking with Elijah. "That's just the thing, Fanny. I promised Elijah that I would look after you."

Fanny doubted any such thing. Elijah would never elicit such a promise from anyone. Fanny was, after all, more than capable of walking home from the Yoders' house. She wondered if Henry was outright lying or merely exaggerating.

"There is no need, Henry. Miriam and Julia..."

He interrupted her. "...seem to have already left."

At his words, she looked around. Neither Miriam nor Jeb were in the room, and it appeared that Julia too was nowhere in sight.

"Still, I prefer the fresh air," Fanny insisted. "But thank you again for the offer."

"Always so modest," he said lightly. "I insist. I will use the bishop's buggy and that, my dear Fanny, is open-topped. You shall have all of the fresh air you would like."

There was nothing more that Fanny could say on the matter without causing a scene. Henry seemed more than satisfied; after all, he had covered every argument that she could possibly offer. What struck her as even more infuriating was the fact that the harder she tried to thwart his pursuit, the more he seemed to chase her.

For the next hour she sat in the chair, barely able to focus on the words of the songs being sung. If propriety was not a problem, she would have snuck out and walked home before the break when, undoubtedly, Henry would signal her that it was time to leave. Anyone who was nearby would see his gesture, for sure and certain. And then the rumors would begin.

Fanny began to feel resentment toward Henry. She didn't want to be in this situation, having people talk about her, and, even more so, she did not want to be riding home with him. Not once had she given him any indication that she favored him. That alone had encouraged him. With all of the other young women pining for him, why on earth would he want the only one who did not?

When the next set of songs ended, Henry started to walk toward the door. He paused, just as Fanny expected he would do, and lifted his hand to catch her attention. She didn't even have to look at the groups of women to know that every single one of them turned and stared, wondering which lucky woman had captured Henry's attention. And, as Fanny reluctantly joined him, she heard more than a few whispers from the other side of the room.

Miriam and Julia walked into the house as Henry and Fanny were leaving. Julia looked the other way, her chin tilted in the air with indignation. But Miriam stopped walking and blocked the couple's way. "Hey now, what is this?" she asked, her eyes meeting Henry's, an imposing look on her face. "The singing isn't over yet, is it?"

Henry regarded her with a cool look, his gaze flickering over her shoulder as Jeb approached. "It is for us, *ja*," Henry said dismissively. He nodded at Jeb and then, in a gesture far too friendly and comfortable for Fanny's liking, he took her arm and guided her through the side door.

Fanny did not need to turn around to know that Miriam turned to watch them, dumbfounded at Henry's unexpected departure.

"It's a wonder that your cousin is here tonight," he said as he helped Fanny into the buggy. "She's to be married quite soon, I understand."

"*Ja*, this is her last youth singing, I suppose."

Henry said nothing as he untied the horse and tossed the lead rope into the back seat of the buggy. With expertise he backed up his brother-in-law's horse, the open-top buggy jostling so that Fanny fell against him. In the glow of the dashboard lights, she thought she saw him smile. As quick as she could, she scooted further away.

"So Fanny Price," he started. "Tell me all about yourself."

Her heart beat rapidly and she stared into the darkness. The air was cold and she shivered. Her coat was not enough to remove the chill that she felt. "There's nothing to tell."

"I've heard tell that you lived in Colorado," he said.

She hated the fact that he 'heard tell' anything about her. Any inquisition that he must have made certainly increased the likelihood that people would talk.

"Tell me about Colorado."

"I'd rather not," she said in a flat voice. "It was a long time ago."

"Were there mountains?"

"*Ja*."

"Snow covered?"

His genuine interest surprised her. "I remember that they were, *ja.*"

He sighed. "I've always wanted to travel," he said. "So many places to see. And I'd love to hike up a large mountain."

"No one hikes that mountain. Not from my parents' community, anyway."

He shifted his weight, his body more open to hers. "Not hike it! That's such a shame."

"I always thought it would be fun to walk to one of the peaks," she admitted. "But I was only ten years old when I left, and what does a child know of such things?"

They rode in silence for a few minutes, Henry seeming to focus on either his driving or the idea of a mountain. She wasn't about to ask him which, so she enjoyed the break in conversation. She couldn't imagine Henry hiking a mountain or traveling to different states or exploring anything else, for that matter. His enthusiasm for the comforts of friendly camaraderie was far too great to entice him to visit such a remote place as Colorado.

"I've decided to move to Mount Hope," he said at last.

She remained silent, uncertain how to respond to such a statement. What would he do in Mount Hope? He couldn't farm and he had no trade. Was Mount Hope so much more appealing than Gordonville?

"Why, that's surprising," she managed to say, hoping that her voice did not give away her true feelings. "Whatever for?"

He smiled and looked at her with a sideways glance. "I have decided that my future lies here, Fanny Price! And I will be purchasing the bishop's small property. There's just enough land there for me to make a living, especially if I clear the wooded section in the back."

Stunned, Fanny sat there and said nothing. His future? What future could he possibly have in Mount Hope? With all of his family back in Gordonville, Pennsylvania, that is where his future should be. Of course, she suspected that he meant he was *choosing* to make his future in Mount Hope, most likely because he suspected his sister would be marrying Elijah.

"And I was wondering..." He paused to take a deep breath of air. "...*mayhaps* you'd let me come calling on you, Fanny."

She shut her eyes and swallowed. Come calling? On her? She knew far too little about this man, and the little she did know, she certainly did not like.

"I—I am not so sure," she forced herself to respond. "I have so much work to do and do not socialize much." She hoped that last bit would soften the blow. She didn't want to hurt his feelings, but she wasn't about to encourage him when he was the last man on the face of the earth that she would consider marrying. And that was where courtship led: marriage.

She pointed up ahead. "There's my mailbox," she said. "You can let me off there, please."

When he slowed down the horse, she didn't even wait for it to come to a standstill before she jumped out. "*Danke* for the ride, Henry," she mumbled and darted toward the lane, hoping that he couldn't see the humiliation that colored her cheeks crimson. She had never been asked to be courted and she had never given it much thought. But she knew that there was only one person she would want to ask that favor, and that one person was most likely riding in his own buggy with Mary Coblentz. Between Henry's awkward question and her own disturbing realization, she couldn't walk fast enough to get to the house. All she wanted was to retreat to the solitude of her bedroom and cry into her pillow.

Why, oh, why, did the one man she despised show such interest in her, while the one man she loved cared for another?

❧ *Chapter 14* ❧

For Fanny, Miriam's wedding day seemed longer than any other day in her life. The morning worship service followed too quick on the heels of Sunday's communion service. By the time that Miriam and Jeb were asked to stand in the front of the room before the bishop, Fanny's back ached and she could barely fathom how she would survive another hour seated on the hard wooden bench.

She knew that she should have paid closer attention as Jeb and Miriam repeated their wedding vows. However, the stress of dealing with Miriam the previous day had sapped what little enthusiasm she could summon for the wedding.

All day on Monday Fanny had worked tirelessly beside Julia and Elijah as they set up the first floor for Tuesday's wedding. While most brides would work alongside their family, Miriam had spent her time crying to Naomi, first with emotion over the importance of her upcoming wedding day, but later when Jeb arrived with the list of unmarried people attending the wedding, her tears turned to distress.

As was common at all Amish weddings, the bride and groom played matchmaker, setting up the evening meal's sitting arrangements for the unmarried guests at their celebration. Fanny was helping bake pecan pies in the kitchen when the first of Miriam's tirades began.

"Henry and Fanny?" she yelled. "No! I will not have them paired together."

Jeb remained calm when he confronted his bride. "Now Miriam, she is the only person that Henry knows here, besides Julia. So you need to decide which one is more to your fancy."

When Miriam realized that she had to choose between the two women—her sister and her cousin—she began crying once again. Naomi was quick to put her arm around Miriam's shoulders and whisper, "Wedding jitters, no doubt" to Jeb.

Regardless of whether or not Miriam felt wedding jitters at all, Fanny cringed when she realized that she would have to be in the company of Henry Coblentz again for the majority of the evening after Jeb and Miriam's wedding.

And now Fanny sat on the bench and watched Miriam stand beside Jeb in her pretty new blue dress, as the bishop went through their wedding vows.

"Can you both confess and believe that God has ordained marriage to be a union between one man and one wife, and do you also have the confidence that you are approaching marriage in accordance with the way you have been taught?"

The bishop turned to face Jeb. "Do you also have confidence, brother, that the Lord has provided this, our sister, as a marriage partner for you?"

When Jeb proclaimed a loud "Yes," the bishop turned back toward Miriam.

"Do you also have the confidence, sister, that the Lord has provided this, our brother, as a marriage partner for you?"

For the briefest of seconds, she hesitated. From the smile on Jeb's face, Fanny could only presume that he mistook the pause for modesty, but from where Fanny sat she could see that Miriam's eyes, though downcast, glanced in the direction where Henry was seated.

"Yes," she responded at last.

Jeb's shoulders straightened and he lifted his head just enough to show his pride in his lovely young bride that had agreed that he, Jeb Riehl, was truly provided by the Lord to be her husband.

The bishop turned back to Jeb and asked, "Do you also promise your wife that if she should in bodily weakness, sickness, or any similar circumstances need your help, that you will care for her as is fitting for a Christian husband?"

Another resounding "Yes" came from Jeb's lips.

"And Miriam," the bishop continued. "Do you promise your husband the same thing, that if he should in bodily weakness, sickness, or any similar circumstances need your help, that you will care for him as is fitting for a Christian wife?"

This time she shuffled her feet as if shifting her weight, a movement that finally spoke of the edge that remained on her nerves. Fanny looked toward Elijah, who sat on the other side of the room with the men, wondering if he had seen Miriam's discomfort. But he was too busy staring at Mary.

"Yes," Miriam answered at last.

The vows ended with the bishop addressing them both for one last question: "Do you both promise together that you will with love, forbearance, and patience live with each other, and not part from each other until God will separate you in death?"

In unison both Jeb and Miriam said, "Yes." Fanny wondered if anyone else noticed how Jeb's face glowed with joy while Miriam's simmered with barely suppressed misery. But she knew that most people were probably feeling just as uncomfortable as she was, tired from so much sitting. The smell of good food from the kitchen had begun to permeate the room, and more than one rumbling stomach revealed that no one was paying as much attention to the vows that had just been spoken as they were to their own pangs of hunger.

With the vows finished, Miriam and Jeb sat down in the front of the room while the congregation began singing the final hymn. Fanny glanced over her shoulder toward the kitchen and saw two young women hurrying about as they began to prepare the food for the first meal of the day. Unable to sit any longer, Fanny quietly stood up and hurried to help them. Normally other members of the church district helped with the preparation so that the family of the wedding couple could enjoy the day. Fanny, however, suspected that she would take greater delight in working than in visiting.

After the service finally ended, many of the men retreated outside to visit with each other while the women set up the room. The wooden benches were quickly converted into a long U-shaped table. White table clothes were spread over them and benches positioned around them so that the guests could sit while they enjoyed their dinner meal. With so many people in attendance, they would have two sittings at noon where roasted chicken, mashed potatoes, steaming hot green beans, and other wonderful foods would be set in the middle of the tables. Miriam would sit to the left of Jeb in one of the corners while the other corner would be left to display the desserts.

Happily, Fanny worked alongside the other women in the kitchen, not caring that she was hungry and missing her own meal. The last thing she wanted to do was to sit still and see any more of Elijah mooning over Mary. She was well aware that far too many couples met at weddings while just as many who already were courting became engaged.

Equally as distressing was the fact that she knew she had been set up to sit with Henry during the five o'clock meal. She couldn't even begin to think about having to sit across from him for an entire meal. Besides having nothing to say to him, and him having nothing of interest to say to her, she just dreaded the thought of people speculating why they had been matched together.

And she was far too aware that Elijah had been matched with Mary. Oh, how she dreaded looking down the table to see Elijah seated across from Mary, the two of them talking and laughing. The rest of the guests would see how comfortable they were in each other's company and tongues would begin wagging, for sure and certain.

"Come, Fanny," she heard someone say behind her. "You need to take a break."

To her surprise it was Martha who forced her to stop working in the kitchen and to sit for a moment with a plate of food. It was the first time in a long time that Martha had taken initiative to care for a member of her family.

Usually it was Fanny caring for her, which made the attention even more endearing to her.

"And you should let the others take care of the evening meal," Martha instructed her in a soft voice. "You don't want to miss the singing and the games with the others, do you now?"

Fanny could think of nothing she would *rather* miss, with the exception of the evening meal!

After sitting down and eating the food which, by now, was cold and not nearly half as good as it had smelled just two hours ago, Fanny glanced around the room at the chairs occupied by the older guests. Most of the young people were outside, probably gathered together in the barn and sitting on hay bales. Jeb and Miriam, however, remained in the house with the others. Now that they were married, they would not interact with the social gatherings of the young, unmarried people in their church district.

For a long few minutes Fanny took advantage of the activity in the room to watch Miriam. After all of the preparation and days of emotional outbursts, Miriam seemed subdued and distracted as she sat next to Jeb. People continued to approach them to offer their well wishes and blessings. While Jeb grinned and beamed, his happiness resonating with every person who came, Miriam sat slouched over, her eyes barely looking at the well wishers. Instead, she seemed to be searching for someone in the room.

Fanny could only imagine what was bothering her cousin now.

"There she is!"

Fanny looked up and saw Mary walking toward her. She stood before Fanny and reached for her wrist, pulling gently to get her to stand up. "You are missing all of the fun, Fanny Price! Come outside. We are playing Around the World and Elijah says that you are the best at that game!"

"I really should help with the..."

"Nonsense! There are plenty of women in here to help with the dishes and cooking for supper! This is our time!" Mary wouldn't take no for an answer, and before Fanny knew what had happened, she found herself in the barn and seated at a makeshift table playing the marble game with Elijah, Mary, and Henry.

Of course, Henry, she thought as she took the only vacant seat left.

"I didn't know you played games!" Henry said, his expression full of delight at having made this wonderful discovery.

"There is much you do not know about me, I'm sure," Fanny retorted. Too aware that her voice sounded sharp and unkind, she forced herself to smile. "But marble games are one of my favorites."

Elijah laughed. "She always loved playing games as a child. When she arrived, I taught her this game and, why, she made me play it with her every Saturday evening!"

His memory made her smile feel less forced.

"Then I look forward to requesting that we team up, Fanny, and play against Elijah and Mary!"

Oh, how she dreaded this matchmaking business at weddings. But she did not want to sound unpleasant or rude so she agreed and found herself in Henry's company for the rest of the afternoon and well into the evening. It wasn't as tiresome as long as Elijah and Mary remained nearby. Even the supper meal was not as dreadful as Mary sat next to her and provided nice conversation during the meal. As for Henry, every time he spoke to her, Fanny would look up see Elijah beside him.

If only they could remain friends, Fanny thought, her eyes lingering on Elijah for a moment longer than they should have. No thoughts of marriage or courting, just friends. Anything that permitted her and Elijah to remain at the Bontrager farm without any interference from either of the Coblentzes.

❧ *Chapter 15* ❧

WHEN HENRY ARRIVED at the Bontrager farm on Thursday evening, Fanny noticed that Timothy seemed to be expecting him. She had been working on a small basket while sitting in her special spot, hidden from the rest of the room. But she heard Henry's voice greeting Timothy and then Elijah, who seemed equally as surprised as Fanny.

"Something wrong at the Yoders?" Elijah asked, the concern in his voice immediately indicating that he worried more for Mary's safety than the bishop or his wife.

"*Nee*, not to fret," Henry laughed. "My *schwester* is fine, since I suspect that is what you truly mean."

From her hidden corner, Fanny grimaced at how forward Henry sounded.

Elijah sounded relieved. "*Gut, gut.* But I do hope all are well in the household." She heard the sound of a friendly laugh with reassurances from the visitor that there were no issues at the Yoder household. "Well then, I'll be quick to run, Henry," Elijah said in a much more jovial tone. "I promised Benjamin I'd go look at his mare. Something's off with her hind leg and he's reluctant to summon the vet."

As Elijah left the room, it dawned on Fanny that Henry had not come to visit with him. Miriam and Julia sat at the kitchen table, both of them working on a tie-knot quilt;

from where she sat, Fanny could not see either of them. Their silence, however, indicated that they were hanging onto every word that had just passed.

After the wedding Jeb had stayed at the Bontragers so that he could help with the clean-up in the morning. And then, after a big noon meal, he had left his new bride and returned to his own farm, pausing to kiss her in front of the rest of the family before he left. Miriam had turned red at his public affection, and as soon as the door shut behind her husband, she had run upstairs, hiding in the room where she had spent the first night as a married woman.

Ever since then, her demeanor had been quiet and sullen as if angry with the world. Seeing Henry walk into the house had done nothing to change that.

Timothy waited in silence, as did the rest of the people in the room, anticipating Henry's purpose for such an unexpected visit.

"I've come to speak with Fanny."

"Ah, *ja*! Right," Timothy said, sounding neither surprised by nor curious about Henry's statement. Fanny, however, wished that she could blink her eyes and disappear. Why on earth would he want to see her?

"Fanny!" Timothy's booming voice clearly indicated that he knew exactly where she was hidden and he fully expected to her to come greet their unexpected visitor.

She shut her eyes, saying a quick prayer for God to give her the strength to maintain her conduct as expected by her aunt and uncle as well as herself. Especially after the disastrous buggy ride home from the Yoder house after the singing, Fanny knew that this visit from Henry Coblentz did not bode well, and she would need God's grace to avoid hurt feelings.

Setting aside the basket, she arose from the chair and slowly made her way into the main area of the kitchen. From where she sat at the table reading *Family Life*, Naomi watched her with an expression of curiosity. Next to her, Julia looked from Fanny to Henry and then back to her. Miriam merely avoided meeting his eyes, but the expression on her face displayed her resentment.

"*Ach*, Fanny!" Henry removed his hat and held it before him. "I stopped by for a visit."

"So I see," she responded. From the corner of her eye, she noticed that Naomi frowned. She hoped that her neutral response had not carried a tone of disdain which, undoubtedly, would distress both Naomi and Timothy.

Henry shuffled his feet for a moment as if searching for something to say.

When it was clear that Henry struggled for words, Timothy cleared his throat. "*Mayhaps* you two might want to go sit on the porch."

With the chill in the weather, the last thing that Fanny wanted was to sit outside, regardless of whether or not it was with Henry. However, she remained obedient to her uncle and walked toward the entry room, pausing to take her heavy black coat from a hook. She slipped her arms into it and was buttoning the front when Henry opened the door and walked through it. He didn't even hold the door for her. Fanny pressed her lips together, the muscles in her jaw twitching as she pushed through the door herself.

Outside, with a kerosene lantern already lit and on the porch, Henry motioned for Fanny to sit on the swing. She didn't want to sit there, especially since she knew that, most likely, he would sit beside her. Too many times that spot had been occupied by Elijah, and while she doubted that there would be many more, she didn't want the memory soiled.

But he insisted.

She took a heavy breath and sat down, staring straight ahead so that she did not have to see Henry as he spoke.

"Fanny, I'm sure that you have noticed my attentions to your person," he said, the words stilted and awkward.

No, no, no, she screamed inside of her head. She wanted to stop him from talking, to beg him to not say the words that she could just feel were lingering on the tip of his tongue. *Not me*, she wanted to cry out.

"I am most impressed with your submissive obedience to the *Ordnung* as well as your modest mannerisms in social dealings."

Fanny couldn't help herself. She turned her head and looked up at him. Submissive obedience? Modest mannerisms?

It was just the gesture that he needed to encourage him. He sat down next to her and reached for her hand. "It was a joy to work beside you in preparation for the communion and to see how hard you worked to ensure that your cousin's wedding went smoothly. I fear that you may not always be treated the way you should be treated, Fanny Price. There is such a gentle sweetness about you."

She felt the urge to speak. "*Nee*, Henry. No more so than most other women."

His grip on her hand tightened. "There is that modesty, so rare and infrequent among others. It is the truth, Fanny, and my affection, which increases with every moment spent in your presence, has grown to the point where I fear the only recourse is to offer you my hand in marriage."

Fanny withdrew her hand from his and stood up, taking a step away from him and shaking her head. "*Nee, nee, nee!*" She spoke the words aloud but she was speaking mostly to herself. "Your words distress me, and I can hear no more of this." She started to walk toward the door but Henry was already behind her, reaching, again, for her hand.

"Fanny—" he said.

But Fanny pulled her hand from his. "Please, Henry," she whispered loudly, avoiding any eye contact with him. "You are crossing the lines of decency."

She turned her back to him and quickly opened the door. She needed to put distance between herself and this man. His proposal shocked her, not only because of how little she thought of him, but also because it spoke clearly of how much he thought of himself. His compliments were not meant to show his admiration, but to finally charm her into falling for him. She suspected she was the one woman he had ever failed to win, and he had fallen in love—not with her, but with the challenge of conquering her.

From the moment she first met him, she had given no indication of harboring any interest in him, and if he had an ounce of honor, he would have respected her wishes and stayed away. If anything he should have been satisfied with Julia, who clearly had fallen for his wily charms.

Timothy looked up as she entered the room. "Fanny? What is the good news?"

Fanny stood there, feeling helpless as the eyes of her aunts and uncle stared at her. "Good news?"

Timothy stood up and walked toward her. The smile on his face, so rarely directed at her, began to fade as he glanced over her shoulder toward the door. "Here now! Where is Henry? Surely he would like to share the news of your engagement with the rest of the family, *ja*?"

At the same time, Miriam and Julia jumped to their feet. "What?" Julia cried out.

Miriam said nothing, but when Fanny looked at her two cousins, she saw that the color had drained from both of their faces.

"Is there to be another wedding, then?" Martha asked.

"Fanny? I asked you a question," Timothy said in a firm voice.

"I—I don't know where he is," Fanny admitted at last.

"You don't know where he is? Why, he was just speaking to you!" Suddenly as if realizing that Fanny's timidity was not due to bashfulness, Timothy's expression darkened. "Am I to take by your demeanor that you have refused him?"

"I did."

"Refused Henry's offer?" It wasn't a question that was asked in expectation of an answer. "For heaven's sake, Fanny, what reason do you give for denying a perfectly suitable courter?"

She bit her lower lip and tried to find the right words to respond. "I—I do not care for him," she said at last. "I do not care for him at all."

"You don't *care* for him?" Timothy seemed to weigh the word in his mouth. He stood before her, a stunned expression upon his face.

Naomi shook her head and scowled. "What does *caring* for him have to do with *marrying* him?"

"How very strange." Frustrated and clearly not quite understanding what had just occurred, Timothy rubbed at his face with his hands. "Fanny, do you realize that Henry Coblentz is a very proper young man with a very good upbringing and he's purchasing the Yoders' property? That is a sound future for a young woman of your means," Timothy said. "Why on earth would you refuse him?"

"He is not a righteous man." Her voice sounded as small as she felt.

Timothy blinked once, his head moving backward as though he had been slapped. "Not righteous? Why, do you think you are above Henry Coblentz? Do you feel yourself superior?" He gave a small laugh that sounded hard and sarcastic.

Naomi pursed her lips and added her contribution to the discussion. "You will never find another man as honorable and righteous as Henry Coblentz."

"I—I beg to differ."

"And what gives you such an opinion, Fanny?" Timothy asked. "Has he treated you ill? Others?"

Fanny wished that she could tell her uncle of how Henry Coblentz had trifled with the hearts of her cousins. She wanted to remind him of Henry's involvement in the *Englische* hymn debacle. And she longed to explain that his ongoing attention to her, despite her efforts to discourage him, spoke volumes about his character. She glanced over at Miriam and Julia, only partially surprised to see that the former scowled at her while the latter looked close to tears.

"*Nee*, I dare not say," Fanny whispered, returning her attention to her uncle.

Timothy walked toward her, his eyebrows furrowed together in cold fury. "Refusing such a proposal is most disappointing, Fanny. It lacks the very good sense and reasoning that I had come to expect in you. My favorable opinion of your character is most suddenly reversed. I have to wonder from where this display of willful behavior comes, not to mention the lack of consideration for your family."

Her mouth opened into a small O.

"Oh, *ja*," Timothy said angrily. "You never once think of your parents—your brothers and sisters—who might have benefited from a marriage to Henry Coblentz! Instead you question his righteousness without any cause. It is folly, indeed, if you believe another proposal from such a man will come your way again! Had he proposed to one of my *dochders*—" He didn't finish the sentence.

Julia jumped up from where she sat and ran from the room, leaving the house through the side door. Miriam glanced at her and, with the greatest of reluctance, stood up and pushed back her chair. "Now look what you've done," she hissed in Fanny's direction.

As Miriam left through the same door as Julia, Timothy began to pace the floor as he shook his head. "Indeed!"

"I'm so sorry," Fanny managed to say.

"Sorry? Well, I hope you are. Despite the past eight years of providing for you, I do not pretend that you owe me the same duty as my *dochders* do, but I would think that you could have at least demonstrated an ounce of gratitude instead of such self-centered concern!"

Fighting tears, Fanny bit her lower lip. "It is less my misery I consider than my inability to make him happy."

Try as she might, she couldn't hold back her emotions, and the tears began to fall from her eyes.

When he noticed that she was crying, Timothy stopped pacing. "Now, now, there is no need for such an emotional display. *Mayhaps* it is just the surprise of such an offer. Time will change this feeling, Fanny. *Ja*, time." He seemed pleased with this thought and the stern expression on his face changed to one of hope. "You need more time to get to know Henry, to see what he has to offer you."

She wished that she could blurt out the truth, that time and familiarity would only increase her antipathy toward Henry.

While Fanny remained silent, not wishing to further damage her uncle's opinion of her, Naomi took advantage of the break in conversation. She clicked her tongue and cast a disapproving look in her niece's direction. "Timothy, you presume Henry will risk further humiliation by asking her a second time."

Her aunt's comment should not have surprised Fanny, as Naomi was always eager to offer her thoughts on matters— especially when she found fault with something related to Fanny. But this time, followed on the heels of Timothy's criticism, the words stung ever more than usual. "I'm suddenly not feeling well," she managed to mumble. "*Mayhaps* I might go lie down?"

If she had displayed ingratitude toward her uncle in rejecting Henry Coblentz, she felt nothing but appreciation when he dismissed her from their company. As quickly as she could, without appearing overly eager, Fanny climbed the stairs and hurried to her room. No sooner had she shut the door behind herself than she collapsed onto her bed, burying her face into her pillow to stifle the sounds of her sobs.

Despite only knowing Henry for just twelve short weeks, Fanny knew that there was no amount of time that would change her opinion of Henry nor her position about marrying him. She had seen the true essence of his character from the very first day she had met him. And while she had done nothing to encourage him, it seemed that that alone was responsible for motivating Henry's ardor. Now that her uncle was convinced of the match's soundness, Fanny knew nothing would stand in the way of his desire to clinch it.

"Come walk with me, Fanny," Henry said, his warm breath on the back of her neck giving her a fright. He smiled when she spun around and faced him. "Did I frighten you?"

She stepped backwards so that she did not have to stand so close to him. "It's too cold to walk."

Attending the Saturday night youth gathering had not been high on her list of to-dos. However, Timothy had once again insisted that she attend. Given the alternatives, Fanny relented and sat in the back of the buggy, Julia seated beside her brother as the three of them silently rode to the gathering.

No sooner had they arrived than Elijah disappeared with Benjamin and Julia seemed to float in the direction of her friends. With no one to talk to—or, rather, no one she wanted to talk to—Fanny had moved to the back of the room, waiting for the right moment to slip out the door and walk home. She planned on hiding away in the barn until she saw the kitchen light extinguished and could sneak into the house, safely avoiding any questions from Timothy.

But Henry must have spotted her and, unbeknownst to Fanny, snuck up behind her as she sat alone at the gathering.

"I must talk with you." His voice was low and sounded unfamiliar. Gone was the overly confident young man, so full of mischief and flirtation. "I confess that I have thought of nothing else but you, Fanny Price."

She caught her breath. Oh, those words. She had longed to hear them spoken but not from the lips of Henry Coblentz.

"I'm sure that is not true," she said.

"Oh, but it is!" Henry gave her a warm smile, the likes of which she had never seen from him. "When Timothy talked to me after our visit, his words of encouragement..."

Fanny interrupted him. "Words of encouragement!" She had suspected that Timothy had gone to the Yoders' house; he had disappeared the following day with no one offering an explanation as to his absence. Later that evening, when he returned, he spoke to Fanny with more kindness than she could have expected. Now it made sense. Her uncle had met with Henry and received encouragement that the young man was still inclined to pursue Fanny.

He continued speaking as if he hadn't heard her. "I simply had not considered the fact that your modesty would compel you to deny that which I offered. But I can assure you that your propensity for such self-effacing behavior makes you even more alluring."

"That is not my intention, I can assure you."

"Your humility..."

His persistence was unbecoming, especially for a man who amused himself by flirting only to disclaim interest when a woman responded to his ploys. She was relieved when the conversation was interrupted by a call to gather for the singing.

To her dismay she could find no way to extricate herself from Henry without causing a scene. And so, an hour later, she found herself seated next to Henry Coblentz in his uncle's open-topped buggy, the last place on earth she wanted to be.

"Are you warm enough?" he asked as he started driving the horse and buggy down the road.

She nodded her head, knowing that he could barely see her in the dim light from the buggy's battery-operated lights. He sat far too close to her and his tone with her was far too familiar.

Unaware of her discomfort, Henry began to talk to her as one would talk to a close friend. He told her about his plans for the Yoder property and how he was interested more in animal husbandry than crops, although he planned on planting several fields of hay.

Her resentment toward Henry built anew. She simply could not understand why he continued to pursue her when she had made it perfectly clear that she had no interest in marrying him.

While she understood that Timothy had gone out of his way to encourage the relationship, what Fanny could not understand was *why*? Was the idea that she might never get married and stay at the farm so distasteful to the Bontragers? She felt a mixture of distress and anger at that thought. She had certainly gone over and above as far as carrying her weight. Not once had she given anyone reason to criticize her for not working, never mind shirking her responsibilities. And while she knew that many couples married without being in love, she didn't know too many that married when one so clearly disliked the other.

When she returned home, Fanny found it surprising that Timothy, Martha, and Naomi were still awake. From the look on Timothy's face Fanny suspected that they were waiting for her. He watched her as she came into the kitchen, an eagerness in his eyes that Fanny suspected came from anticipation of an announcement of an engagement.

She took her time removing her black coat and hanging it on a hook.

"Well?"

Fanny's feet stopped moving. Frozen, she quickly weighed her options. Clearly Timothy had believed that she was, indeed, being modest. But could he truly believe that in one buggy ride she would have changed her mind, even if she *could* be so inclined?

Her silence gave Timothy his answer.

"This is mind boggling," he said, jumping to his feet. He began pacing, his hands behind his back and his eyes on the floor as if deep in thought. "You have no idea what you are doing, Fanny. What you are throwing away!"

"I think that I do." Her voice, soft and almost inaudible, surprised even her. Had she truly just spoken back to Timothy? "I do not want to marry Henry Coblentz."

Martha sighed and, for the first time, spoke up. "Fanny, you really should reconsider."

Her contribution startled Fanny. For so long Martha's mental faculties had deteriorated, the overbearing nature of

225

her older sister simply wearing her down. Now, of all times, Martha suddenly expressed an opinion, and one that clearly showed no understanding Fanny's character.

"Do you so want to get rid of me?" Fanny cried out at last. "Has it truly been so awful that I have been in your care? *Aendi* Martha, would you not miss me and the help that I provide?"

"There are some things more important, Fanny," Martha said, choosing her words sparingly. "And we will not always be here to care for you. It really is about your future that all of us are so worried."

Naomi took a short, sharp breath. "Ungrateful girl."

Timothy shut his eyes. "Impossible," he grumbled as he continued pacing. "Just impossible."

For a long moment Fanny stood there, waiting in the silence. She knew that Timothy was not finished with her. She suspected that his disappointment in her refusal of Henry as a husband disturbed Timothy for different reasons than Martha vocalized. It wasn't her future that Timothy cared about, but his reputation in the community. Had he promised Henry that Fanny would marry him? Was he looking for more esteem in the eyes of the bishop? Clearly Timothy was more concerned about himself than Fanny's care.

Finally he stopped pacing. A thought seemed to occur to him and he turned to look at her. "Fanny, you have become far too comfortable," Timothy proclaimed. "It's time for you to gain a finer appreciation of what has been given to you."

"I do appreciate—"

He raised his hand to stop her. "Silence!"

Startled by his booming voice, Fanny ceased talking, her mouth still partially opened from her unfinished sentence. From the corner of her eye, she noticed a movement in the mudroom. Elijah. He must have just returned from spending time with Mary. She glanced in his direction and saw that he stood there, not hidden but not entirely out in the open, listening to the exchange between Fanny and his father.

"After all this time," Timothy said, struggling to maintain his composure, "I had hoped you might have gained a finer sense of righteousness. Clearly, the change in your environment—even after eight years!—had no impact. It was always our hope, Fanny, that bringing you to Ohio would give you that opportunity to transform into a virtuous person, an opportunity you never would have had in Colorado living in that..." He paused as if looking for the word to express the contempt that his facial expression displayed. "...that settlement your parents moved to."

Naomi clucked her tongue. "You'd think she might have learned from the example of Miriam and Julia."

Timothy glanced at his sister-in-law, contemplating her words. He pointed at her as he turned back to Fanny. "She's right. You've never quite integrated yourself into the social circle which we afforded you! Why! You barely attend singings or even work outside of the house! What contribution do you bring to this family?"

Fanny stood there, in the center of the room, the color drained from her face. Contribution? How many times had she fulfilled orders for baskets, took on Miriam's chores, or tended to Martha? "If I had integrated myself into Miriam and Julia's circles," she said in a small voice, "I would never have received an offer from such a man as Henry Coblentz."

Timothy gasped. "You dare to question the morality of my daughters?"

"*Nee*," Fanny said, lifting her chin and forcing herself to meet his gaze. "But I do question Henry's. He is a man who wants the challenge of acquiring that which is not easily obtained. And for that reason—and that reason alone!—he has decided to make such an offer, an offer that I could never accept. The only thing worse than being forced to be someone you are not is being with someone who pretends to be someone else entirely!"

The sudden look of anger that flashed in Timothy's eyes frightened her. "You!" He shook his finger at her. "You will learn! You will learn what we have given you. What we saved you from! You will return to your family, see what you came from! I don't care if it takes one week, one month, or one year! But you will not return to Mount Hope unless you accept the marriage offer from this virtuous young man. You will learn the one thing I have apparently failed to teach you, Fanny Price!" He glared at her. "Humility!"

"Uncle, please!"

He shook his finger at her. "*Nee*, you are not my family, Fanny Price. But where you belong is with your family. You have forgotten why you came here, why your parents cast you aside, and why we opened our doors to you. But as God is my witness, you shall be reminded!"

Fanny trembled, not fully understanding where this rage was coming from. Just because she had denied Henry's offer of marriage? She saw Elijah step forward, concern etched in his forehead. He started to approach his father, to speak out on Fanny's behalf, but his father ignored his son's protective gesture.

Instead Timothy rose to his full height. Straightening his shoulders and lifting his chin, he pointed to the stairs and in a stern, booming voice gave his final instruction to her.

"Go pack your things, Fanny! You will be returning to Colorado to see exactly what we have sacrificed in order to give you such wonderful opportunities. *Mayhaps* then you will see that Henry Coblentz has presented an offer to you that could provide a future you would have never had elsewhere! Perhaps then you will realize how selfish a creature you truly are!"

❦ *Chapter 16* ❦

A	s the driver approached the long, flat road that led toward a small house, Fanny felt a rush of anxiety. The house sat in the middle of a valley, nothing around it but other scattered houses. The property was outlined with post and wire fencing, separating it from the neighbors. No one had pretty white fences or large white farmhouses. Some of the houses were made of logs, while others seemed built haphazardly from different material.

Eight years had passed since she had seen her parents. Eight long years that confined her relationship with her family to sporadic letters written in her mother's shaky hand and with words that sounded more like a school child. She hadn't heard much about her siblings, only that her father was still struggling. With the property surrounded by *Englischers*, it was a lonely life for the Price family in Westcliffe, Colorado.

Colorado.

Fanny tried to remember something, *anything*, of the dry, vast-looking land where her parents' farmhouse broke the horizon. She knew that her father had a mere thirty-two acres, but it looked much smaller. There were no trees to break the line of vision, no rivers or rolling hills to guide her eyes to look somewhere else. Just small farms that sat in the shadow of a mountain range already tipped with snow.

The car came to a stop in front of the log house. Three young children watched curiously from the porch, the smallest one looking about five years of age. An older girl, dressed in a dark brown dress that was almost similar in style to what young girls wore in Holmes County, motioned to the three children to go inside. She stayed, however, and stared at the van.

Fanny opened the passenger door and hesitantly got out. Her legs ached and her ankles were swollen from sitting so long, first in the bus and then in the car. But her eyes could only stare at the familiar face that watched her from that porch.

"Susan?" Fanny finally said. "Is that you?"

Her sister started to nod her head but, as if thinking better of it, stopped. Susan had been no more than eight years old when Fanny had been sent to Holmes County. Now at sixteen she looked like a young woman, yet her shyness suggested that her lack of exposure to the outside world kept her trapped in a child's mind.

The door opened to the house and an older version of her mother walked outside. Her thin, gray hair was pulled back under her stiff but worn *kapp*. Her face looked aged and weathered. It took a moment for Fanny to realize that the woman standing before her was, indeed, her mother.

"*Maem*?"

There was a coldness to her mother's expression. Fanny hadn't expected a warm reunion, but she hadn't expected indifference.

"Heard they were sending you back." Her mother's eyes did a quick assessment of Fanny, taking in her pretty green dress and buffed black shoes. Fanny couldn't tell if the cold look on her mother's face was from discomfort over her own shabby dress and bare feet or complete disappointment that her daughter had returned to burden them with her care. "Best come in, then. You can help with supper."

Eight years and that was her greeting? Fanny sighed, realizing that Timothy had known exactly what he was doing when he had sent her back to Westcliffe. He might never have been to Colorado, but he had somehow known that Mount Hope, Ohio, was much more modern and full of conveniences that even she, a simple Amish woman, would miss. The message was clear: a life with Henry or a life of misery. But Timothy didn't understand that, to Fanny, a life with Henry would have been just as bad, if not worse, than a life of misery in Colorado.

She took her bag from the driver, thanking him but avoiding his eyes. He had witnessed the chilly greeting from her family and seemed as uncomfortable as Fanny felt. Inside the house Fanny took a moment, standing in the doorway and looking around the large room. Only it wasn't large. It was small.

And dirty. Cobwebs hung inside the corners of the windows and the floor was covered in a fine layer of dust. One of the kitchen cabinets was broken and hung in a haphazard manner, the hinge having been twisted in an odd manner. And there were remnants of flour and dirt caked in the crevice where the counter met the wall.

Only vaguely did Fanny remember anything about the house: not the black wood-burning stove in the corner or the small kitchen table that certainly could not house the entire family in one sitting. The only thing that she did recall was the one thing that was missing: the scent of pine from the soap that her mother used to clean the hardwood floors and cabinets.

"Oh, my," she whispered.

"Take her to her room," her mother said in an emotionless voice to Susan, who leaned against the wall, her big eyes staring at her older sister. "Best be getting changed, Fanny. No sense ruining such a fine dress."

Obediently Susan pressed off from the wall and led Fanny down a small hallway to the two bedrooms shared by the children.

Fanny took her bags and followed her, on her way catching a glimpse of her parents' bedroom through their open door. Unlike the kitchen, it wasn't as messy. Clothes hung from the pegs on the wall and a faded quilt covered the bed. The contrast between the two rooms startled Fanny. Was her mother sending a message to the rest of the family? That her own space was worth keeping neat and tidy but her children didn't deserve such consideration?

The bedroom was small with two bunk beds built into the walls. It was familiar to Fanny and she set down her bag as she reached out her hand to touch the wood. Fanny remembered sleeping in this room, sometimes spending more time in here than in the kitchen, especially during the cold, dark winter months. Her eyes drifted to the very bunk, the top one on the right, where she used to sleep. Unlike her parents' room, the four beds were mussed, not having been made yet, even though it was three in the afternoon.

"Which one?" Fanny asked.

"The little ones sleep here now. *Daed* built a lean-to when Joseph was born. Jerome and Peter still sleep in the other room because *Daed* wants them well rested to help him on the farm. The little ones wake them up sometimes. So you'll sleep in the lean-to with Ruth and me," Susan said in a quiet voice and then walked toward a door that Fanny hadn't noticed.

It was made of rough-hewn vertical boards, four to be exact, with two smaller boards nailed horizontally to keep them in place. Unlike the wood for the rest of the house which was sanded and covered with a thick protective layer of shiny polyurethane, this wood looked like it must have been found in the old barn. When Susan opened the door, Fanny took a step back, seeing nothing but darkness on the other side.

"*Kum*." Susan beckoned to Fanny. "Sometimes Caren sleeps here too but *Maem* said she needs to stay in the bunk room." She jerked her thumb toward the first bedroom. "At least until her cold gets better."

When Fanny looked at the small beds in the lean-to, she noticed that the quilts that lay in crumpled heaps were thin, not like the thick quilts at the Bontrager farm. Already it was cold in the lean-to room, which was probably why their father had not put in a window. With only a wood-burning stove to heat the house, it was bound to get even colder in the wintertime. Fanny didn't remember being cold as a child, but she felt it now.

"What's it like?"

Fanny looked up. "Hmm?"

"Ohio." Susan scratched her ankle with her other foot. "What's it like there?"

"Oh, *ja*, Ohio." Fanny set down her bag, and now that her eyes had adjusted to what little light spilled in from the other room, she looked at her sister. "It's nice, I reckon. The houses are bigger and brighter." As soon as she said those words, Fanny regretted it. She hadn't intended to make a comparison, especially one that sounded as if Ohio was superior to Colorado. "I mean they're just different, that's all."

Susan almost smiled, and Fanny wondered if that was a rare reaction for her sister. "There are bigger and brighter houses out here too," Susan said lightly. "But we're just poor."

"Oh, I don't know about..." But Fanny could not complete her sentence. The truth was that her parents *were* poor.

"*Daed*'s been trying to sell the house for five years, you know. No one wants it. It's too far away from the other Amish community, and *Englische* people want a house that is big and bright." She emphasized the words *big* and *bright* but not with malice. Fanny wondered if Susan considered her to be more *Englische* than Amish. "*Daed* can get a bigger farm on more fertile soil if he moves. But no one wants this old place.

"It's—it's really not that bad," Fanny said.

This time, Susan did smile. "*Mayhaps* no. But it sure would be nice to live with the others. It's ten miles away from here, you know."

"I wouldn't know that."

Susan took a deep breath and nodded. "I forget that you were sent away so young. *Ja*, *vell*, it's too far for all of us to go to worship; we only have the one buggy. We take turns."

Fanny frowned. This would have been her life had she not been sent away.

"And the little ones have to study at home."

Without being closer to the community, Susan wouldn't be able to attend youth gatherings or make friends. How on earth would her sister ever get married if she couldn't court a young man? Westcliffe wasn't like Mount Hope, where there were so many different families, both in the town as well as surrounding areas.

"I don't see why someone wouldn't buy this place," Fanny said.

"The people around here know that the crops aren't growing. Plus they can get more land a bit further out. Doesn't matter to them. They all have trucks to drive to town."

Fanny looked at Susan. "The crops aren't growing? Bad soil?"

Susan shrugged. "*Mayhaps.* Or *mayhaps* it's just that *Daed*'s a bad farmer. Either way, he can't buy a new farm if he can't sell this one."

"Oh help!" Fanny whispered.

Her thoughts shifted to Henry Coblentz and for a moment, just a brief hesitation in her mind, she considered that she may have made a mistake. But a second image, this one of Elijah, pushed Henry away and she lifted her chin, resolute in her determination that she would not be bullied into a marriage with a man she did not love, even if she knew that she could never marry the one she did.

"I think I best go help with supper," she mumbled, not wanting to criticize her sister, but not wanting to hear Susan say anything else regarding their father.

"Aren't you going to change into your work dress?" Susan asked.

Fanny gave her a soft smile and lifted her shoulders in an apologetic shrug. "This *is* my work dress."

"Oh."

They walked back into the kitchen where the three younger children huddled together near the stove and stared at her, their eyes big and filled with curiosity. From the looks of things the children seemed introverted and her mother appeared overworked. Depression and tension lingered between the four walls of the house. Without a nearby school and with the church so far away, their social interactions were certainly limited, and that did not make for a happy future for any of the remaining Price children.

Fanny hesitated before approaching her mother. She could see that the past few years had not been kind to her mother. Despite having sent away William and Fanny, her parents had added two more mouths to feed, Caren, and Hannah, and Joseph, new siblings that Fanny had never met before: family and strangers at the same time. She felt conflicted knowing that they watched her as she waited for instruction from her mother.

And Fanny longed for Mount Hope.

"May I help then?"

Her mother turned around from the stove. Right away, her eyes traveled from Fanny's head to her toes. When she realized that Fanny had not changed and was still wearing the shiny shoes, her lips pursed in a familiar and disapproving way, one that reminded Fanny far too much of Naomi. Yet her silence favored Martha's personality.

"I'll just slice the bread," Fanny mumbled and moved toward the two loaves that rested on a cooling rack. Even though the kitchen still carried the sweet scent of yeast in the air, the loaves were cold to the touch. Her mother must have baked them earlier that morning.

Susan slipped into the room and began to busy herself with the younger two children. Sitting on the large chair near the glass window that faced west, she pulled out a children's book, and with one sibling on each of her legs, started to read to them. Fanny was thankful for the distraction.

"Who is this, *Maem*?" eight-year-old Ruth whispered.

"That's your eldest *schwester*," their mother said at last. "Fanny."

Susan stopped reading for a moment and looked up from her book. "You were a baby when she left," she said in a maternal tone. "But I remember her. And your *bruders* Jerome and Peter will too."

Fanny continued slicing the bread. Jerome. Peter. The names didn't even sound like family to her ears, though they'd been five years old when she left. She had been cast out from the Bontragers' lives as if she had never belonged. All of those years that she had wanted to be a part of their family—and perhaps had tricked herself into thinking that she might be!—had been wasted on a foggy dream.

By the time that the sun started setting behind the mountains, the house took on a different kind of chill. The younger children were fed first so that by the time their father and older brothers returned home, they would be able to eat at the table without interruption.

When she heard the male voices outside, followed by the sound of heavy boots thumping up the steps to the porch, Fanny turned and braced herself. Already she had gotten over her disappointment with her mother's lack of warmth, compassion, or plain emotion. She could barely anticipate what would happen with her father.

The door opened and a rush of cold air flooded the room.

"Oh now!" a male voice boomed from the open door. "I thought I saw a car coming down the lane. Must be that Fanny's returned."

To her surprise, her father seemed much more jovial and lively than she had expected. He removed his hat and placed it on the counter, unaware that his wife scowled as she moved it to the peg on the wall. He ran his fingers through his thinning hair and stood there, blocking entry for his two sons that eagerly peered over his shoulders.

"There she is!" Her father gave her a crooked smile and she saw that he had lost a tooth. His face looked more weathered than she remembered it, but otherwise he hadn't aged nearly as much as his wife over the past eight years.

He approached her at last, leaving the way open for Jerome and Peter to hurry inside and shut the door behind them. The chill of the November evening air lingered in the air.

"Look at you, *Dochder*!" He placed his hands on her shoulders. "Turn around then." He helped her move in a circle. "My, my, so grown up." He grinned again and looked over at his wife. "It'll be good to have another girl here to help you, *Maem*." He withdrew his hands and made his way over to the table. "I hope you've made plenty, *Maem*. I'm ravenous after the day we've had."

Her mother said nothing as she set the food on the table before him. Jerome and Peter joined him at the table, and Susan hurried to help her mother bring over the basket of bread and plate of butter. Beside the boiled potatoes and carrots, there was only a thick slab of pork that, from the looks of it, had been overcooked. There was no sauce or gravy to keep it moist.

"Ah, look at this!" her father said cheerfully as he picked up his fork and jabbed it into the plate of meat. "A feast fit for a king."

Fanny hesitated before sitting down at the far end of the table next to her brother Jerome. She wondered when they might pray, but as her father began to eat, she realized that he had not forgotten but merely did not consider the bounty, the one that he claimed fit for feeding an earthly king, fit for thanking a heavenly one.

"That back field," her father said with his mouth full. "This spring it will be our saving grace, I tell you."

Fanny watched as her mother took her place opposite her husband. She bowed her head and silently prayed, despite the fact that her husband still talked.

"Spreading that manure now will make it more fertile and we'll make a go of corn once again." He looked over at Jerome, pointing at him with his fork. "Corn, my *bewe*! That is the answer. With just one good year, we will have enough money to move at last. Why, every farmer will be begging to buy this place. Mark my words!"

Fanny looked up, staring at her father with complete surprise. "Corn, *Daed*? In Colorado?"

"Ah ha, my girl!" He laughed and hit his hand against the table, thumping the top three times. "Your education has certainly paid off. Why, you are the only one with sense at the table!"

Her mother made a slight noise and began to cut the small portions that were on her plate.

"I don't see it as a matter of education or sense, *Daed*," Fanny said, forcing herself to address the man seated at the head of the table. "It's just simple common sense that no one in Colorado, at least not in Westcliffe, plants corn."

"See?" Her father delighted in her response. He slapped Peter on the arm joyfully. "She understands that we will be the only ones to do it!"

Fanny frowned. "I think you misunderstand. No one plants it here because it is not possible at such high elevation."

"*Ach!*" The smile faded from his face. "Such nonsense! Why, corn can grow everywhere. Just because some farmers fail, especially in Westcliffe..."

Fanny glanced across the table at Susan. When their eyes met, Fanny realized what her sister had meant when she had criticized their father's capability at farming the land. His determination to succeed in planting corn was a misguided dream and, perhaps, the very reason that the family suffered in such a state of destitution. If he had only abandoned the dream years ago and developed a skill or, at least, begun farming acceptable crops, they might have moved and become an integrated part of the Amish community at last.

If only her uncle could see that Henry in his own way was just as unreliable as her father! But Timothy's blindness to issues of character—even the character of his own daughters—and his focus on material comfort and rule-keeping had left him unable to discern the difference between righteousness of the heart and the pseudo-righteousness of appearance. If Timothy had thought that sending her to Westcliffe would change Fanny's mind toward Henry, he had been wrong. Now, Fanny was more determined than ever that she would not fall into *his* misguided dream of seeing her wed to a man who, undoubtedly, shared both her father and her uncle's propensity for misplaced ambition.

❦ *Chapter 17* ❦

I N FANNY'S OPINION there was very little to like about Westcliffe and even less about being at her parents' home.

For the first few days Fanny never saw another person. Her days were spent trying to clean the house when her mother wasn't watching; Fanny feared insulting her. Often, in the afternoons, her mother would lie down for an hour, sometimes two. Fanny would take that time to scrub the walls and floors, often with Susan at her side helping. Fanny took advantage of those moments to teach hymns to Susan and any of the other children who cared to listen.

One surprise that impressed Fanny was Susan's aptitude for learning. With the three younger children being homeschooled—and not a lot of time for that!—they were all behind in their reading, writing, and arithmetic. On her third day in Westcliffe, when the chores were finished, Fanny took over the schooling hour, more to try to help them rather than to give her mother a break. The older two boys, thirteen-year-old Jerome and Peter, were rarely home during the day, but the other children loved to listen to Fanny read stories from the Bible.

The children loved the story of baby Jesus. One night, Caren asked Fanny to point out the star of Bethlehem.

"That was only there to guide the wise men!" Joseph said.

"But his birthday is coming up so the star has to come back!" Caren retorted with a fierce determination in her cherubic face to prove him wrong. Fanny smiled, listening to Caren try to argue with her six-year-old brother and watching four-year-old Hannah's eyes dart back and forth from one sibling to the other.

Finally on the fourth night, Fanny decided to write a letter to Elijah. Sitting at the table, her head bent, Fanny wrote about reuniting with her family and her alarm at prospects of any future for her siblings, especially Susan. It was the closest she could come to saying how much she missed Mount Hope.

Not wanting to belabor the terrible situation that her parents were in, she added her thoughts on how different the climate was from Mount Hope. The air seemed thinner and the valley in-between the mountains looked desolate. She paused and turned to look out the large window near the wood-burning stove. The sun was already setting behind the mountain range, a tinge of orange-red color outlining the mountain. By day the mountain was covered in snow, but during the sunset it looked as if it were on fire.

"Wha' ya writin', Fanny?"

Fanny didn't even lift her head. "It's you, not ya, Ruth, and I'm writing a letter to..." She paused. She had almost said the word *home*. But Mount Hope was no longer her home, was it? Timothy had made that clear. In the eight years that she had lived with the Bontragers, she had given them not one reason to complain about her behavior or work ethic. Yet the first moment she stood her ground, and about something as important as marriage, Timothy had quickly banished her from Ohio, a cruel reminder that she was not truly a part of their family and their house was never going to be her home. "...friends," she finally said.

The next morning, she walked to the mailbox and slid the envelope inside of it. She lifted her face to the sun, her back to the mountain range, and shut her eyes. Breathing in the crisp November air, Fanny wondered how she could possibly stay in Colorado. The cramped house offered no warmth, spiritually or emotionally. While she enjoyed the children, she felt no familial bond with them.

Susan, however, was different. With her natural intelligence, Susan had potential to escape a life of poverty. But not while living with her parents. She had too little education and even less social interaction. At best she might marry a man she hardly knew, but Fanny couldn't imagine much happiness in that type of arrangement.

"I'll be going into town today," her mother said when Fanny returned to the house. "You might as well ride along and let Susan watch the little ones."

It was the closest thing to a friendly effort on her mother's part since she had arrived!

Fanny saw the look of desperation on Susan's face. While Fanny wanted nothing more than to see the town, not to mention other people, she knew that such opportunities probably came infrequently to her sister.

"I can watch them, if Susan wants to ride with you," Fanny offered, sending a soft smile in Susan's direction. Her sister lit up, her eyes glowing in anticipation.

"If that's the way you want it," was the only reply their mother gave.

When her mother and Susan left in the buggy, Fanny sent Joseph out to muck the barn and took the opportunity to clean the kitchen, scrubbing months, if not years, of grime from the floorboards. Ruth and Caren helped her by drying the floor when she was finished with each section. By the time that she finished and moved onto the cabinets, almost two hours had passed and she knew that she needed to start cooking the evening meal.

"Oh help! I wonder what *Maem* wanted to make for supper," she asked as she dried her hands on a towel.

"Potatoes, carrots, and meat," Ruth offered.

"We had that last night."

Caren tossed a damp towel into the sink. "We have that every night."

Fanny frowned. "That can't be true." But it was true, at least during the past week that she had been there with her family. Some nights there were different variations of it such as stew instead of dried-out ham with no gravy. "Where does *Maem* keep the canned goods?"

Ruth took her outside to a small storage room in the barn, where glass jars of pickled and canned foods filled the rough-hewn shelves. On the floor were baskets heaped with potatoes and onions as well as a crate filled with carrots. Fanny picked through them and realized that there was not enough food for the family to survive the winter. Something needed to be done to help her siblings get better nutrition.

"*Mayhaps* we can ask *Maem* if we can make some pasta tomorrow, *ja?*" Fanny suggested as she selected potatoes to cook for dinner. She grabbed an onion and several carrots as well, wishing that there was a greater variety of food.

As she headed back to the house, she noticed a vehicle in the driveway. A man approached them. She looked at her sister Ruth, who shrugged.

"You got a Fanny Price here?" the man said when he drew near.

"I'm Fanny Price," she said.

The man pursed his lips and stared at her. "Never seen you before," he said. "You visiting?"

She nodded.

"Someone should've told me," he mumbled. "You got some mail. Almost didn't deliver it today, since no one else on the route this way had mail. But I made the trip anyway." He thrust two envelopes toward her, and without waiting for her to thank him, he turned and hurried back to his truck.

Fanny stared after him, watching as he turned around his truck and practically flew down the driveway.

"That's Mr. Belz, our mailman," Ruth said as they walked up the steps to the porch. "*Maem* says he doesn't like the Amish."

Knowing that the letters would be a distraction when she had supper to make, Fanny tucked them into the pocket of her dress without looking at them. Back in the kitchen, she set her sisters to peeling and chopping the carrots and potatoes while she handled the onions. Thankfully, by the time *Maem* and Susan returned, Fanny had a beef stew prepared and bubbling on the stove. *Maem* went to her bedroom to rest, and the three youngest children escaped outside to play. With Susan knitting quietly by the cookstove, Fanny took advantage of the rare moment of peace in the house to sit at the kitchen table and look at the envelopes.

"One is from Mary Coblentz!" Fanny said to herself in surprise. Quickly, she opened the flap of the envelope and withdrew the single sheet of paper.

> *Dear Fanny,*
>
> *I pray this letter finds you well and that your visit home to Colorado is all that you expected. You are missed in Mount Hope and I hope that you return soon. One particular person seems to miss you more than others. If you might send a note with some kind words for Henry, it would help to lift his sadness at your abrupt departure.*
>
> *Regardless of your decision, I consider you a friend and, hopefully, one day soon as family.*
>
> > *God bless you.*
> >
> > *Mary*

Fanny scowled. Why should Mary send her such a letter, she wondered, unless to gloat that Elijah was soon to propose to her. She couldn't help but wonder if Elijah already had. After all, the letter was postmarked four days earlier, and her comment that it didn't matter whether or not Fanny married Henry indicated they would be family one way or the other. Surely Mary was counting on an upcoming wedding, and that wedding was to be hers into the Bontrager family.

She tucked the letter into her pocket and looked at the other envelope. The handwriting was familiar, and with a feeling of dread, she opened the envelope.

My dear Fanny,

How strange to know that you are so far away! The farm is not the same without our Fanny Price.

Soon after you left, Miriam insisted on moving to the Riehl farm, and Jeb readily agreed so as to keep the peace. Naomi is fretting because Miriam didn't wait until spring as most young brides do. With both you and Miriam now gone, Mother is desolate, her melancholy deepening as the winter approaches. Julia is quieter too, although I have reason to believe she might be stepping out with someone. And brother Thomas remains the same. There is nothing more to add on that front.

As for me, reflecting on my future has helped me see that there is a hole in my heart. Like every man, I know the need for lifelong companionship, a woman who is righteous, nurturing, and kind. It is time for me to settle down and take a wife. I intend to make my offer as soon as I see her again.

I just pray that she says yes.

With all of God's grace,
Elijah

Fanny shut her eyes and breathed deeply. How could it be that Elijah's words cut through her, filling the hole in his heart but creating a deep one in hers.

"What news, Fanny?" Susan asked in a soft voice.

"The worst kind, I'm afraid." Opening her eyes, Fanny looked at her sister. "Elijah's going to ask Mary to be his *fraa*."

Susan stared at her with large eyes. Starved for companionship as well as eager to develop her relationship with her sister, Fanny had confided in her younger sister shortly after her arrival. Susan had eagerly listened to Fanny's stories about the Bontrager family as well as Henry and Mary. With great reluctance, Fanny had also shared the reason she'd been sent back to Colorado in the first place. Although Fanny had not said anything overtly negative about Mary, her disapproval of the young woman had been hinted at when she spoke of her rejection to Henry.

"*Ach*, Susan!" Fanny fought the tears that threatened to fall from her eyes. "If only..." She couldn't finish the sentence. She dared not confide her feelings about Elijah to Susan, even though her outburst had probably already betrayed too much. Her sister was too young to understand the kind of love she had for Elijah. She folded the letter, taking care to slip it back into the envelope. Rather than put it in her pocket with Mary's, she held onto it. Standing up, Fanny turned to Susan and tried to smile. It was forced. "I suppose I shouldn't second guess. God has his plan, and who am I to question it?"

❧ *Chapter 18* ❧

ANOTHER LETTER, THEN?" her brother, Jerome, said when he and Peter trotted through the door. He tossed an envelope at her. "Why, aren't you the popular one!"

"Bet it's from your beau back in Ohio!" Peter snickered. At dinner a week ago Ruth had chattered about Fanny receiving mail, and Fanny had been forced to explain who sent her the letters. Hearing that one of the writers had been a man, Peter had drawn his own adolescent conclusions and was merciless in teasing her about Elijah.

Fanny frowned at him. For so many years she had been the youngest member of the Bontragers' household. Now that she was back on her parents' farm, she was the oldest. While she always had gotten on well with the younger children in the church district, she found it almost intolerable to have all six of her younger brothers and sisters around her. Besides the fact that the house was so small, their manners lacked the refinement she had come to expect from Amish children.

She presumed that their tendency toward being overly rowdy and mischievous came from living so far away from the other Amish households. Without access to school or town, the children had learned to amuse themselves with little to no external influence with the exception of the occasions that they managed to go to church services.

When the two boys scampered out the door to play, Fanny finally looked at the letter that she held in her hands. At first she smiled, for one glance at the handwriting told her who had written the letter: Elijah. And then, just as quickly, the smile faded from her face.

Only last week he had declared himself ready to marry, so Fanny could only presume that he had made his offer to Mary and this letter would inform her of his engagement. Fanny let her hands fall to her lap, the letter still clutched in her fingers, and shut her eyes.

Oh, how she had dreaded this moment! To read the news of Elijah's engagement to Mary Coblentz would crush her heart to pieces! While she knew that Elijah considered her as part of his family, she always hoped that he could see beyond that familial relationship and finally recognize her as not only his "cousin" and friend, but a potential wife as well. But there could be no doubt that any chance she had of capturing his heart had disappeared from the moment Mary Coblentz had walked through the doors at the worship service last August.

For several moments Fanny sat by the cookstove, the letter in her lap and her eyes staring out the large window that overlooked the mountains. She recalled the way, as a child, she had always looked at that same mountain and wanted to go to it. Yet she never had. *I shall walk to them*, she told herself, getting ready to put the letter into her apron pocket. *I shall finally do what no one else has. Walk to the mountains and pray for God to give me the strength to receive the news of Elijah's engagement.*

She could envision herself sitting among the trees, a coat wrapped around her shoulders, as she held the letter in her hands. While she sat upon a rock and looked out at the valley, she would open the letter and read his words. Only then and there could she accept the sorrow she would certainly feel to learn that her Elijah was committed to wed another. Surrounded by God's majestic grace, she might be able to reconcile herself with the loss, forever, of the only man she had ever loved.

She shut her eyes, her hand still on the letter that was now safely stowed in her pocket.

"Fanny?"

Her thoughts interrupted, Fanny opened her eyes and saw Susan walk through the open door, her apron full of eggs from the chicken coop.

Susan walked to the kitchen table and gently began to place the eggs in an awaiting carton. "I saw the boys run in here with a letter. Since *Maem* doesn't get too many, I presume it was for you then?"

Fanny sighed. "*Ja*, it is."

Shaking the dust and hay from her now empty apron, Susan walked over to where Fanny sat by the window. "You don't look none too happy 'bout it. Was it bad news?"

Fanny nodded her head. "I'm afraid so. Elijah is probably announcing that he is to marry."

"Probably? And that's not bad news."

When Fanny did not respond, Susan seemed to suddenly understand. "Oh," Susan said in a soft voice.

For a long few moments, neither one of them spoke. Fanny turned her head back to look at the mountain. With the sun beginning to dip behind it, the light that shone through the window began to hurt her eyes. Wincing, she looked away.

"In the Book of Mark, Jesus told us, 'Truly, I say to you, whoever says to this mountain, "Be taken up and thrown into the sea," and does not doubt in his heart, but believes that what he says will come to pass, it will be done for him.' If only I could have no doubt in my heart…"

Susan looked at her with a questioning expression on her face. "Doubts about what, Fanny?"

She looked at her younger sister and tried to force a sad smile. "That he isn't making a mistake, I reckon."

"You don't like his fiancée?"

Fanny pursed her lips to the side and looked up at the ceiling as if searching for the answer. "It's not that simple, Susan," she started to explain. "It's not that I don't like her, I reckon, but I don't like her for *him*. If he must marry another woman, then I would want to wish him happiness, for I would be remiss to want us *both* to be unhappy. This Mary is everything that Elijah is not. I cannot bear to think of the years of sorrow he may encounter in trying to change her."

Susan leaned against the arm of the chair. "I'm sorry, Fanny." She glanced over at the table and then back again at Fanny. "Where is the letter? Did he at least mention that you should return to Ohio?"

Fanny shrugged. "I don't know. I haven't read it yet."

At this comment Susan looked taken aback. "You haven't read it yet? Why, Fanny, you don't know what the letter says then! You might be trying to ask the mountain to move into the sea without realizing that it's already there!"

Susan lifted an eyebrow as if silently encouraging her sister to open the envelope and actually read the letter.

With great reluctance Fanny withdrew the letter from her apron. After casting a quick glance at Susan, who nodded for her to continue, she slid her finger under the flap on the envelope and withdrew a two-page handwritten letter.

> *Dear Fanny,*
>
> *I hope this letter finds you well. Unfortunately it brings some news that might be rather distressing to you. I am sorry that I am the one to tell you and pray that your grief will be tempered by your strong faith.*
>
> *The family has faced some distressing times. Evil has been lurking in the shadows. And the community is in an uproar.*
>
> *I am sorry to have to tell you that Thomas has taken ill. While his sickness is of his own reckoning, we are distraught that he is not recovering.*
>
> *Perhaps just as distressing, Fanny, is another situation of a very sensitive nature. My sister—and your cousin—Miriam Riehl, was found in the company of Henry Coblentz by her husband, Jeb. I must, unfortunately, leave the details of that discovery to your imagination, as they are of such a delicate nature that I am embarrassed to write the words on paper...*

Fanny's mouth opened, her jaw almost touching her chest. "Oh, help," she whispered, lowering the page.

"What? What's happened?" Susan asked, starting to lean over Fanny's shoulder as if to read the letter. But Fanny got to her feet and began to pace, the letter clenched in her hand. "Fanny! What is it?" Susan insisted.

"I—I can hardly believe it!" Fanny glanced at her sister. She was thankful that her mother and the other children were not in the kitchen, a rare occurrence but perfectly timed. "Thomas has taken ill. Gravely ill it seems. And while that is bad enough, he writes that Miriam has—" Fanny hesitated. Elijah's words had explained the situation as well as could be expected, given the delicacy of the situation. But Fanny almost could not believe what he had written. Rather than explain it to her sister, she merely held out the first page of the letter. "You read it! I don't even want to say what I fear Miriam has done! Certainly I'm misreading it!"

Susan snatched the page and her eyes scanned the handwritten words. "Oh, my!" Her eyes grew large and she quickly passed it back to Fanny. "And that is the man they wanted you to marry? That Henry?" She shook her head. "You don't think that Miriam has…"

Fanny finished the sentence for Susan. "…broken her wedding vows? That appears to be the insinuation. Oh, how dreadful! How terribly awful." She turned to the second page and continued reading. "There's more here about Thomas. Elijah must have added to the letter after writing that page," she said before reading the rest of the letter in silence.

Susan waited patiently for her to finish.

"Oh dear! That poor Thomas!" Still reading the letter, Fanny nodded her head. "Seems his sickness is of his own doing. He was racing his horse with his friends at night. He fell off and no one seemed to notice." Or care, she wanted to add. She knew far too well of the types of people with whom Thomas socialized. "Elijah writes that Thomas broke his ankle and hit his head. He was outside for hours and now he has pneumonia."

"Pneumonia! Two people died out here last winter from pneumonia!"

"He's young and strong," Fanny said, setting down the letter. "He should pull through, I imagine. However, surely we will pray for him. He needs God's love now more than ever."

They both bowed their heads and prayed silently for Thomas Bontrager's recovery from his injuries and his sickness. Fanny could only hope that Thomas had asked for forgiveness from God and Jesus for all of his sins. *Perhaps*, she thought as she finished praying, *Thomas will learn from these mistakes.*

"Is that all it says, then?" Susan asked.

Fanny looked back at the letter. "There's a little more." Silence followed as her eyes scanned the remaining two paragraphs. She frowned for a moment and had to reread the words.

"What is it, Fanny?"

She looked up from the letter, an incredulous look on her face. "Why! Elijah says I am to return to Mount Hope and he insists that I bring you with me!"

"Me?" Susan's eyes widened. "He says that?"

Fanny nodded and pointed to the paragraph. "Right here, Susan."

Her sister leaned on her shoulder so that she could read the section of the letter indicated by Fanny. Her face lit up when she read it. "Oh!"

"They have a driver fetching us on Monday! We're to catch a bus in Denver!"

Fanny set down the letter and stared at the window. The majestic beauty of the mountain contrasted sharply with the turmoil of emotions she felt from having read Elijah's message. While she had mixed feelings about returning, she knew that there was no other option. Staying in Westcliffe meant burdening her parents with more expenses, and from the short time she had been there, Fanny knew that she, like her siblings, had limited prospects in Colorado.

Yet Fanny still felt with wounded pride the sting of her banishment from Ohio. Was she so easily discarded, her contributions so unworthy of any appreciation? Now, to be beckoned back, not because she was wanted but merely needed? She felt disparaged and maligned once more. Truly Fanny did not expect—nor did she want!—to be commended for having discerned Henry's true colors long ago. He had proven himself to be everything Fanny suspected.

But there was no word in the letter about that. No blame given to Henry nor to Miriam—just the stark facts of their mutual fall.

Suddenly Fanny wondered if the family would blame *her* for the unspeakable situation. After all, no one had ever acknowledged Henry's faults, nor had they taken note of Miriam's flirtatious behavior. Perhaps the family believed that, by refusing Henry, she had broken his heart and driven him to find comfort in Miriam's arms.

"Oh, Susan!" she said, crumpling the letter into her hand. "What if they blame me for what Henry and Miriam did? How will I ever face them again?"

"*Nee*, Fanny! You've done nothing wrong." Susan forced Fanny to stand up. Placing her hands on her older sister's shoulders, Susan stared into her face. For the first time since Fanny had been there, she saw a look of excitement in Susan's eyes. "Don't you understand, Fanny? They are sending for you. They realize you were right. They realize you are part of their family. You do not have to worry about facing them; *they* have to worry about facing *you*!"

Fanny wasn't entirely convinced.

Susan laughed. "And we are leaving here! They are going to give me the same opportunity!" Like a child, Susan spun around in delight. "No more of this!" she said and waved her arms. "No more isolation. No more living hand-to-mouth. No more worry about the future!"

Fanny's worry began to transition into happiness for her sister.

"And you know what?" Susan said suddenly, grabbing Fanny's hands. "There is one thing that I've always wanted to do. Dreamed of doing. But I never had the nerve."

"What's that, Susan?"

Susan turned toward the window and pointed. "There. That mountain. I may never see it again, Fanny, but I have always dreamed of walking to it. To climb it, even if only for a few yards or so. Why, all of my life I have been staring at the mountain. Now I want to see what it stares at for all of its life!"

Fanny stood up and placed her hand on her sister's shoulder. They stared at the mountain, so majestic and glorious as it rose from the earth and climbed toward the heavens. The snow at the top looked pure and virtuous, clean of any sin from man. *Yes*, Fanny thought. She wanted to go to it too. For she knew that she would never return to Colorado again.

"Tomorrow," Fanny whispered. "Tomorrow we will say goodbye to Westcliffe properly." She pointed toward the mountain. "From there."

❧ *Chapter 19* ❧

FANNY AND SUSAN sat in the kitchen, both of them feeling uncomfortable but for different reasons. Susan kept wringing her hands, quietly looking around and taking in the vast differences of the Bontrager family's home. Ever since their arrival the previous evening, Susan appeared uncomfortable, certainly feeling out of place and less confident than she had been in Westcliffe. But Fanny remained grateful for her company and the opportunity the Bontragers offered to provide her with a better future, even if the timing of their arrival coincided with Miriam's unfortunate turn of events.

Julia had left the house just after supper, Fanny presumed to go visit her friends and to escape the heavy tension that encompassed the house. Meanwhile Elijah had spent the better part of the day and the early evening in the barn. When he finally entered the house and headed to the bedroom to sit with Thomas, he paused only to glance in Fanny's direction and offer the slightest of smiles. He too appeared distraught and grief-stricken by the recent turn of events.

Fanny worried about Elijah more than she worried about Thomas or Miriam. Certainly Henry's involvement with Miriam would negatively impact Elijah's relationship with Mary. She couldn't imagine that it wouldn't. How could he possibly marry Mary, Fanny thought, after her brother had ruined Miriam's marriage? *No*, she corrected herself, *both Henry and Miriam ruined it*. But it didn't matter. Elijah certainly could not bring Mary Coblentz into the Bontrager family now. She would be a constant reminder of what had happened, the link between the two families that would never go away.

Where are Henry and Mary now? she wondered. She had not dared ask, fearing the question would only rub salt in the wounds that needed far more time to heal.

Fanny stood up and walked over to the stove. Without being asked, she poured some coffee into several mugs and carried them over to her aunts and uncle. Timothy shook his head and Naomi scowled at her. Unconcerned, Fanny handed one of the mugs to Martha and took the other two over to the table.

As the two sisters sat at the table, Fanny on a chair and Susan on the bench with her back to the sitting area, Fanny focused her attention on Martha. She held the coffee mug in her hands, her shoulders hunched up to her ears and her head hanging so that her chin almost touched her chest. Naomi, however, paced back and forth, rambling on about Miriam and what could have caused her favorite niece to commit such a heinous act.

The more Naomi talked, the farther away Martha drifted.

Fanny wondered where she was. A meadow, perhaps, she thought, looking at dried stalks of goldenrod along the edge of the back field, just barely visible in the evening gloom. Or perhaps Martha had returned to her past, remembering a much simpler time in her life, when she too was young and perhaps a little foolish. She had, after all, married Timothy.

"And to think," Naomi said, her voice wavering between angry and distraught, "that I introduced her to Jeb Riehl! Why, my reputation will be sullied as well!"

Fanny glanced at Susan, who sat quietly across from her. Neither one of them spoke. There was nothing to say.

"*Your* reputation?" Timothy shook his head. He stood by the window, his hands clasped behind his back, and stared across the empty fields. "I imagine it will be none the worse for wear," Timothy mumbled.

Naomi ignored him—or perhaps she just chose not to hear!—and continued pacing as she complained about Miriam and Henry. "Such a match between Miriam and Jeb!" Naomi shut her eyes as she sat down in the rocking chair. With a big sigh, she rubbed her temples. "How could she possibly have engaged in such dishonorable behavior?"

"Possibly?" Timothy said in a sharp tone. He turned around and glared at Naomi. "Why, Jeb walked in and caught them holding hands! In his family's hay loft, of all places! She even had hay on her clothing. The way Jeb described it, they most certainly had at least kissed. Lord knows what else they may have done. And just weeks after she wed Jeb!"

Martha sighed and shook her head. "A disappointment, indeed."

"Disappointment?" Naomi huffed. "You are very lackadaisical about this situation. Why, that daughter of yours is a full-blown disgrace, Martha!"

"Susan," Fanny whispered as she leaned over to her sister. "You should get ready for bed, *ja*? You must still be tired from our long journey yesterday. I'll be up to join you soon."

The look of relief on Susan's face didn't surprise Fanny as she quickly stood up, leaving her untouched coffee where Fanny had left it, and hurried to their bedroom so that she could escape the tension in the kitchen. Fanny was glad that she thought to send her younger sister away. While it was not an ideal situation for Susan, meeting the family while everyone was dealing with such a stressful circumstance, she didn't need to be exposed to hearing the details.

"What will happen to her?" Naomi asked, wringing her hands and staring at Timothy as if hoping he had a solution for the situation. Focused on her own woes, she didn't even notice that Susan had left the room, nor care that a young newcomer had witnessed the family's disagreement.

"And Julia!" Martha suddenly spoke up. "Who will want to marry her?"

"Oh, hush, Martha! It isn't as if Julia broke her wedding vows!"

Naomi's scolding left Martha silent and suddenly devoid of any interest in the conversation. Instead, Martha set her jaw and stared at the wall, her eyes glazing over. Clearly Naomi had just added insult to injury.

"Will she be shunned, Timothy?" Naomi asked, redirecting her question to him. "Has Jeb said anything? Will she be permitted to stay with the Riehls or will they send her back here?"

It struck Fanny as odd to hear the genuinely worried tone in Naomi's voice. Usually her aunt sounded so confident and in control. She gave directives and rarely asked for advice. Now the color was drained from her cheeks as she stared at Timothy, looking to him for guidance when, not so long ago, it was she giving the advice to him.

For the first time as Fanny studied the older woman, she noticed how old Naomi looked, her hair grayer and wrinkles deeper than she ever observed in the past. No one had ever before dared to betray Naomi's good opinion. Miriam had certainly achieved that with her wayward conduct with Henry. How frightened she must be, Fanny thought. She was a widow living off the goodwill of her brother-in-law. Despite her years of promoting how righteous and good her husband was, his death had not left her in a good financial situation. The only thing she had to hang onto was her previous position in the community as the wife of the bishop. She used that to her advantage far too often to have the stain of scandal mar her reputation.

"She will most certainly be shunned," Timothy admitted, his voice catching as he said the word *shunned*. "And Jeb will surely expect her to leave his home. I'm surprised that he hasn't kicked her out already! No man wants a wife who has shown a propensity for such scandalous behavior."

"Shunned?" Naomi looked horrified at Timothy's words that were spoken with such conviction. "This is horrible. Dreadful. Surely she will return to us then and such a position that will put us in! Living with a shunned woman. And why? All because of a situation that could have been avoided," Naomi snapped, her previous concern about Miriam's precarious position within the community shifting to concern over the inconvenience to the family, or, more likely, to her in particular.

"Avoided?" Timothy turned to look at his sister-in-law. His eyes studied her, an incredulous expression on his face. "I fail to see how," he said.

"Why, it's quite simple, Timothy. None of this would have happened if only Fanny had accepted his marriage proposal!" Naomi said at last, turning her attention toward her niece. "How tragic that you could not see the ramifications of your denying him!"

"Me?" Fanny could hardly believe her ears, even though she'd been expecting this accusation. Still, the forwardness of Naomi's allegation and the vindictiveness of her tone shocked her and she felt the heat rise to her cheeks.

Timothy turned to look at her. Her heart pounding, she braced herself for his tirade. If only Susan were here! Surely he would not have berated her in front of her sister.

But Susan was not there. Fanny had sent her sister upstairs. And now Timothy's attention was on her.

"Fanny," he said in a soft, even voice. The word wasn't directed at her, but more as if he was merely thinking of her. "It is true that Fanny rejected Henry Coblentz, *ja*."

Paralyzed, Fanny stared at the steam still rising from Susan's deserted coffee mug, waiting for what seemed an eternity to have him turn on her and accuse her.

But he didn't. So Naomi renewed her attack.

"*Ja*, Fanny! You!" Naomi snapped. "You thought only of yourself when you turned him down, and now look at the consequences of your selfishness."

Timothy lifted his chin as his eyes shifted toward Naomi. He held up his hand as if to stop her from speaking. "*Nee*, Naomi," he said in an equally sharp voice. "You judge Fanny in error. If anyone should be blamed, it would be *you*, for not watching over Miriam more closely in my absence. Clearly this flirtation had been going on for a long time, long before the wedding. Miriam made a bad decision, while it appears that our dear Fanny made the only good one in this family!"

Our dear Fanny. How Fanny had longed to hear those words spoken from his lips. During her formative years Timothy had been the closest thing to a father that she had. His endearment startled her. Since her return just the night before, Timothy had barely looked at her, never mind spoken to her. Neither had Naomi. Now Fanny knew why. While her aunt sought to blame Fanny for contributing to Miriam's situation, Timothy had exonerated her from all blame. In fact, based on what he had just said, Fanny now realized from the way that he averted his eyes from her that he felt shame for himself, not blame for her! Had he truly seen the error of his accusations that she was ungrateful and unappreciative? Did he now realize that Fanny had known all along that Henry was a wolf in sheep's clothing? It appeared so!

"*Mayhaps* I should go check on Thomas," Fanny said in a quiet voice as she stood up and started to walk toward the master bedroom door.

"Such disappointments," Timothy muttered. "The lot of them!" And she knew that he was referring to all his children who had fallen from grace.

As she opened the door, Fanny saw Elijah seated beside the bed. He was hunched over and, from the looks of it, either dozing or reading. The kerosene lantern cast an orange glow onto the walls. Quietly Fanny shut the door behind herself and tiptoed over to the bed. Immediately Elijah looked up from the Bible he held in his hands.

"Fanny," he whispered as he stood and motioned toward the chair. "Sit, please."

"How is he?" Once seated, she leaned forward and pressed the back of her hand to his brow. "Oh, help. His fever hasn't broken yet?"

Elijah shook his head. "*Nee*, not yet."

"Poor Thomas," she said. "To think he could have frozen to death! God was surely protecting him."

Elijah knelt down beside Fanny's chair, his knee brushing against hers. "Protecting him from himself, *ja*. So foolish! Racing horses at nighttime! And to think his friends just left him there!" He stressed the word *friends* with such contempt that Fanny glanced at him. But Elijah was only staring at his brother.

Last night Elijah had met Fanny and Susan at the bus station, having accompanied the hired driver who waited in the parking lot. There was something different about him. Fanny saw it right away. He avoided her eyes and seemed nervous in her presence. After his initial inquiries about their journey, they had traveled the rest of the trip from the bus station to Mount Hope in silence. Elijah offered no commentary about Miriam's situation nor an update on Thomas's condition.

"With friends like those people..." Elijah added, watching as Fanny dripped a cloth into the basin on the nightstand. She glanced at him as though waiting for him to finish his sentence, but Elijah merely looked away.

"It seems that some people we consider friends," she said cautiously, "are not friends at all. Such a shame to put our trust in people only to find out how deceitful they can be."

He didn't respond. Not at first. But after a few long seconds, he nodded his head. "Mary..."

Once again Fanny braced herself. She wasn't certain if she was ready to hear what he had to say about Mary. She swallowed and looked at him, waiting for his words.

He averted his eyes from her and licked his dry lips. When he didn't continue talking, she knew that something was wrong. Had he already proposed to her? Perhaps before Miriam and Henry were caught in the hayloft?

"Elijah? What about Mary?" she heard herself ask. "You can tell me." But she didn't really want to hear it. Inside of her head she felt as if she was screaming, begging him to not say it, for she wasn't prepared to hear him professing his love for another woman.

"This is very difficult, Fanny."

For me too, she thought.

He cleared his throat, glancing at Thomas to make certain that they were not disturbing his sleep. "When Thomas fell ill," he said in a slow, drawn out, and calculated manner, "her main concern was what would happen if he died."

"I'm sure that was everyone's concern."

Elijah gave a shake to his head. "That's not what I meant, Fanny. She was concerned about my own prospects if he lived."

She frowned. "I don't understand."

He raised his hand to his face and rubbed his eyes. "She thought that, since *Daed* wants me to take over the farm, he would give Thomas a property of equal value. Or money to start a business. To be equitable."

Fanny squinted her eyes and stared at him, still confused. "Why would she be concerned about that?"

"Because she doesn't want *Daed* to do that."

She almost laughed. "Oh, Elijah! That makes no sense!"

"That's what I thought. When I pressed her about it, she got defensive and said Thomas didn't deserve any help from *Daed*, given his character. But I knew that was just a ruse to cover her true motive."

The idea of laughing quickly faded from her mind as she realized what Elijah was saying. "Do you mean...?"

He nodded his head. "*Ja*, I do."

"Surely you are mistaken," she whispered, her eyes wide. As much as she did not care for Mary and her pull on Elijah, she certainly did not want to believe what Elijah was telling her.

"Her concern was not for his recovery, Fanny, but for her own prospects if she joined this family."

With a gasp, she clasped her hand over her mouth. Mary had wished for Thomas to die? It couldn't possibly be true. How could any person be so evil?

"You speak of trusting people and learning how much they can deceive." He took a deep breath, his chest heaving upwards. There was sorrow etched in his face and Fanny knew that the realization of Mary's true nature, especially on the heels of Miriam's indiscretion, had come at a hefty price: he had lost faith in people. "I have been blinded so that I did not see just how deceitful people could truly be."

"Not everyone is like that, Elijah. Not all people are so..." She couldn't finish the sentence. There was no word for what Mary had implied, though *wicked* came to mind.

"Plenty of people are that way, Fanny." Elijah paused, deep in thought over something. Patiently, Fanny waited for him to continue. When he did, there was a hint of anger in his voice. "Look at the family. Why, there is not one of us who is not guilty of self-indulging behavior! Even *Maem* with her ceaseless—and very self-serving, might I add—depression!"

"Elijah!"

"It's true, Fanny. It's easier for her to withdraw into herself than to stand up to *Aendi* Naomi. Not once has *Maem* stood up to her, not before she moved into the *grossdawdihaus* and certainly not after. If she had not permitted *Aendi* Naomi to oppress her, and if she had taken her own daughters in hand instead of leaving them to Naomi's care, we might not be in this situation today."

There was truth to Elijah's words. For many years Fanny had watched as Martha sank into listlessness and despair, yet she had done little to help herself climb out of it. And not only she but her daughters also had suffered the consequences of her failure.

"But as I have been pondering all of this," Elijah added, his voice losing the bite so evident in his comments about Martha, "I have realized something else. You are not like the rest of us. Despite the supposed inferiority of your background that *Daed* and *Aendi* Naomi so often held against you, you are the only one that has lived a life that honors God." He paused. "You always have."

She blushed and looked at the floor.

Her modesty in accepting a compliment caused him to look over his shoulder at her. "Just think, Fanny, all these years my *daed* has prided himself on his children's upbringing in this community, even lording it over you. Yet the only one who has held true to the principles and values of the church—and our upbringing!—is you."

"I—I'm as much a sinner as anyone else," she whispered.

"Your response just proves the very point that I made." When he said this, his voice was low and his eyes narrowed as if he studied her, seeing her for the very first time. "What a disappointment the Bontrager children must be to our *daed*."

"Not you!" Alarmed, she reached out and touched his arm. "Why, you are a righteous man, Elijah. Your hard work on the farm is only second to your faith in God. Surely you cannot feel as if you are a disappointment. Your *daed* is most proud of you, for sure and certain."

But Elijah turned away, his eyes falling upon the sleeping form of his sick brother. "*Mayhaps*, Fanny, but the one thing I will never be is Thomas. He had such high hopes for his firstborn son and such great disappointments as a result. I'm not certain his pride in my following the faith will ever balance out his dismay in Thomas losing sight of it."

The sorrow in his voice struck her heart as if it were pierced. Was it possible, she wondered, that Elijah lived in his own prison of trying to live up to the expectations his father held for Thomas? Had Elijah felt the same disappointment in Timothy that she felt for the past eight years? And if so, how could Timothy favor Thomas? After all, Thomas showed no signs of committing to Jesus, the one thing that Timothy seemed to hold in greater value than anything else.

"Elijah," she said in a soft, compassionate voice and gently placed her hand on his shoulder. "You are misconstruing your *daed*'s concern for and attention to Thomas as displeasure with you. I think you are mistaken. You have proven yourself a most righteous son, and if he does not show you the same love and concern that he shows Thomas, it is only that, as Jesus did, he longs to bring back his lost sheep."

He glanced at her hand and then his eyes traveled up her arm to look at her face. He gave her a smile that simply said, without words, that he appreciated her support but did not truly believe her. He placed his hand atop hers, letting it linger for a moment, before he turned his attention back to his brother.

"Oh, Thomas," he sighed. "If only you could find your way to God."

They stood there, her hand upon his shoulder and his hand upon hers, as they watched Thomas sleep. Without speaking, Fanny knew that Elijah was praying for his brother's recovery just as she had done throughout the day. She watched him, his head bowed just enough so that she could see his lips move as he prayed.

Oh, Elijah, she thought, *if only you could find your way to me.*

❧ *Chapter 20* ❧

F ANNY!"

When she heard Elijah call out her name, Fanny stopped walking and turned to see what he wanted. Should she return to the house? Did Naomi want something of her? But Elijah did not beckon her to return. Instead, he stepped off the porch and jogged down the walkway in her direction.

With her black wool shawl wrapped around her shoulders, for the afternoon air was cold, she stood in the road, shivering as she waited for him to catch up with her.

Thanksgiving dinner had been a subdued event at the Bontrager household. Unlike past Thanksgivings where the family invited others in their community to join them, this year the family ate alone. Fanny suspected it was partially by choice, although she wondered if they were also afraid to invite others to join them. Certainly Bishop Yoder and his wife would not have accepted, and they always were seated at the Bontrager table for holidays. At least the Yoders wouldn't have to dine with Henry or Mary either, as Fanny had learned that they'd quietly returned to their home in Gordonville.

Also absent were Jeb and Miriam. Fanny hadn't seen Miriam since her return from Colorado, and she couldn't help but wonder where, exactly, Miriam would spend the day. Certainly Jeb's family would have issues inviting their new daughter-in-law to celebrate a holiday that commemorated giving thanks when they probably felt little gratitude this year.

Thomas too was absent from the table. Though his fever had broken, he was too weak yet to sit up for any length of time. But this Thanksgiving offered at least one thing to be thankful for: the prospect of a full recovery. Physically anyway. His spiritual fate, however, remained uncertain.

After the dishes were washed and the extra food put away, there was too much tension in the kitchen. The blue sky and still air beckoned Fanny. So when Susan declined her suggestion of a walk, opting instead for a nap, she decided to go alone. The fresh air would do her good, especially after the less-than-festive Thanksgiving dinner atmosphere. After so much had happened, she needed time to be alone and to think. Between Thomas's illness, Miriam's fall from grace, and Mary's dismissal from Elijah's future, there was much to reflect upon.

But for Elijah she would happily give up her solitude.

Out of breath when he caught up with her, he took a moment, his hands on his knees as he gulped for air. "I didn't know you went out for a walk," he said at last. "I would have accompanied you if you had asked."

She gave him a soft smile and began to walk slowly, Elijah falling into a familiar step beside her. "You are now," she teased.

With what Fanny thought was an unusual degree of nervousness, he laughed but averted his eyes. For a few moments they walked in silence, the only sound the crunch of the macadam under their shoes.

She glanced at him and saw that his coat was unbuttoned.

"You'll be the next one sick," she said as she reached over and tugged at his open coat.

Startled, he glanced down at her hand, which she promptly removed.

Ever since their conversation at Thomas's bedside, Elijah had been even more pensive than usual. Of course Fanny understood his reticence to talk. All of his hopes and dreams had been set on his marriage to Mary Coblentz. And while Fanny was not sorry that Mary had been dismissed, she did feel sorry for the hurt in Elijah's heart. The pain of a trust betrayed seemed far greater than the pain of unrequited love. Ever since she received his letter, her morning and evening prayers had focused on Elijah. If only he would lean on his faith, she thought. God's plan was not for Elijah to marry Mary Coblentz, and for that, Fanny was thankful. While Elijah had considered marrying her for love, clearly Mary had wanted to marry him for his prospects.

"You—you are doing well?" Elijah asked at last.

Fanny nodded. "*Ja*, but I suppose I should be asking that question of you."

Elijah frowned for a moment and then, realizing her meaning, quickly responded, "Oh, *ja*, for sure."

He didn't sound convincing to Fanny.

"You know, Fanny," he said slowly, kicking at a stick in the road. "So much has happened, so much has changed."

How could she argue with such a statement? "Indeed." Her voice carried her own inner turmoil. Naomi's words still lingered in Fanny's memory. She often wondered how many others blamed her for the situation, but lacked the forthright nature to speak their thoughts. It was a worry that kept her awake at night long after she had prayed for Elijah's heart. She knew that Elijah couldn't and wouldn't blame her for Mary's self-serving nature or Henry's illicit behavior. But she worried that he might fault her for not warning the family more clearly of the dangers that the brother and sister presented. Perhaps he believed that, like Martha, Fanny should have done more to prevent what had turned out to be a terrible tragedy for everyone in the family.

"If only you had—" Elijah began.

"Oh, Elijah!" she said, abruptly interrupting him. She simply couldn't bear to hear the words of blame come from his lips too. "Please don't. I cannot conceal my emotions over the situation for one more minute."

He stopped walking and turned to face her. "Do you feel the same way, then?"

Tears threatened to fall from her eyes. She could not look at him so she stared at the ground. "I have wondered at my role for the past week, Elijah."

"Fanny—"

"Please," she begged. "I have suffered enough."

He smiled at her, a reaction that she did not expect. "*Ja*, Fanny, I know that you have. And I have to tell you that I love you for it."

Love. The one word she had longed to hear from his lips but never thought would be spoken. He loved her for ruining his relationship with Mary? She couldn't make sense of that and forced herself to look at him, questioning him with her eyes.

"If only you had been here and not been sent away," he began again, "I could have dealt with all of this so much better."

His words startled her and she glanced at him. "I'm sure you handled it just fine, Elijah. You have always had more prudence than the others when it comes to situations that require strength and sense."

"Prudence," he repeated softly. "Unfortunately there is one area where I failed tremendously in what you claim such high esteem."

"Oh?"

He nodded. "I never would have realized that my judgment was overtaken by my imagination."

For a few long, drawn-out seconds, Fanny didn't respond. She suspected he was referring to his revelation about Mary Coblentz, but she didn't want to mention it. Surely his self-regard had been as injured as his heart.

But Elijah did not hesitate to continue discussing the matter. He frowned and looked toward the horizon as he spoke. "I had thought so highly of Mary Coblentz. And while she hadn't thought so highly of me when she thought I was to be a mere farmhand, she grew more interested when she realized I, and not Thomas, would inherit the farm. Why, she was no better than Miriam loving not Jeb Riehl but his 150-acre farm!"

"One-hundred-sixty acres," Fanny corrected him in a soft whisper.

He laughed, the tension fading from his eyes. "*Ja*, 160 acres. And look where that has landed Miriam! Shunned by the church, her family, and her husband!" He raised his hand and shielded his eyes from the sun as he glanced toward the horizon. "*Nee*, the person I imagined Mary Coblentz to be…a loving wife, nurturing mother, and best friend…is not who she truly is. You, Fanny Price, have saved me from a lifetime of unhappiness, for surely I would have discovered the truth quickly."

"I'd say that I'm relieved to hear I was helpful, but there is still so much pain in the family and community. My guilt outweighs my gratitude for your words."

Elijah frowned. "Guilt?" He took a step closer to her. "Whatever do you have to feel guilty about?"

"I…well, if I had spoken up—"

"Oh, stuff and nonsense!" He waved a hand in the air as if dismissing her words. "You tried to warn us, but none of us would listen! You have more sense than the entire family, Fanny. You saw the self-serving falsity of Henry Coblentz long before the rest of us did! Why, a man like Henry has no one to blame but himself. And as for my *schwester*, she too is equally culpable for her downfall! *Nee*, Fanny, you have no guilt on your head."

A car drove down the narrow road and Elijah took her elbow in his hand, gently guiding her to the side until the car passed.

"You know, Fanny," he continued, "I missed you while you were in Colorado. Two weeks you were gone, and those were the longest two weeks of my life."

She tried to smile. If she could only tell him about her long nights, weeping into her pillow as she shivered under the thin blanket and wished she were back in Mount Hope. "I missed you too, Elijah." She smiled at him. "Guess what Susan and I did before we left?"

He raised an eyebrow. "What was that?"

"We got up early and hiked toward that big mountain, the one that I always told you about, remember?" He nodded. "And when we got there, we climbed up it a spell. There are trails, you see. We got to a large rock and we stood there, watching as the sun rose on the other side of the valley. It was funny, though, Elijah. All of those years when I lived there, that mountain overshadowed our house and farm. But when you stand on the rocks and look into the valley...well, you can't see our house at all!"

He frowned.

"We are insignificant in its glory, I suppose," she said softly.

"I realized something while you were gone," Elijah said.

"Oh, *ja*?"

He nodded. "Your absence was more than physical. I missed talking to you. You are my best friend."

At this, she leaned over and nudged his arm with her shoulder. "You are my best friend too, Elijah."

He raised an eyebrow. "All of the talk about your possible marriage to Henry got me thinking. Of you as a wife and mother, I mean."

Her heart beat faster, and she looked away.

"I had never thought of you that way before," he continued, "and I couldn't help but wonder how you would be as a mother." When she blushed, he laughed. "So modest."

"You are embarrassing me," she said lightly.

"The thought of you having a *boppli*, why, Fanny, it made me realize how nurturing you would be."

She felt the color on her cheeks deepen.

"And then," Elijah said, lifting one finger into the air as if he had an idea, "it dawned on me that there is something else you would be." He paused, waiting for her to look up at him. "A loving wife."

For a moment she doubted her ears and worried that she read too much into his words.

"*Ja*, Fanny. You are a best friend and would most certainly be a loving wife and nurturing mother. The only problem is that..." He deliberately hesitated, his eyes softening as he gazed down at her. "...I don't want you to be those things with anyone else."

She felt a wave of panic. Had she misunderstood him? Surely this was a dream!

"When I learned of Henry's interest in you, I started to realize the truth," he confessed. "And then *Daed* sent you away. Without you here, Fanny, I felt lost. There was a hole in my world without you. The more distant I became, the more aggressive Mary grew. And then the situation with Henry and Miriam—why, she called it all folly. And as the word repeatedly left her lips—folly! folly! folly!—I knew. All of those characteristics that I imagined Mary possessed were only because I denied myself the truth."

"The truth?" Fanny didn't quite understand what he meant.

He took a deep breath as he placed his hands on her shoulders. The warmth of his touch caught her off guard. Here she had been expecting their conversation to follow a very different direction, one that would lead to tremendous heartbreak. Instead, the way that he looked at her, such an affectionate glow on his face, she realized that her fears were not to be realized. God's plans did not include Elijah—*her* Elijah!—mourning Mary Coblentz or blaming Fanny for not warning him of her character.

"The truth, Fanny, is that Mary had none of the characteristics I envisioned. I was blind to her faults because I projected on her the traits I had enjoyed and taken for granted these last eight years!" He paused. "Fanny, I merely wanted to recreate *you*!"

She raised her hand and covered her mouth, shocked at his words.

"When I said I love you earlier, I really meant it. I meant it not as a brother loves a sister but as a man loves a woman." He smiled and gave a small laugh. "Oh, how much I love you! Why, the thought of Henry pursuing you and you possibly marrying him nearly drove me mad!" The way he emphasized that word startled her. "And then listening to my father talk with Naomi about what a good match that would be for you—Fanny, I could scarcely think straight. I was almost relieved when you were sent to Colorado, for I knew that there you would be safe from that man!"

"I—I had no idea."

"*Ja*, Fanny, it's true." This time, he laughed, his delight so apparent in the sound. "Oh, how true it is!" He looked at her again, still smiling, and said, "You've been my best friend since you've arrived. Honorable, righteous, and loyal...sometimes to a fault. When I thought I might lose you, I realized that I didn't want to! So I am asking you, Fanny Price, if you would consider staying my best friend for the rest of your life in the role of loving wife and nurturing mother?"

"Oh, Elijah," she whispered. "Is this possible?"

"Do you doubt me?"

"*Nee*, of course not." She shook her head. "You are always true to your word."

"Then tell me," he said, bending his knees just enough so that he could look into her eyes, "do you love me enough to marry me?"

A tear fell from her eyes and she wiped at it with her fingers as she gave a soft laugh. "Oh, Elijah, I could never love anyone as much as I love you."

He put his arms around her waist and lifted her into his arms, spinning her as she laughed at his display of enthusiasm. "You have made me the happiest man!" he said, setting her back on her feet. "And I will spend all of my life ensuring that you are the happiest woman!"

He leaned forward to brush his lips gently against hers.

"I already am, Elijah," she whispered just before he kissed her. "I already am."

❧ *Epilogue* ❧

THE WARM SMELL of freshly baked bread filled the kitchen as Fanny shut the oven door. Carefully she set the two pans of bread onto the cooling rack and removed her oven mitts. She leaned over and inhaled, the yeasty scent filling her with happiness.

Ever since her wedding to Elijah, that was how she felt: happy. They had married in December, urging Timothy and Martha to allow a smaller celebration, rather than the traditional large service with hundreds of guests visiting throughout the day and evening. No one wanted to be reminded of the other wedding that had taken place just six weeks earlier.

To her surprise, Timothy had seemed unusually complacent when he learned that Elijah and Fanny were to marry. She had worried that he would be offended anew, this time at the idea of his son marrying someone that he'd grown up with, but she was relieved and gratified that he respected and even seemed to approve his son's decision. Even better, he welcomed Susan into his home, showing her the attention and concern he had withheld not only from Fanny, but also from his own daughters.

Truly the man's spiritual awakening amazed everyone in the family, especially Fanny.

Timothy's wedding gift to them was the farm, for he had finally come to accept what he had long ago realized: Elijah was the more deserving of his two sons. Even if Thomas changed his ways and became a more responsible member of the household, Elijah had proven himself to be consistently righteous and principled and, therefore, the more deserving of the two sons.

In fact, after Thomas recovered from his illness, he appeared a changed man. While he still refused to take the kneeling vow, he showed his appreciation for his family's care by awaking early enough to help with morning chores. He also no longer demonstrated any of the rebellious ways from his prior self.

After the wedding Fanny had fully expected to move into Elijah's bedroom in the large farmhouse. But when Naomi, shamed by Timothy's accusation, went to live with her sister-in-law in Indiana, Elijah suggested that they move into the *grossdawdihaus* instead. It had seemed a logical solution, allowing them to start their lives together in the comfort of the smaller attached house.

As for Miriam, Timothy had refused to let her return to his household, which left her in a quandary and living in virtual exile at the Riehls' household while she endured her shunning. The bishop had urged Miriam to repent and exhorted Jeb to forgive, and the two, realizing they had no other choice if they were to remain in the community, agreed to his counsel. Whether they could yet build a happy marriage after such an unhappy start remained to be seen.

Julia seemed to breathe easier now that Miriam was gone from the house and Henry was no longer in Mount

Hope. Without her sister, Julia became friendlier to both Fanny and her sister Susan; and with the newfound attention of her father, Julia seemed to grow in self-confidence and maturity. Not only that, she appeared to be more genuinely happy, with a glow to her eyes and a quickness to her step that left Fanny wondering if she was, at last, courting someone.

One night Fanny thought she heard a buggy in the driveway late on a Friday night. Outside the window, she could make out two voices, a man and woman who talked as they walked away from the house. The voice sounded vaguely familiar, and Elijah wrapped his arm around her as he whispered into her ear, "Benjamin's come calling for Julia at last."

As for Martha, with Naomi's departure and Timothy's softened attitude, the fog that had gripped her slowly lifted. Her attention now focused on patiently teaching Susan how to weave baskets. Fanny often found them laughing as they worked at the kitchen table of the main farmhouse.

But today Fanny hadn't joined them. Instead, she was finishing the preparations for the noon meal.

She glanced out of the window and saw Elijah walking toward the house from the barn. He was whistling, a sure sign of his good mood. Within a few minutes, she heard him on the porch, and after kicking the dirt from his boots, he opened the door.

"Mmm, fresh bread!"

She smiled as he approached her. With no one else in the kitchen, he leaned over and gave her a warm kiss, his arm around her waist. She placed her hand upon his shoulder, and when he pulled back, she stared into his face. "Finished then?"

"Until tonight, *ja*." He glanced over her shoulder at the clock on the wall, a wedding gift from him to her. "It's nice out today. The air not so cold. *Mayhaps* we have time for a ride?"

"Oh, Elijah!" Just the thought of riding together, one last time through the empty fields before he planted the corn, made her glow. "That sounds right *gut*!"

"I thought you'd like that."

"But..." She paused and let her hand fall from his shoulder to her stomach. "Is it safe?"

He laughed and hugged her once again. "*Ach*, Fanny, what a *wunderbarr maem* you will be!" He kissed her forehead. "*Nee*, you're fine. Why, you're only ten weeks pregnant!"

Fanny glanced at the floor, not wanting to be argumentative with him but wanting to protect her unborn baby...no, *their* unborn baby. "Still..."

"*Ach*, none of that, Fanny," he said in a gentle voice. "No hiding your face or your opinions from me. You are my *fraa*, and as both your husband and your friend, I value what is on your mind. Your concerns are my concerns. If you have any doubts, we can go for a nice, slow walk instead."

He placed a finger under her chin and made her look at him again. The hint of a beard along his jawline still looked out of place for the face that had been so familiar to her for almost nine years. But she didn't mind. In fact, she liked seeing the growth, for she knew it meant that he was hers and no one else could ever claim him.

Taking a step backward, he held out his hand for her. She gave him a tender smile as she reached out to take it, feeling the warmth of his skin touching hers. He led her toward the door, pausing to take down her black coat from a hook. As she slipped her arms into it, he turned her around and helped her with the buttons.

"Fanny Bontrager," he said. "I am a happy man, and all because of you."

"And God," she added.

"And God," he affirmed. "When you first arrived, your dress soiled and your shoes torn, I never would have imagined that God's plans would have led to this moment. But I thank Him every day that He knew what we both needed."

"Each other."

He leaned down and gently kissed her lips before he repeated, "Each other" into her ear.

She felt the all-too-familiar butterflies in her stomach as he took her hand. Together they walked outside and headed down the lane toward the road. Elijah lifted his hand as they passed by the kitchen window of the main house, his mother standing at the sink and smiling as she observed them.

With the sun beginning to lower in the late winter sky, beautiful colors of red, orange, and purple filled the horizon. A few birds flew overhead, squawking as they did. Soon the sun would set later in the evening and the trees would begin to bud. Spring was just around the corner, and with it came the rebirth of life on the farm. While Fanny always favored spring, this year it would be even better, for she would have Elijah by her side.

Just as God had planned.

❧ *Glossary* ❧

ach vell—an expression similar to *Oh well*

aendi—aunt

Ausbund—Amish hymnal

bann—the shunning of a church member

boppli—baby

bruder—brother

daed—father

danke—thank you

Englische—non-Amish people

Englischer—a non-Amish person

fraa—wife

g'may—church district

grossdawdi—grandfather

grossdawdihaus—small house attached to the main
    dwelling

grossmammi—grandmother

gut mariye—good morning

haus—house

ja—yes

kinner—children

kum—come

maedel—older, unmarried woman

maem—mother

mayhaps—maybe

nee—no

Ordnung—unwritten rules that govern the g'may

rumschpringe—period of "fun" time for youths

schwester—sister

wie gehts—what's going on?

wilkum—welcome

wunderbarr—wonderful

❦ *Other Books by Sarah Price* ❦

THE AMISH CLASSIC SERIES
First Impressions (Realms)
The Matchmaker (Realms)
Second Chances (Realms)
Sense and Sensibility (Realms)

THE AMISH OF LANCASTER SERIES
Fields of Corn
Hills of Wheat
Pastures of Faith
Valley of Hope

THE AMISH OF EPHRATA SERIES
The Tomato Patch
The Quilting Bee
The Hope Chest
The Clothes Line

THE PLAIN FAME SERIES
Plain Fame (Waterfall Press)
Plain Change (Waterfall Press)
Plain Again (Waterfall Press)
Plain Return (Waterfall Press)
Plain Choice (Waterfall Press)
Plain Christmas (Waterfall Press)

OTHER AMISH FICTION BOOKS

An Amish Buggy Ride (Waterfall Press)
An Empty Cup (Waterfall Press)
An Amish Christmas Carol
Amish Circle Letters
Amish Circle Letters II
A Christmas Gift for Rebecca
Priscilla's Story
Secret Sister (Realms)

For a complete listing of books, please visit the author's website at www.sarahpriceauthor.com.

❧ About Sarah Price ❧

THE PREISS FAMILY emigrated from Europe in 1705, settling in Pennsylvania as the area's first wave of Mennonite families. Sarah Price has always respected and honored her ancestors through exploration and research about her family's history and their religion. At nineteen, she befriended an Amish family and lived on their farm throughout the years.

Twenty-five years later, Sarah Price splits her time between her home outside of New York City and Lancaster County, Pennsylvania, where she retreats to reflect, write, and reconnect with her Amish friends and Mennonite family.

Contact the author at *sarah@sarahpriceauthor.com*. Visit her weblog at http://sarahpriceauthor.com or on Facebook at www.facebook.com/fansofsarahprice.

CONNECT WITH US!

CHARISMA HOUSE

(Spiritual Growth)

Facebook.com/CharismaHouse

@CharismaHouse

Instagram.com/CharismaHouseBooks

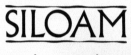

SILOAM

(Health)

Pinterest.com/CharismaHouse

REALMS

(Fiction)

Facebook.com/RealmsFiction